OUT OF OBLIVION

HOW I LEFT OB-LOM

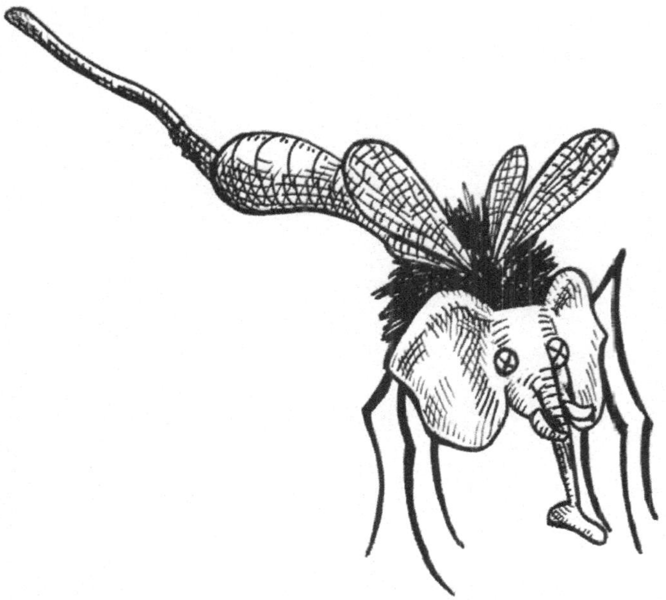

OUT OF OBLIVION

HOW I LEFT OB-LOM

KRISTINA BIRK

Edited by Sarah Kolb-Williams
www.kolbwilliams.com
Illustrations by Alina Galaktionova
www.agalaktik.com

ISBN: 978-1-7363897-0-6
Printed in the United States of America
First Printing: 2021
25 24 23 22 21 5 4 3 2 1

Book design and cover illustration by Athena Currier
www.athenacurrier.com

To order, visit www.kristinabirk.com

To Ma and Pa—Larisa and Oleg Karpovich

MANY THANKS TO:

Babushka Lucy, who taught me to read at age four;

Miroslava Karpovich, for teaching me to live in magical realism and play the most surrealistic games at all times;

Krylov Aleksey Igorevich, for helping me fall in love with English;

Zaretskaya Elena Naumovna, for teaching me how to fight against totalitarianism and follow logic, freedom, and creativity of speech.

PART I

DETSTVO[1]

In recalling my childhood I like to picture myself as a beehive to which various simple obscure people brought the honey of their knowledge and thoughts on life, generously enriching my character with their own experience. Often this honey was dirty and bitter, but every scrap of knowledge was honey all the same.

—Maxim Gorky

1 From Russian, meaning "childhood."

CHAPTER I

RODINA

Ibant obscuri sola sub nocte per umbram.[2]

I WAS ABOUT FIVE AND A HALF when my height reached the level of the only windowsill in our apartment and I learned to sneak out of my bedroom, where I had to stay about ten hours a day in complete solitude for "safety purposes." Two extra inches were enough for me to locate the poorly pronounced streak of somber moonlight coming from the thoroughly concealed window in the living room. I was convinced that catching a quick glimpse of the world outside by breaking my parents' rule would help me finally understand why being as quiet as a mouse outside of my behind-the-wall bedroom was so critical (they even made it a point to teach me to sneeze noiselessly), why we had to speak to each other through inconvenient tin can telephones, and why none of the other rooms behind other walls were ever available to me.

One day, before getting myself into a great deal of trouble, I asked Mama about all of the above, but her answer was vague and nowhere

2 From Latin—"They went in the darkness, beneath the shadow of the lonely night."

near satisfying. Without looking me in the eye, she repeated in her cold professorial tone: "For safety purposes." Papa's reaction was the same as always—he just nodded lugubriously to everything she said. I knew he had so much more to add based on the shape of his eyebrows (they had a tendency to angulate like two electric eels in moments of indecisiveness or unfinished trains of thought), but he conspired with his beloved *dama* against his will quite often, because . . . well, because his temper was sweeter than condensed milk.

Of course, "for safety purposes" was my least favorite answer. What an amorphous thing to say to a child! What an unreasonably *clear* way to convince a young offspring to act capriciously!

"What safety purposes?" I asked both my parents from the doorway to my bedroom, hoping to get a better explanation. The impatience in my voice made the tin can telephones in my parents' hands shake like freshly caught sardines.

Instead of answering, Ma gave me one of her well-known killer-iceberg looks, after which she immediately came up with an urgent task and pattered her way out of the room. It was the first time she hadn't even attempted to distract me with a different topic or her collection of embroidered kitten images. Pa, bent in a half-glum, half-irritated posture similar to that of a frozen shrimp, dragged his feet after Ma's little frenetic steps at a harmonious distance.

My repeatedly offensive inquisitiveness had enlarged itself to the size of a supremely frustrated hippopotamus. At that point, the urge to see what they had been putting out of my sight was beyond my control.

I waited till nobody was around to unwrap the firmly sewn-in opaque curtain on our only window and see what the outside was all about. Dealing with the rough, dusty fabric while slurping borscht from an old jar, I did not notice that Papa had entered the house until a long, eloquent sigh filled the air. He leaned against the wall, calmly watching me try to release my face from the half-empty jar it was stuck inside.

Instead of grounding me like he would if Ma were around, he eventually slid the jar off my face and let me finish eating. His eyebrows angulated for a whole minute before he was done processing his thoughts.

"Okay, *Malenkaya*," he addressed me in a distant, nervous tone, "I can't do this to you anymore . . . I will show you why safety purposes are important in this house. But you must promise me you won't tell Mama."

I nodded with so much enthusiasm that my head almost fell off. Pa grinned and shook my hand.

"Well then, let us seal our newly made pact," he said.

Making secret pacts with a superlatively official handshake was a regular ceremony back then, performed strictly between the two of us.

"Our job is to save Mama's nerves. She has been through a lot," he said.

Unlike all the innocent mischief we had done before, I could feel that our new adventure was fraught with real danger.

"You go ahead and lull them with the Fifth Symphony," said Papa inaudibly with his lips before stapling them with an old squeaky stapler.

I obediently hummed the most complicated piece of classical orchestra music straight to the floppy wide-open ears on the wall. My father's face lit up with pride while he continued taking out multiple pieces of moth-bitten furry garments from the only closet in the house. We bound each other with at least twenty of them.

"Wait until these *stukachi* stop moving," whispered Papa, explicitly despising the stubborn spying ears.

Once they finally dozed off, Papa tied me to the abdominal section of his *tulup*—his military jacket—as if I were a baby wallaby.

"Put these in your pockets. They will keep you warm," he whispered into our tin can telephone, handing me two freshly boiled potatoes wrapped in gauze.

When he had made sure I was properly equipped to go outside, he added in a nervous, gruff tone, "Pinch me when you are ready to go back. And remember, you must stay quiet the entire time. Nobody can hear you. Want to show me your quietest sneeze?"

I tried to nod, but there were too many layers of clothes on me, making me look like an immobile penguin. I quickly tickled my nose with the yellowish feather sticking out of Pa's tulup and demonstrated how well I could suppress multiple sneezes.

"Very nice," said Papa. "We are ready to go."

Seeing my *Rodina*—my home country—for the first time was rather disturbing. I will never forget the frigid air, reeking of dog piss and intoxicating fermentation, forcing itself into my nostrils through the little hole of the missing button in my father's tulup.

"Psst—it's all clear. Hop out," Pa whispered, though not a single soul was around.

As soon as I crawled out of Papa's jacket and put my feet on the impossibly slippery, icy ground, surrounded by giant ominous constructions, the visible world spun in an odd kaleidoscopic circle. Papa caught me while I was in the air, put me back on the ground, and pointed at the giant construction in front of us.

"This is why," he murmured through the right corner of his mouth.

Wide-eyed and dizzy, I stood next to my father, with my hand in his, in the midst of a gargantuan frozen State called LIM, also referred to as "Lunar Immaculacy." The frosty land was dully lit by amoeba-looking stars perched in the dark purplish sky, unstable flickers of the belligerent-looking Moon, and about two hundred poorly operating streetlights. (Maybe thirty-two of them worked, while the rest could easily be mistaken for mangled silverware.)

My eyes became used to the dim streetlight as soon as everything stopped spinning. Then and there, I made out the most prominent element of the local environment Papa was pointing at: through the murky, monotonous winter, I saw an outrageous, horrifying citadel, situated at the farthest compound of LIM. A handful of identical people were carefully promenading back and forth at its base, despite the fact that nothing in that architectural monstrosity's intensely glowing adornment signaled it was safe to be anywhere near it. Brighter than anything around, it came across as some exotic reptile, the aposematic patterns and colors of which warned other species about its deadly poison. The giant had a built-in clock on its top, sending a sinister, hypnotic series of militant tapping to the entire State. Every new tick-tock-tuck inside the clock's face sounded as if some heavy-handed warden had just hit a shallow tin drum with his fist to announce a funeral procession: "Tick-tock-tuck. Tick-tock-tuck. Tick-tock-tuck. Tick-tock-tuck."

Have you ever forgotten to take off your watch before turning in for the night? Remember the moment you heard it next to you and could no longer think about anything else? The ticking disrupted your sleep so much that even after you put away the watch, you still heard it just as distinctly? Something similar happened to me that day. The ghostly mechanical echo ingrained its excavated rhythm into my mind, not for just a day but for the next two decades of my life.

Papa's voice brought me back to reality.

"Are you all right?" he asked.

My breath came to a motionless halt. Suffocated by a vortex of snow, I could control my spasmodic trembling no longer. Intense flushes of adrenaline washed through me. No longer wishing to absorb the torturous rhythm or the repetitive blocks of LIM's imperturbable compounds, I pinched Pa with a great deal of effort. He tucked me back into his tulup.

His walk was different this time; accelerating in reverse, he was sliding and stumbling along the roads, trying to behave as casually (monochromatically, rather) as he possibly could. It felt as if I had suddenly awakened in a strange country.

CHAPTER II

WARDWORKERS. WARD.

PA RUSHED BACK INTO OUR HOUSE, clumsily untangling me from the ice-covered layers in the same fashion Ma used to dissect freshly harvested heads of cabbage, leaf by leaf. His shaky but deceitfully rapid hand movements made it seem as though, for a moment, he had somehow obtained a few extra limbs.

Something even more peculiar happened to the color of my father's face the moment he looked at my feet: it turned three different shades of blue, until it became entirely pale.

"Your slipper . . . it's gone," said my devastated Pa.

I shrugged, showing zero awareness of the degree of misfortune and distress the slipper accident was going to cause.

"What do I do. Whatdoido, whatdoido," Pa repeatedly roared under his nose, trying to contemplate a solution while walking around the apartment like a lunatic, startled by every hint of noise.

It was disorienting to see my generally rational father shake from fear, bite his hands, and tear parts of his clothes and hair.

The sound of someone's footsteps entering the building made Papa stop walking in circles; he squeezed me so tightly that I thought he intended to turn me into a mashed potato. His eyes looked like two eerie blood bubbles.

"Ouch!" I squeaked into his chest.

He hurriedly dragged me into my behind-the-wall bedroom, mumbling a sporadic series of nonsensical thoughts out of which I made out this one: "Your mom will never forgive me."

The footsteps in the building were coming closer and closer. We crawled under my bed. The moment somebody reached our floor, Pa tightly pressed my pale face against his chest.

Ten-second pause.

Somebody walked into our house and unlocked my room. The wall squealed and moved an inch forward with a pitiful "uuu-aaa-eee."

Pa's bright green eyes turned gray, almost black. He was gasping for air. The ugly LIM-wig he had to wear on top of his own thick curls daily—to come across as perfectly normal—fell off his head. The brown in his hair turned white in an instant.

"No-o-o-o-o! Papa, what is happening to you?" I burst out screaming. The spying ears on the other side of my room woke up and began to shriek, moving like monstrous tentacles.

Then Mama's anxious, high-pitched voice entered my realm through the deafening waves of the spying ears' alert. The footsteps we were hiding from belonged to her.

"*What have you done?*" she yelled at Papa.

Without thinking twice, she ran around covering up the doorknobs that led to all of the hidden walls, doing at least five other things at the same time. She was sweating heavily, pushing various objects inside the walls to revert the apartment to its uneventful emptiness.

"Be quiet. If Wardworkers get anywhere near you, hold your breath like we do when we play *vodolaz*," she warned me before she completely ran out of breath.

I knew all about playing frogman, though the word *Wardworker* was new to me. There was no time to ask questions. Ma hurriedly pushed me into the room I had never been inside.

"Quiet as a mouse. Like a vodolaz," she repeated in a harsh whisper, a frantic look on her face, then fastened the wall with one click.

While rehearsing my vodolaz abilities, I noticed several tunnels stretched into the unknown darkness in front of me, their entrances surrounded by piles of books.

Where am I? What a wonderful place, I thought.

In what felt like a minute, wet, heavy boots entered the building and walked up the stairs directly to where we lived. Through the tiny hole in the wall, I saw how a group of sallow-faced individuals in drab grayish tulups tagged as "WARDWORKER MILITSIA" strode into our place. They kicked the door unapologetically with their dirty *valenki-kaloshis.* Freezing-cold air came in with them, like a spooky fragrance. Then my lost slipper, hung on a pair of pliers, was presented to Ma and Pa, whose knees shook at the sight of it.

No matter how innocent and unsuspicious they tried to remain, the drumming rhythm of their hearts was as loud and vivid as the ticking of the giant clock from outside.

Pa looked like he was about to faint. Ma, on the other hand, stood straight. She had the bravery to look the strangers in the eye and show them her beloved doll Zosya (childless people in LIM were allowed to own toys that resembled toddlers), whose plastic feet could easily fit in my shoe.

"I will admit. We are guilty. Victor and I enjoy taking Zosya outside on occasional promenades, regardless of the fact that we are not supposed to, for which we wholeheartedly apologize. We accept our punishment," she explained while loosening the staples on her mouth for better oral communication.

Pa nodded, having obvious difficulty keeping his eyebrows perfectly straight and motionless.

The strangers punched the staples back into my mother's lips. One of them yelled in a dry, throaty growl, "Quiet! Where is the other slipper? Give it to us! *Now!*"

The other slipper was behind the wall, under my bed. As a result, Ma's excuse didn't convince the invaders one bit.

Wardworkers were surely preparing themselves to detect something criminal in our guest room, based on the raving anticipation all over their steaming faces. They beheaded Zosya and continued examining every millimeter of the apartment and its surfaces with a magnifying glass and a handful of mosquito-elephant-looking vacuum cleaners. The mechanical monsters with dotted red eyes were moving like well-trained predators ready to pounce.

The men refused to stop searching the place one hour later, regardless of the fact that their specially assigned vacuum cleaners had nearly come apart at the seams after the multitude of dominant pushes, indicating that they had not found anything worth paying attention to. One more push. Two more kicks. The flabby machines fell on the floor.

"Eeeh-geeegh," squeaked the door grumpily. A tall, square-headed Wardworker-General walked into our apartment and ceremonially unbuttoned his ornately embroidered overcoat with a crimson side pocket, where he kept his other hand warm. The bright insides of his side pocket were intimidating and could easily be mistaken for an open wound.

The man took out a mushy plastic receptacle that resembled an IV solution bag from the crimson pocket and poured the bag's contents into the only two tin mugs in the house.

"*Svetlana and Victor*" read the sloppy cursive letters on the mugs.

"Bottoms up!" bellowed the square-headed man.

There was so much spleenful hatred in the sound of his voice that the staples gashed his mouth. All the other workers supported his command with dutiful eagerness and a series of sardonic grins.

Without any arguments, Pa forced the contents of the mug through his chattering teeth and momentarily collapsed on the Wardworker-General's feet, like a brittle marionette.

"Get out of my way!" roared the Wardworker-General, seizing my sleepy dad with a humiliating dagger look, after which he continuously kicked him into the hallway with his muddy valenki-kaloshis.

Ma squeezed her nostrils and brought the sizzling mug closer to her lips. Suddenly, she changed her mind and spit half the mug's contents in the men's faces. She yelled out their names and was ready to add many more personal invectives when one of them hit her on the head with a wiry chair, acting like he was performing the most ordinary action. Ma gracefully landed in the same doorway my father had been swiped away from seconds before.

I hope they are going to be okay, I thought hastily to myself through drops of rapid tears. *I really, really hope they are going to be okay . . .*

The Wardworker-General returned from the hallway and stumbled over my mom's body. His face changed.

"*Go search the kitchen!*" he yelled at the grinning militsia men.

When no one was around, he gave my unconscious mother a somewhat gentle look full of sorrowful sentimentality. Before leaving the room, he put his giant paw-hand on her thin neck, as if intending to choke her, but instead of squeezing it, he planted a grossly wet kiss on her lips and bosom, leaving big drops of grayish saliva all over her skin. Then his body shook like an old car engine. The intensifying noise and chaos of the other square men's investigation brought the Wardworker-General out of his trance.

"Have you found anything yet?" he yelled.

"Come here, General!" one of the Wardworkers yelled back to him.

The man threw Mama back on the floor, readjusted his mustache, and walked away.

It became quiet. I loosened my hands, letting an uncontrollable, soundless sob out of my chest.

Through rivers of tears, I noticed a bizarre pair of shiny blinking eyes emerging and vanishing from one of the far corner tunnels. They floated closer to me. I wished to move as far away from them as possible, but even the most poignant fear didn't make me neglect my responsibility to remain as quiet as a vodolaz. I buried my face in my knees, wishing for everything to be over.

I took one more deep breath, like Papa always showed me in moments of utmost anxiety, as Wardworkers approached the wall in large, decisive steps . . .

Suddenly, the siren outside informed all of LIM about the beginning of the Collective Marching Hour Gathering, also known as the CMHG. A skittish, chubby black cat with yellow eyes sprung out of nowhere, like a bullet, at the exact same time the siren went off. The creature was clearly overreacting to the sudden noise coming from outside—it landed on my head, releasing its long claws into my scalp and skin. After overcoming my short-lived heart attack, I immediately pulled the maniacal cat out of my hair and threw it into the tunnel in front of me.

Luck was on my side: the Wardworkers didn't hear the deafening meowing through LIM's screaming siren. The worst was over. For the most part.

The intensifying siren made the men hurriedly squelch their way out with a gross "chvyak-chvyak," leaving large puddles of brown chunky dirt on the floor. Before exiting in a state of disappointment and blistering anger, they collectively spit on Ma and Pa. Halfway out of the building, they remembered they had left the fatigued vacuum cleaners napping on our floor.

"E-e-e-k," hiccupped the door cantankerously, in response to being pushed by a large gloved hand that dragged the pile of benumbed machines outside. "E-e-e-k," the door repeated with a lot less apprehension, as if happily returning to its previous uneventful position.

When Wardworkers were nowhere near, Ma propped herself against the wall and vigorously rubbed her injured forehead. Dark lines of blood had already coagulated on the sides of her head. She coughed once, twice. A couple of teeth fell out of her mouth, but she didn't seem to mind.

"Spit it out, Victor. They are gone," said she to Pa.

"Ooooh," Papa exhaled as he began to roll on the floor, back and forth, left and right, in a wormlike wiggle, propelled by some tremendous internal force. His unstoppable spitting turned the already dirty-slushy floor into a bigger swamp mixed with Ma's blood. The more he spat and coughed, the more clarity lit up his blackened, lackluster eyes, until they regained their naturally emerald-green color.

Seeing Ma's wounds made him forget about his own pain. He hurriedly brought a large briefcase marked with a sloppy red cross and put stitches on her forehead. Mama pointed at the two missing teeth in her mouth without saying a word.

"Oh no! Again!" exclaimed Papa. "Here, take these. They will fit you as well as the ones I gave you last month."

"*Da,*" confirmed Mama passively.

"Maybe you ought to stop spitting at them . . ." Papa suggested in a gentle voice.

Instead of replying, Mama gave Papa an adamant look. He lowered his eyes and turned away.

In about two minutes the State's loudspeaker announced my parents' misconduct to the masses: "The delinquents will be deprived of edibles and the colored rug on their wall for seven consecutive days for reasons of quietude disruption, illicit promenades with the inanimate child named Zosya, and complete disrespect to the glorious CMHG."

It's a good thing my mother was a resourceful lady with a constant urge to pickle everything edible to prepare ourselves for the occasionally reoccurring famine. We had enough pickled supplies to get us by stored in one of Pa's briefcases marked as "Zakvas" somewhere deep inside our kitchen floor. That's how I survived the first State-related misconduct in my life. It was difficult to eat pickled items exclusively for seven days, but we managed. On the other hand, not having the most visually entertaining item in the house with patterns and colors was quite intolerable.

"*Spasibo,* Victor. It's more than enough. I don't need any more iodine," Ma hissed irritably through her new chattering teeth as soon as the loudspeaker finished announcing the verdict. "Where is our *dochka*?"

After crawling around Dom for a while, Pa concluded: "You may have thrown her into *Biblioteka*."

They unlocked the wall and found me bent like a question mark on top of a pile of books, ogling thousands of fascinating objects and tunnels. Pa, motionless and decrepit, though victorious, with a guilty look on his face, watched my mother strangling me with her hugs. Her new teeth made a strange clicking noise. Slowly, our worried hearts reached an acceptably healthy pace and our jumpiness dissolved, and she let Pa join us.

We embraced for the rest of the day, quietly drinking cups of hot water, staring at the empty spot where our colorful oriental rug used to hang. Even though I always secretly thought oriental rugs were a bit grotesque, I never refused to scrutinize the rug's busy complexity in my parents' company. My eyes entered the sown labyrinths so meticulously that the rug's pattern with its specks often transformed itself into groups of sad elephant tortoises swimming in an inky river, a crowd of absurd human faces with animal features, or, in moments of acute hunger, one of Ma's soups. I suppose it was the severe boredom, the lack of color and playmates, that boosted my imagination to an otherworldly degree.

I broke the silence hours later, around bedtime, after Ma finished playing a new symphony on her ancient, out-of-tune fortepiano behind one of our walls. "*Mamulya*, what was it? Are you going to tell me?"

Ma lowered her eyes despondently, sighing for a whole minute. Then she took me back to the windowsill.

"Open it," said she, pointing at the torn black curtain.

Through the window, I saw the same monstrous construction in the heart of LIM. Ticking.

Despite being just as intimidating and hideous as it had been to me the first time, the creation gave off a strangely soothing glow with a sickening scent of infallible protection, similar to antiseptic liquids found in hospitals. With every new announcement the citadel issued to the masses through its hexagonal loudspeaker, causing a tremendous din, a furtive whiff of frigid air broke free from its dank hermitage and spread itself like fungal spores in every squatty corner of LIM's sickening compounds. The sight of the citadel, strapped in a bright red velveteen mantle like royalty, displaying LIM's mascot of crisscrossed plunger and stapler, made Ma's heart race like a wild moose. She covered my eyes with her hand and whispered in my ear, "Enough for today."

After a long motionless pause, she added in a different tone, "Ward. They call it Ward."

CHAPTER III

LIM. DOM.

Before I proceed with any further narrative about my extremely secretive family history, let me share a few more memories with you about where I grew up. For some inexplicable reason, it was always impossible to tell what time of day it was in LIM, my endlessly large home country, since everything there looked the same every day, afternoon, evening, and night. The same could be said about the local weather, since the never-ending dreadful winter, which we referred to as *zima*, was the only season there.

To make the unfortunate environmental sameness—along with people's daily confusion caused by it—harmless to the production cycle and overall workflow, LIM issued plainly made mechanical pocket watches with mini-calendars glued to their backs. We called them *operativnye chasy*—operational watches. Everyone had to carry them in small square pockets sewn next to their hearts, to avoid causing all sorts of collective dysfunction or untimely delays of the scheduled rituals. Forgetting to keep operativnye chasy in your chest pocket, or coming more than forty-five seconds late, was penalized as an inexcusable violation that led to sixty extra consecutive days of harsh physical labor.

The State was primarily occupied by supremely thin, anemic, mathematically gifted citizens referred to as *LIMers*. Their flawless white complexions, tightly stapled mouths, identical mustard coats (or gray for special workers) that resembled kitchen rags, valenki-kaloshis, and furry hats shaped like disheveled poodle heads—all were the required attributes of the locally established human normalcy. The explanation for why LIMers had their mouths stapled most of the time was a simple one: most commonly, nobody needed to speak to anyone back then, or rather, everything was arranged in a perfectly quiet manner, eliminating a need for the unnecessary transaction of confusing words and alert suspicions. Hardly audible whispers were utilized only in moments of unmanageable situational confusion, out of acute necessity for verbal communication.

Despite being the biggest piece of land in the world, marked as a single State that offered an abundance of work, free *kommunalka* spaces, and pocket watches, LIM's population was catastrophically low. This demographic disaster was most likely caused by the fact that the deathly low temperatures and constant food scarcity had a negative effect on people's courting behavior. Hungry locals refused to dally and take their clothes off before each other (!), like is done in many parts of the world as a flirtatious form of human behavior that leads to mating.

Since zima and the constant absence of natural light never promised to ameliorate and imposed a risk of complete human extinction, the State had to invent a special "survival" potion called *Wardwater*. Many believed it was made out of moonlight, as belligerent as the Moon's face, largely because of its pungent flavor. The liquid was distributed from the same factory everything was distributed from: the Gastro Chambers of Distribution, or GCD for short.

Besides Wardwater, every consumable product in LIM contained a variety of soothing valerian drop elements that kept everyone reasonably content, modest, and composed at all times. Wardwater had to be consumed by the population daily, thanks to its undeniable ability to add extra body heat, loosen stapled lips before bedtime, and grant people a half-hour period of delusional merriness turning into a six-hour dreamless night's sleep. LIM's hexagonal loudspeaker was programmed to announce the exact times of day when citizens measured out and drank the assigned amount of Wardwater. Such an irrational drinking ritual was traditionally followed by horrific, high-pitched celebratory seallike squalling (vaguely similar to our noisy doors) as a form of respectful cheering. Some citizens abused the potion behind the State's back, which led to the inevitable brain malfunction or, in some of the most extreme cases, fatality.

Whenever too few individuals were left in the State, LIM-Leaders would resort to adding a few additional "courting elements" to the Wardwater and sustenance that inevitably inspired males to flirt with females quite aggressively (rarely the opposite). The fabricated courting behavior resulted in a four-hour-long flow of confidence and a burning desire to play chess with the opposite sex, eat potatoes together, and sign a special communal agreement (the way marriages worked back then) instead of going to work. (Rest assured, the State agreed that skipping workdays for those crucial occasions was imperative.)

Then, finally, after about twenty-five days of reading, stamping, and signing 349 papers of the *BRAK*-agreement that nobody was ever allowed to break, the specially selected men and women received official permission to take their clothes off and touch each other in ways to save LIM from being entirely deserted. Just like it is done in many places in the world! There was no question about allowing men to court, eat potatoes with, or play chess with other men, if you know what I mean. There was absolutely no chance of women doing the same with other women. Nyet. Nyet. Nyet! Besides feeling more peaceful and, at times, supremely erotic, indulging in the bloodcurdling potion helped everybody forget their unfortunate doubts about being the luckiest people alive.

All of the notably extreme LIM governance decisions were made by a group of chubby, schnitzel-fingered rulers known as LIM-Leaders. They couldn't be mistaken for anybody else, because they were the only individuals found locally who happened to be overweight and dressed in wide-boned animal skins, on top of their snowflake-embroidered crimson uniforms, for warmth. Even though their words created unified control, the fat rulers, for some strange reason, never showed the slightest inclination to speak with articulatory agility. Instead, they barked like angry dogs on most occasions.

To justify their obviously inappropriate size, vocal habits, and appetite, they let the public know that their need to eat so much was a courteous act, performed for obtaining enough physical strength and influence to take the best kind of care of the scarce human population and the abundant and commonly hard-to-manage *mishka* migration. (In case you need to know: yes, there were far more bears walking the streets of LIM than human beings.) As you can perhaps tell by now, LIM-Leaders were solid believers in reaching a state of complete equality and identity between the citizens, along with integrating the immaculate control of every action, ritual, spoken word, dish, shoe, and thought. I have always had a creeping suspicion they hoped we would all turn into obedient *nyevalyashkas*—roly-polies—one day.

Amid all of that nonsense, there was our *Dom*, the old communal apartment I grew up in. I wholeheartedly believe that there is a certain value in breaking down the contents and consistency of Dom's cloddish carcass to you, since its images and details carry the most powerful ability to paint an odd representation of those solitary, investigative days of my early life and where it all began.

I cherish all the significant and insignificant memories of Dom and can access them clearly even in my adulthood, perhaps because I studied every surface and corner of it with the same kind of propinquity I dedicated to Ma and Pa's beloved oriental rug and the harmonious smells in the kitchen: old paper, dill, freshly boiled liquid glue, fried potatoes, and *hoz mylo*.

Even my mother's notes left in her impeccably elegant handwriting in our family photo album confirmed that from an early age, I was eager to observe and study everything in Dom "with the same precision and accuracy a pathological anatomist would use to study a corpse." Ma had a unique way of classifying people's traits, you see. A pathological anatomist, of all things! Perhaps she knew a few things about pathological anatomists thanks to her grandparents. Both of them studied and cut corpses open, if requested by the State, for about half a century.

Dom was a seemingly unimaginative, oddly built dwelling, one of three kommunalka units originally shared among two other families. Sadly, none of them survived Dom's unfavorable conditions: numbingly cold floors, occasional cockroach invasions and phlegmatic biting spider occurrences, rusty tubs, curvy yellow delineations on the ceilings, rarely available brown tap water, and excruciatingly squeaky doors that talked, whined, barked, snored, meowed, hooted, and even grunted on certain days.

The constantly spying ears attached to some of the walls didn't make people's life any easier. They were present not only in our Dom but also in every human-occupied place in the State. Their membranes had been invented to gather information and send it directly to those who needed it to keep the State under control.

Despite all the inconveniences, discrepancies, and catastrophic failures, nothing has ever held a more special place in my heart than Dom, for which I must thank both of my remarkably intelligent, fastidious, and, at times, paranoid parents and their unique interpretation of our surroundings.

Both my parents were avid admirers of poetry, illicit fiction, allegories, metaphysics, typewriters, visual oddities, and holding one's breath as a form of interpersonal competition and flirtation. Also, as you already know, they had a deep affinity for oriental rugs. They wore ugly "controlling" LIM-wigs every single day, due to their unmanageable weather vane–like hair that had an expressive tendency to reshape itself about ten times per hour—not by the wind, but by the conflicts within their thoughts. They were writers in disguise, and the things they avidly admired made their lives a living nightmare. You will know why very, very soon.

No matter how involved my parents wanted to be with many extraordinary things, they had no choice but to remain believably decent, hardworking citizens. Obliged to depart every morning to serve LIM till late evening, they left me in the annoying company of two creepy nyevalyashkas named Rosa and Fialka six days a week. But when the main door would squeak "ee-eek" around the same time every day, informing me of their return, I could easily forget about the stupid toys and everything else unfavorable in the world and jump on Pa's neck to shower him and Ma with hundreds of affectionate kisses. Then I would help them go through the aching daily routine of unstapling their mouths. The act of removing the little metallic fences from their lips allowed them to smile so big that they made the kerosene lamps and leftover candles around Dom glow like little constellations.

There was always a lively dialogue between my parents and me. We could speak to one another for hours behind those imperfect walls while sharing horrific-looking edibles at our handmade square table (Pa built it from a piece of the broken airplane he recently found in the snow). Papa loved to challenge me with riddles and explanations of the meaning behind every object, event, and action. Mama helped me learn to appreciate theatricality and music. She and I could hum hundreds of symphonies accompanied by the moaning of her piano, the sounds of which were akin to those of an old locomotive. She adored engaging me in performances with scripted roles and a fair amount of clumsily choreographed feints, deaths, flights, and fights in costumes constructed from old worn undershirts. To make our shows even more believable, Pa decorated them with papier-mâché-and-old-socks forests, mermaids, sea creatures, and tinfoil masks.

My most beloved times were when Mama and Papa took turns reading *skazki* to me before bedtime, beautifully handwritten fairy tales that lived inside an ancient-looking brittle book. These stories were about different planets, flying homes, little children traveling to magical kingdoms on the backs of geese, talking fish, bears, and other curiosities. I knew it was the reading hour whenever one of my parents would ritualistically shut the door of my bedroom and thoroughly cover all the holes and crevices in it. The main safety rule in Dom was for one of them to stand outside my room and hypnotize the spying ears. For some unknown reason, they were especially sensitive to the sound of my parents' voices reading aloud.

I will never forget listening to the radiant symphony played by Ma's soft fingers, intricately flipping pages, gracefully sliding down the letters of long sentences with her index finger, and her versatile, multitoned act of reading, as light and ancient as the sound of hundreds of feathered nomads gliding in the clear peaceful sky. I will never forget Pa's strong hand holding the book like a weightless goblet filled with wizardry. Thousands of different pitches, exclamations, and streams of lively "ahs" that Pa read to me seemed to dilute our glum reality to no end. No starvation punishments, negative announcements, draconian regulations, forever-dreadful zima, dirty snow, or rabid stray dogs always waiting patiently outside (enticed to bite more passersby after tasting their first spurts of blood) could compete with the excitement reading was giving him. Sometimes, just watching my parents' faces was even more exciting than listening to the stories. It would be fair to say that my mother and father were great characters whose features, mannerisms, and looks could easily compete with the ones described in the book. They were my wizards.

I remember my mama as a quick, elegant, rebellious dama full of arcane sensibilities. Half of her being was similar to the ladies you see in medieval paintings—by all means encompassing something dramatic, snobbish, and timeless. Her long, thin neck, tiny ears, and round face with rosy cheeks (she had to bleach every day before going to work) were a serious work of art on their own, and they had the ability to provoke instant infatuation and respect among people with hearts of all levels of softness. My mom's always slightly fatigued hazel eyes were decorated with golden specks that framed the pupils like unpredictable streams of hurling sulfur. She was as tall and thin as a fishing rod. She loved Papa and me more than pickles, her old incurably-out-of-tune fortepiano, aromas, shadows, kitten embroidery, and drama—her absolute favorite.

Papa was a shorter, slower, and simpler person with fewer portrait-worthy qualities than his spouse. His impeccably clear, wide, owl-like eyes that had turned from gray to mossy green in the first few years of loving Ma, extremely mobile brows, and eager attitude made him look like a mischievous child. Papa was a fantastic secret keeper, a logical speaker, and by far a much sweeter, more patient parent than Ma. I remember him as a warm, harmlessly eccentric man with a pair of huge crafty hands gifted with all kinds of construction abilities. I believe he had every tool known to mankind in his secret briefcase stash. He loved Mama and me more than sauerkraut, saxophones, building everything, colors, whirligigs, and fables—his absolute favorite.

My appearance was largely a combination of my parents': my wide cheekbones and prim nose were my mother's, my round green eyes and parsley-looking curls were my father's, and my wide head that somehow looked bigger than the rest of my angular body, chicken legs, and pointy knees—they were all someone else's. I toppled over inconveniently at times.

If you walked past my parents standing next to our ambivalent compatriots at the main factory building of LIM, you would notice a number of drastic differences in the way they looked and carried themselves. There was something radioactive in their quiet disagreement with those around them.

I grew up to become the same.

CHAPTER IV

FAMILY ARCHIVES

SINCE THE DAY I LOST MY SLIPPER on the streets of LIM, life in Dom seemed to become continually harder. Everybody was onto Ma and Pa. We convened significantly fewer drama performances or reading hours in order to remain quiet, though Ma and Pa's occasional tin-can-phoneless melodramatic fights caused even more penalties and starvation punishments. Somehow, they disagreed with each other a lot those days. During this period, I mastered camouflaging my existence behind one of Dom's walls with impressive efficiency.

Soon enough, I outgrew the height of the only windowsill in Dom by a couple of inches. The tick-tock-tuck had grown three times louder in my head since the day I'd heard it for the first time—especially when I was alone. Dom's doors worsened, and their barking and hooting (the noises had become morbidly sinister) didn't make anything any better either. In short, everything around seemed to drip the worst kind of anxiety.

"Settle down! You have gone too far with your strategies, Victor!" I heard Ma scream one day in the hallway.

"'Poltroons don't get to drink champagne!' You used to say it yourself, didn't you?" was Pa's childish defense.

"Don't be silly, Victor. I liked to say that when I was an irresponsible teenager, to make everyone angry. Besides, they banned champagne thirty years ago!"

"Naturally . . . you were quite good at making everyone angry," said Pa in a cheeky tone.

"You are making me angry right now!" yelled Mama.

Tick-tock-tuck.

"Keep your voice low, Sveta. You don't want them to hear you again," said Papa.

Tick-tock-tuck.

"I know, I know," she whispered very, very quietly through her tightly shut teeth. "Unlike you, I remember that we have a child. Unlike you, I am trying to take every precaution there is. I would rather serve the State and keep everything sub rosa than put my dochka through the hell we have suffered."

Tick-tock-tuck.

"You don't want to serve the State, Svetlana! What nonsense!" yelled Papa. His cheeks turned bright red, and his eyes lit themselves with fluorescent fury. He looked angrier than I had ever seen him.

Tick-tock-tuck.

The LIM siren went off. Earthquake. Screaming. Whistling.

Tick-tock-tuck-tick-tock-tuck.

Sheer chaos. "Chvyak-chvyak-chvyak"—the same heavy footsteps entered the building.

"You are right, Victor . . . I am just so fatigued and lost," said Ma, completely ignoring the sound of the siren and its resultant mayhem.

"Can you tell me one thing? You don't intend to keep your only child behind these walls for the rest of your life, do you?" whispered Pa, also disregarding the obnoxious noises caused by multiple Wardworkers running upstairs.

Tick-tock-tuck-tick-tock-tuck.

"I suppose I only would if there were absolutely no other option," answered Ma after a short pause with a sad smile on her face.

"It's time to change things," Papa said decisively with an atypical hint of virile pride.

Tick-tock-tuck-tick-tock-tuck.

"Perhaps I am not as brave as I used to be," said Ma as she absent-mindedly proceeded to wax the threshold of Dom to make the mob of Wardworkers slip and fall, like they always did in different areas of Dom. Leaving traps for Wardworkers and finding various ways to injure them without planning anything ahead was my parents' specialty, the kind of telepathic collusion people achieve only after years of knowing each other.

"Please don't spit in anyone's face this time, Svetochka," whispered Papa. "I don't have any extra faux teeth left for you."

Tick-tock-tuck-tick-tock-tuck.

Mama displayed one last artificial smile and handed him a stapler. They stapled each other's lips. I swear the act almost came across as something deeply romantic.

Tick-tock-tuck-tick-tock-tuck.

Wardworkers stormed back into Dom with an earth-shattering "Boo-boom!" Half of them ended up lying on top of each other with Mama's malicious wax smeared all over their uniforms. Aggravated and purple, the Wardworker-General performed the same humiliating "punishment procedures" with the same weary mosquito-elephant vacuums.

I locked my wall and prepared myself to be as quiet as a well-trained vodolaz. It would be a lie to say I wasn't frightened of them anymore, but as you know, when you do something frightening more than ten times in a row, it becomes predictable. And predictability, in some ways, inspires a feeling of false security.

Six months later, when I became a few inches taller than the only tea table in Dom—when I believe I was about six—my parents finally stopped fighting. I was happy to see how they picked up their dusty tin can telephones again and verbally exchanged all their concerns and unruly thoughts with melodious passion instead of explicit yelling. They also made it a habit to write down the most private information on pieces of paper and put them in the "box of complaints and potential solutions," behind the squeaky eighty-five-year-old *komod*—a clunky chest of drawers. In their late-night suppressed conversations, I made out the word "escape" blown through the plastic phone cords more often than other words. Eventually, it occurred to me that Ma had, after all, agreed with Pa's strategies. I knew what the words "escape" and "strategy" meant, though I wasn't aware yet of the fact that there were other places in the world people could strategically escape to.

The next day, at breakfast, which consisted of undercooked buckwheat and potatoes (the stove gave up after ten minutes of Ma's huffing and puffing), Pa's eyebrows were moving so nonsensically that Ma and I had to look away.

"Okay, Papa, what is going on?" I finally asked through our reactivated tin can telephone.

Ma gave Pa a brief clandestine look.

"I think the sooner we do it, the better," he uttered.

"Certainly," Mama answered in an indecisive voice after stirring her teaspoon in an empty tin mug for a whole minute, "but we are going to be late to the factory if we don't leave in seven minutes. Seven minutes is clearly not enough, Victor."

"Oh! Time flies when I am in your company, ladies," muttered Pa, hurriedly wiping his mouth.

He kissed me on the forehead and, rubbing his hands like someone with a piece of conspiracy waiting to sprint of the tip of his tongue, he said: "All right then. Tonight will be a very special night, you'll see. Just wait for it."

I didn't move a finger or touch my half-eaten breakfast for as long as Mama and Papa were gone, daydreaming at the kitchen table about what could possibly be so special about my night to come.

"Khoo-oooot," reluctantly hooted the wall-door of Biblioteka. I woke up with my cheek resting uncomfortably in a tin bowl of cool buckwheat. Mama's fortepiano was being awoken too by someone who had clearly never used one before. Various items were falling behind the walls in the

Gosti room—our guest room. The floor wiggled as if from an earthquake, making the spying ears listen to everything in the room more carefully. I hoped it wasn't the crazy black cat coming back to jump at me again.

"Cats don't play fortepianos like that," I reassured myself and immediately felt much braver. The instant my symphonic humming returned the ears on the walls to their nonthreatening dormant state, I unlocked Biblioteka with my mom's bobby pin.

A contagious, jubilant laughter came from behind the old clock in the far corner.

"Hey, whoever you are, you need to stop this, because they are going to hear you," I politely addressed to the clock.

The laughter disappeared. I looked everywhere, but I found nothing except little dirt marks left all over the floor—someone's handprints that were slightly bigger than mine. They led nowhere. The last bit of them was in front of the clock, as if the person who had left the messy chunks of dirt had disappeared in that particular spot. Whoever it was, my nose detected that he or she had left a light floral smell in the room. I couldn't trust my nasal judgment entirely though, since the only time I had actually smelled real flowers before was when Ma accidentally found a bunch of lilies in one of our tunnels. It was hard to walk away from the heavenly scent bursting with cheer and playful flightiness.

The door on the other side of the wall bark-squeaked like a middle-aged half dog, half seagull. Mama and Papa walked into Dom, and I hurriedly covered the dirt marks with some books and tiptoed into my room. Ma's gentle humming elegantly entered the space. Pa was beaming behind her back with proudly flared nostrils and a freshly lit candle. I have never seen Pa's eyebrows raising themselves any higher on his forehead in those spasmodic leaps.

"This day has come," he said. "From now on, you will have far better companions than Rosa and Fialka. I believe you are too big to play with them anyway."

Ma floundered, not knowing what to say. She picked up Rosa and Fialka and gave them an empty look.

"Let's eat dinner first," she whispered and threw the toys into a dusty chest full of clothes twice her age.

I helped her chop some cabbage while Papa cursed into his tin can telephone and dramatically threw his arms up over the stubborn stove's poor performance. It broke in less than two minutes.

"*Mooduck!*" He barked the insult into his tin can.

We sat at our wiggly table and silently ate the pathetic amount of half-cooked *tushenka*, the fried cabbage my father was especially fond of. Papa thoroughly scraped off the old pot that could easily be mistaken for a rusted bathtub.

"Before we do this, you must promise me you won't dig through any of the tunnels," said Mama.

I didn't know what she meant, though the urgency in her voice told me to give her my most angelic nod.

"It's a pact then," said Pa in a tone far more serious than normal. He didn't even bother shaking hands with me, which seemed inexcusable in that awfully humorless moment.

"Too bad we don't have any copies of *SLFFGR* left for her," whispered Ma to Pa conspiratorially.

"Are you sure all the copies have been burned?" asked Papa.

"Yes . . . I am sure of it . . . of course I am sure of it," Ma muttered. "You think all this would be happening if—"

"Okay, okay, Sveta. I am sorry for asking again," apologized Pa.

Mama unlocked the wall with her bobby pin, just like I had earlier. She was sighing more than usual.

"Uuu-aaa-eee," quacked the wall-door as if telling us how jaded it was from being constantly moved around.

"Welcome to our family Biblioteka," said Papa.

"It's so very momentous," whispered Mama, suppressing a dreamy smile.

It was the first time I had officially been allowed to walk into that freezing-cold, dark place behind the thickest wall of Dom that contained more secrets than I could ever imagine. That chamber of literary secrets that protected my parents' minds from the dangerously comforting totalitarian trance whose roots grew deeper and deeper inside its frozen ground and human consciousness.

The origin and history of Biblioteka will perhaps come across as scandalous. As improbable as this may seem, not everyone in LIM followed rules or was affected by the regime that subjugated the majority of people. It began with Mama, who, earlier in life, was educated to secretly ignore the State's rules by her parents, my *babushka* and *dedushka*, whom I never got to meet in person. The poor things had been removed from LIM for the time being a long time ago, due to starting an absolutely unthinkable underground literary exchange among a slowly expanding group of like-minded individuals who not only wrote freely, without constraining their honest opinions, but also invented ways to attain other books from outside of the State through the tunnels behind the walls of Dom and their own residences. They had the audacity to build and maintain an unlawful channel of forbidden literature, censured by LIM-Leaders. The kind of literature the State conceptualized as temerarious and obligatory to burn.

(If the uncovered books were of any potential value due to their ancient nature, though not conceptually appropriate for the population, they were generally sent to the thickest, coldest woods, to a deep cave protected by the leviathan iron door with hundreds of locks on it. The cave was patrolled by rarely awakened melancholic old mishkas and scrawny wolves affected by some anonymous medical condition.)

I have no idea how Babushka and Dedushka carried themselves, nor do I know what they liked to eat, though seeing their portrait hanging in the middle of Biblioteka gave me an idea that they must have been wise people who carried an invisible laughter in their warm, all-questioning, adventure-seeking eyes. Their unruly hair, unconcealed in the portrait by the ugly State-issued wigs, was as wild as Mama and Papa's. The many colors their ceremonial attire consisted of made them appear extremely foreign.

"Incarcerated for multiple acts of rebellious nature, disrupting the overall mental order of society members, and a lack of conformity," were the words written in their expired identification forms below the portrait.

The day Babushka and Dedushka were removed from society, LIM-Leaders were informed of their illegal meeting by Ivan Ivanovich, an exemplary citizen, one of the most inquisitive neighbors in the building, with terrible eyesight and a fantastically giant pair of spying ears on the walls of the kommunalka he used to share with his paralyzed-from-cold-and-constant-emotional-distress mother. He eavesdropped on his queer neighbors' discussions through a hardly noticeable hole in the wall the spying ears had once pushed him toward. The hole separated two apartments, made by some morbidly starved rodent (rat, most likely, the looks of which could easily be mistaken for Ivan Ivanovich's). A whole army of Wardworkers stormed into Babushka and Dedushka's Dom, where they found two accompanied by a large group of oddly dressed people, all typing their fictional and nonfictional narratives on unnaturally quiet typewriters.

Every single one of them was arrested, tortured, and eventually expatriated to an unknown part of the world, where not a single human had a chance of survival. Ivan Ivanovich was awarded two extra-large tin buckets for taking more convenient baths, two consecutive days of extra potato supplies, and a leading-edge fur hat. Three days later, he was found dead, happily holding on to his buckets filled with frozen water he had boiled with a decaying water-heater stick, hoping to take a superior bath after eating potato soup at the end of the day. The fact that Ivan Ivanovich had accidentally tossed rat poison into his potato soup became apparent as soon as Wardworkers searched his Dom.

What neither the LIM-Leaders nor Ivan Ivanovich had known was that Babushka and Dedushka had hidden plenty of books behind our walls: improperly emotional memoirs, autobiographies of other LIMers, books about logical equations, novels, poetry, and more, all camouflaged and untouched for many years until they were rediscovered by Pa, who signed the BRAK-agreement with Ma and came to live with her in Babushka and Dedushka's empty kommunalka space. There, in the strange hollow space behind the Gosti room wall, Pa found the immensely valuable literary treasures he would have never had the slightest inkling about if he hadn't met Ma.

Thanks to all sorts of worldly jewels and rich fictional expressions living in Dom within the books, Pa reinvented a new bastion based on Dedushka's former knowledge of architecture and Babushka's whimsical nature that had woven the old Dom's structure into an exclusive kaleidoscope, an assembly of carefully pieced rooms filled with literary magic, built in an uncommonly convertible way that was unfathomable to anyone with basic knowledge of standard construction. The special rooms could transform from LIM-issued grayish bare squares with two tin chairs, one rough bed, two soup bowls, two cups, and two spoons into brightly lit secret chambers, divided by tall ruffled curtains, hung in the air on threads as thin as spiderwebs and serving as protective shields to myriads of stories behind them.

"Watch your step," said Papa in his full voice as soon as we closed the wall, "and avoid touching the books in the corners. They are full of spiderwebs."

Ma seated me comfortably at the table, in the middle of Biblioteka. Pa's crooked candle projected amber flickers onto a pitifully thin book cover entitled *Bukvar*.

"I am sorry we don't have a better-looking book for you to learn to read from," said Pa with one of his brows performing tango.

The book he put in front of me was filled with a battalion of shapely little creatures inside rough stained pages. They were running amok, occasionally giving me nonchalant glances.

"*Privet*," I said in a polite greeting.

They blinked at me with a thin laughter and immediately scattered in ten different directions, stumbling and colliding into hopelessly discernible blobs I thought I would never be able to comprehend.

CHAPTER V

THE ALPHABET

FROM THAT DAY ON, AROUND THE SAME TIME in the evenings—which could naturally be mistaken for mornings—the bright light generated by Ma and Pa's return from work and their thousand-times-remolded crooked candle brought us back to Biblioteka.

"Your turn, little one," said Papa, offering me the old *Bukvar* after showing me how to read the Cyrillic alphabet one more time.

The smell of the book's dusty pages was so intimidating. I couldn't say I was especially thrilled about the whole process.

I wonder why anyone needs to know how to do this, I thought to myself. *Why can't they just continue reading to me like they always have?*

"C'mon now," Papa encouraged me.

I slowly reopened the book and continued learning to guess the letters.

Papa was ecstatic watching me squint at the old pages with my index finger glued to the same line of letters for much longer than needed. Mama's feelings were apparently as mixed as the piles of books in Biblioteka—her face showed the widest range of emotions I had ever seen.

There was pride, nervousness, curiosity, and a hint of mischievousness in her lukewarm and skeptical eyes. Every once in a while, her forehead looked way too tense for the calmness she was trying to display whenever I looked at her for feedback.

"I will go boil some water," said Mama when her operativnye chasy showed eight o'clock.

"We will keep working on some more reading here," said Papa, pulling his chair closer to me.

"What's wrong?" he asked me as soon as Mama had exited Biblioteka.

"Nothing," I lied. I didn't want to upset my father by telling him that reading seemed boring to me.

"Look," said Papa, rubbing his temples hard, his eyebrows looking like a supremely crooked hypotenuse, "are you ready to hear the biggest secret there is?"

"Of course!" I exclaimed, dropping *Bukvar* on the ground.

"These books will give you special powers . . . let's just leave it at that," said Papa very, very seriously.

The next few days, reading continued to be just as difficult. The more I chased letters with my eyes, the more chaotically they ran around the pages, as if escaping a tiny island during a fatal storm. They didn't like me any better by the end of the first week, though somehow their skepticism had switched to giddiness.

"Papochka, why are they such brats?" I asked Papa before he kissed me goodnight.

"Who is a brat? And who taught you this word?"

"The letters are brats! They don't want to be comrades with me."

He sat by my bed a while longer, tapping his fingers on my pillow, lost in a tremendously deep thought, until a kind smile lit up his face. His eyebrows, acting like a pair of tightrope walkers, balanced each other into a perfect line.

"They only misbehave because they don't know you well yet, Malenkaya. And you do not know them well either."

"Not too well," I agreed.

"When I was little, my mama drew words that began with the letters I couldn't remember," he said. "We should draw!"

Instead of going to sleep that night, we spent many hours drawing a crooked series of tentative squiggles that represented each letter I had failed to memorize earlier. I wanted special powers to come to me very much, despite the fact that I wasn't sure what they were going to be.

Little by little, the letters welcomed me to their sophisticated realm, where they stood straight and tall in those yellowish iodine-smelling pages, showing me their nobility and wholesomeness. Some were still snobbish and inscrutable, but all in all, I made my acquaintance with them.

These were our first alphabetic drawings, not to mention a whole lot of other mnemonic identities I registered for each letter, strictly for my own understanding.

A: Pa's compass.

B: The glorious queen bee from one of Pa's stories.

C: Ma's earring.

D: Pa's belly after dinner. Sometimes mine.

E: A pigeon's foot.

F: Ma saying, "Stop it!"

G: A snake chasing its own tail.

H: Ma and Pa dancing slowly.

I: Me, acting like a fishing rod (one of my family nicknames).

J: A shrimp; Pa's nose.

K: My very own pair of big scissors.

L: Valenki.

M: Two pelicans kissing.

N: A big flat worm zigzagging.

O: My face.

P: A saxophone.

Q: Pa showing his long tongue.

R: Ma's threaded needle.

S: Ma's cabbage turnover.

T: A great big bird in flight.

U: A pair of big horns.

V: A roof, but upside down.

W: Two thin mountains, but upside down.

X: A sand clock; a bow tie; a handstand.

Y: A funny cup on a stem.

Z: The sad duck, Zizzy, a fictional character from one of Papa's stories.

The new bond I forged with the letters led my thoroughly collected physical and sensory images to a wonderful materialization and completeness. Not overnight, of course. It took some time. In a few months, I became enchanted by how the letters could design whole words and spectacular stories. Despite my mother's fear and skepticism, thanks to my father's efforts, I became an avid reader and—later in life—a writer too, happily devouring and making up one story after another built in confluent, uncanny streams of words. Even though my parents told me not to read anything besides what they had offered me and demanded that I stayed away from Biblioteka without their supervision, I couldn't help myself.

"See you soon, Malenkaya!" they always said before leaving Dom.

As soon as I heard the main door singing "e-e-e-k" to remind me of the ten or more hours of complete solitude ahead of me, I went straight to the beautifully spooky Biblioteka (I always thought of it as a glorious dungeon inside a magical castle, smelling of vanilla-like benzoin, dry mushrooms, and birch brooms) to see what else there was for me. Who wouldn't? At that stage of my early life, breaking rules, making secret pacts, eating borscht, and reading skazki were my absolute favorite things.

Looking back, it's easy to see that I was a very lonely, hungry girl who spent hundreds of hours of her childhood devouring the fantastic and prosaic contents of thousands of hand-copied stories. The more pages I read, the less reality or my constant hunger mattered, and the more my hair was beginning to turn into curious weather vane constructions, not exactly the same as Mama's and Papa's. Mine were being shaped into greater varieties of items at a slightly faster pace. Was it because my mind constantly generated questions that I was never allowed to ask? Or was it because it didn't know what to do with all the newly blossomed thoughts I had to live with but couldn't spit out to someone? Both, I would say. On the only two special occasions—my birthday and *Novyi God*, the only largely celebrated holiday in LIM—Ma had to put bricks on my head to calm the wild shapes my hair was entwining into.

"How I hope you learn to manage those ideas of yours when you grow up. Harmlessly," said Mama, pressing a heavy-duty brick against my head.

"She will," argued Papa instantly.

Of course, I had no clue what my parents were arguing about. Unfortunately, they had gone back to arguing about a lot of things again. I just continued reading everything I could lay my finger on, continuously feeding the inner volcano of the first saplings of my literary thoughts.

The only section I stayed away from for the longest time was near the old squeaky clock in the far corner of Biblioteka, next to Babushka and Dedushka's portrait, buried in a ridiculous amount of soil, feathers, and soot. "Cave ab homine unius libri"[3] were the letters feverishly engraved into the right corner of their portrait.

Even though the intimidating furry pile made me think that the words written in its pages were unlikely to be of a delightful nature, one day I moved some of the folders and sheets surrounding the dust towers with my foot to see if there was anything worthy there for me to read. The two fluffy, evil-eyed spiders on top of the first gray pile convinced me to come back another time. But when I turned around, I slipped on a gorgeous red book with an image of a plunger and stapler printed on every page that made me sneeze about three hundred times for about three hours. Don't worry—I did it very, very quietly.

My achoos blew the dust off most of the books and sheets, revealing disorderly lines of thinly scripted notes printed on a regular typewriter with a few missing consonants. *LIM Konstitutsia* read the title of the

3 A Latin phrase meaning "Fear the man of one book." Some books in Biblioteka were written in Latin. Latin phrases were also used in some fictional books as magical spells to fight the evil.

book. The notes I was reading described all the torture people of different ages were sentenced to in LIM. My mother's name was on the list of the youngest rule-breakers of the State. The more I read into it, the more fear took over. Ticking and tocking were rapidly entering my mind. Panic attack.

Tick-tock-tuck.

The nearly melted candle flickered as Ma and Pa nervously entered the room. The wall chuckled in its grumpy voice that for some reason had recently changed to something like "keeck-keeck."

"Aaaah!" exhaled Mama before she fainted into Papa's arms.

He stood there in a stupor, silently watching me as I flipped the last few pages of the crimson book in the gray misty corner where charcoal ashes were settling in my hair. The reflection in the old mirror hanging in front of me made me drop the red book—the white dust in my hair and on my face made me look exactly like Babushka in the painting above my head. The spiders scurried away as the remaining dust settled back into the same nooks and crannies of the space.

Papa sat on the ground, carefully placing his dama on a moth-bitten winter coat by his side. He stared at me for a few more minutes without saying anything.

"You know what? You are grounded," he said, breaking the silence. "Go to your room now. No, wait, let me wash your face first."

"But Papa, please don't be mad at me!" I tried to argue with him while he was scrubbing my cheeks with a kitchen rag.

"You may have some bad nightmares tonight," Pa said coldly. He tore the red book apart and set it on fire. "Great choice of literature, Alexandra Victorovna."

Let me assure you: it was the first time my father had ever addressed me by my full first name and patronymic.

"Don't feel sorry. You taught her a good lesson. She never listens to us! And . . . how on earth did that *chertova knizhka* end up in Biblioteka?" said Ma the next morning while attempting to boil a pot of water inside our miniature lab (Pa built it so tiny that we managed to keep it inside a briefcase), since the kitchen stove had at last passed away for good. Instead of talking to me about anything, she demonstratively flared her nostrils as wide as two puffy raisins, plopped lumps of chunky buckwheat into a hideous tin pot, and proceeded writing something to Papa's attention in their book of concerns and potential solutions. The runny pen fell out of her hand a few times while she persisted writing something of worrisome nature.

Ma left the kitchen without touching her meal. I could hear her cry. Before leaving the kitchen to comfort her, Pa leaned closer to me and whispered in a conspiratorial baritone through his worn-out tin can telephone: "Ma has every right to be worried. She doesn't want you to know about all the horrors of LIM."

"Papa, are there other children around here?" I interrupted.

"Oh . . . you read the chapter about that too, I see. Yes, there used to be quite a few of them in the building, but unfortunately, they have been sent away," he said.

"Are they being tortured?" I asked Papa.

"Yes. In a very manipulative way," he said.

"What is *manipulative*?" I inquired.

"Unfair and . . . rather confusing," said Papa.

"So . . . I am the only *devochka* in LIM who is not being tortured in an unfair and confusing way?"

"Yes, you are the only little girl. At least in our compound. I don't know about other ones."

I hung my head and sighed. "Can we help them?" was my next question.

"Oh dear . . . it's very, very complicated. But you know what? Everything is going to change soon. We found some help behind these walls. We have comrades on our side."

"Who are you talking about, Papa?"

"People like us. I will make sure to introduce you to them. You just wait for it!" said Pa with a flicker in his eye as he checked his operativnye chasy.

CHAPTER VI

GOSTI

THE NEXT DAY, MY PARENTS' COMRADES, also referred to as Gosti, arrived. Quite frankly, I had never seen a stranger group of adults in my life. They kept popping out of thin air from a variety of walls and tunnels in Biblioteka. Mama and Papa, dressed in their best checkered overcoats, beamed happily in the middle of it all.

To my surprise, there were dozens of book-affiliated delinquents in our building and several other buildings in the compound, who had secrets perhaps more dangerous than a giant snake (I fear snakes the most). Not only did Ma, Pa, and their comrades invent their own way of unstapling their lips, speak out loud to one another through tin can telephones, read prohibited literature, and write their rebellious prose in long, at times rude, sentences; they also found a way to evaporate the deceitfully soothing contents of Wardwater and other local essentials in Papa's little briefcase labs.

Every single one of them was a LIMer except for Morris, a foreign saxophonist who secretly came from afar to study LIM in all of its strangeness. Morris happened to be enamored with Malvina, an extraordinary young lady with blue hair (of course hidden under an ugly LIM-wig during the regular work hours), full lips, and always deliberately ruffled dresses. Malvina's former spouse, a ghostly, amorphous individual, had passed away from chronic depression a few months prior to her discovery of the secret tunnel in her kommunalka. Ever since she'd met my parents, Morris, and others, her droopy grin had turned into a beautiful smile. Malvina was best at writing romance and prose, the genres that had been banned at the LIM publishing house—also known as the LIMPH—for about a century.

I am sure you are well aware that feelings of infatuation make people commit all sorts of follies. The day Morris saw Malvina, his heart grew so big that he could no longer live happily without visiting LIM as much as he could manage, breaking every bit of law of the LIM border control. He would crawl miles and miles through the thin tunnels with his saxophone wrapped in thick protective cloths to be able to come to us and look at his beloved dama. I remember watching her beautiful eyes blinking at him with a hint of coquetry. Especially when Morris played his saxophone like some outlandish deity. That man of many unique tal-

ents never ceased to impress us with his ability to speak our native tongue with only a slight hint of a charming accent.

Unfortunately, the Gosti didn't have any children I could talk to about my own concerns in any of the known forms of communication or perform any literary exchanges with. Every single one of them had already sent their children away to LOB on their seventh birthdays. Age seven was the established length of childhood in LIM. After a few days of medical injections, eyesight inspections, and over one hundred specific questions designed for kids to make sure they had been properly raised and prepared, the State transferred them to the nearby town, LOB ("Lunar Obtainment"), separated from LIM with a giant soundproof cube. There, every child was expected to memorize, recite, and perform several millions of specially prepared texts and marches. If anyone disobeyed or performed at a lower capacity than requested, a sickly, elderly clown accompanied by a depressed roller-skating mishka was called to torture the delinquents with physically painful exercises, bloodcurdling singing of the local anthem, and long lectures dedicated to artistic insanity as a form of punishable protest.

Physical education played an extremely important role in LOB and had a thoroughly planned-out gender division: boys were trained to run very fast, hold their breath (for ice melting and national flood emergency cases), and hit and throw rocks and sticks at plastic figures of foreign men's torsos and featureless faces for protective reasons. Girls, on the other hand, were trained to hold their breath (for the same emergency cases) and become exceptional ballerinas through the most intense militaristic training you can imagine.

A number of Gosti, whom my parents considered their oldest comrades, were petrified to hear that I was kept away from going to LOB, regardless of the fact that my seventh birthday had passed. I often had to stop them from pinching my cheeks, kissing me on the face, and suffocating me with extremely tight, affectionate hugs. I was the only human around who was as short as a kitchen table, with cheeks as puffy as a couple of ripe peaches.

Even though it was hard to be in their company for long periods of time, I generally liked the Gosti very much, merely for who they were. They were special people with exotic names (which I later learned were pseudonyms), tall hairdos, and resplendent attire. Some of them had slick hair covered with broad hats that made their shadows look frightening and glorious. Their perfectly polished typewriters had both local and foreign letters engraved on them. A number of them spoke languages I couldn't understand. Their heads had a tendency to knock down many things, due to their large size, though they managed to walk relatively straight and harmless in their environment on most occasions.

Soon after meeting the Gosti, I learned the word *konfidentsialnyi*—confidential. I knew the word had something to do with conspiring against LIM, since every time I heard it in a sentence, it had something to do with the secrets kept away from everyone outside of Dom. I must admit: I found it slightly annoying that during the Gosti's weekly meetings, the word *konfidentsialnyi* was used in practically every sentence. It saddened me to be left out of the whole konfidentsialnyi act once again.

Who am I going to say konfidentsialnyi things to? I thought to myself as my weather vane hair twisted itself into a cactus-looking knot. *Will I have my own Gosti one day?*

Even though I had developed an agreeable personal connection with every Gost and mastered faultless pronunciation of some of their difficult faux names, I could never fully participate in the late-night confidential conversations held in Biblioteka, where lots of dangerous words were communicated. Through the thick wall that separated me from them, everything they said sounded like ethereal whispers. There were nights I couldn't sleep knowing that something of great importance was being discussed in Dom, right behind my back. I would tiptoe to the wall, press Ma's glass measuring cup against it, and listen very, very attentively. To uncover their riddles was my new biggest wish. A few times, besides hearing the word *konfidentsialnyi*, I made out other subjects—they had something to do with maps and curvy tunnels the group had to redraw.

Later that week, Ma and Pa welcomed a slouchy new Gost who arrived at their next meeting from a tunnel that had never been found before. I wasn't introduced to him right away, though I heard his voice through the same measuring cup, pleasantly repeating the same cadence the conversation was held in. The man introduced himself as Timofey. After a short-lived konfidentsialnaya discussion, my parents and their Gosti accepted the man to their ensemble with honor. Ma treated him to a nice bowl of cold borscht and a few minutes of heartfelt poetry. I closed my eyes and listened to her melodic voice rising and falling in the rhyming narrative of lyrical pirouettes. Suddenly, a chubby ball of fluff jumped out of nowhere, landed on top of me, and bounced off my chest into the far dark corner. The creature left four streaks of blood around my neck. I looked closer at it and recognized the same loony cat I had seen in Biblioteka before. The cat's yellow eyes were gleaming at me in the dim light of my room. Its tiny neck pendant's long cursive letters read: Boris Borisovich.

I stretched my arms to him and said: "Boris Borisovich, please don't be afraid. I love cats very much. You are the first real cat I have met in person. All other ones I only know from my mom's embroidery."

The cat grinned and stepped an inch forward, revealing an impressive, bow tie–shaped white spot on his chest. I carefully petted his rough unwashed head. The loud purring Boris Borisovich vibrated with gave me the confidence to lift him off the ground and squeeze him with affection, but it wasn't such a good decision after all. He scratched my face and victoriously jumped back on the floor, walking around me in alarmingly aggressive half circles as if preparing to eat me. The movements angulated by the animal's body were hypnotic—without knowing it, I ended up outside of my room, facing someone's pointy knees. That person was standing there all alone, seizing me like a hawk with his gray eyes as cold as LIM's air.

"Oh my, look who you've found! A child! When was the last time you saw a child, Boris Borisovich? Thank you kindly for your assistance," he whispered to the cat with a respectful nod and turned to me in a single smooth motion. "You can call me Timofey Grigorievich, child."

The man was nearly as tall as Dom's ceiling. I had to lift my head all the way up to look past his long skinny legs, dressed in a pair of fantastic yellow pants. His whole attire was as extraordinary as the other Gosti's, though it had its own mismatched contradiction of orange stripes and green polka dots randomly scattered on his yellow trousers. Frankly, his patterned clothes made me dizzy. Timofey Grigorievich's skeletal hand crawled out of his pocket and moved toward my head. I nervously slapped it and ran away from him, stumbling over Boris Borisovich interfering with my escape.

Upon storming back into my room and blocking its secret entrance with a pile of books I was allowed to read, a feverishly-written note fell out of one of them, filling the misty air of my space with smells that obviously came from the past. I carefully folded the note and put it under my bed in the treasure box named "My own konfidentsialnaya box." Some of the sentences you are reading here were first written and collected in that box. Papa once told me that lonely, observant girls who are good at keeping secrets tend to become writers.

CHAPTER VII

PRAVDA[4]

Ten fingers would be sufficient for me to count every type of dish we consumed in Dom when I was little. For that reason, the lightless gloomy morning that followed the previous gloomy day was special and exceptionally memorable—our breakfast consisted of something different from the usual water-based buckwheat. Morris generously brought us quail eggs from his secret tunnel. I had no idea how he managed to crawl through the tunnel without breaking them.

Skipping the morning greeting of *Dobroe utro*, I immediately informed Ma and Pa, who were mixing some kind of raw quail egg cocktail from the six tiny eggs, about meeting Timofey Grigorievich and how frightening he was.

Due to another severe gas shortage in our building at that time, and the fact that our mini briefcase lab refused to function, Pa suggested that we eat the eggs uncooked, like his mother used to when chickens hadn't been banned for their loud demeanor yet.

---

4 From Russian, meaning "truth." *Pravda* is also the former official newspaper of the Communist Party of the Soviet Union.

"She called it Gogol Mogol," he said with a harrowing display of sentimentality. A single tear trickled out of his wandering green eye.

The thing was, Pa had lost touch with his family ever since he had ventured off with my young Ma, regardless of his parents' request to sign the BRAK-agreement with Natalia Petrovna, who was one of the most well-behaved LIM-Damas in the village and whose pirouettes were impossible to compete with. My papa's parents were so disappointed in their son's choice and misconduct that they signed the LIM-boycott form (also referred to as the LBF), in which they bitterly declared their decision to boycott their son and his dama for the rest of their lives.

While clumsily spilling egg yolks all over his face, Pa reassured me that Timofey must have been on his way to the kitchen to get extra borscht and that it had nothing to do with me, since he hadn't had the slightest idea about my existence.

"To be honest, at first, I was cautious about having a new Gost too, but the man's mind is exquisite! Besides, he wouldn't have known of the konfidentsialnyi tunnel if he hadn't been one of us."

"But how about his evil cat Boris Borisovich?" I tried to argue while blocking myself from the slimy chunks of Pa's concoction.

"Do we have any sugar left anywhere?" Pa addressed to Ma enthusiastically while wiping his yellow nose with a horrific kitchen rag.

"It's under the most tattered piece of linoleum, Vitya. Under the table. They will never find it there," she answered to Pa, victoriously uncovering her sugar stash.

"You must have imagined him, dear," concluded Pa, redirecting his scattered attention to me. "We have absolutely never encountered any cats that came along with Timofey. You must have seen too many pieces of your mother's cat embroidery."

Ma gave him several concerned looks, hugged me, and whispered in a wonderfully sweet tone: "Don't worry, dear, there is nothing to be afraid of. Timofey is a good man. His numeric agility will help us calculate our escape. He is the only precise Gost we have ever had in our group.

The only thing he may need to readjust is his attire. The poor thing positively doesn't know how to dress."

There was nothing else I could do to prove my righteousness. Even the scratch marks on my shoulders and neck left by Boris Borisovich looked like all the other scratches I had given myself while crawling around Biblioteka for investigative purposes. I was defeated.

Ma tasted Gogol Mogol first. After thinking for a minute with her eyes fixed at the crumbling ceiling, she put wooden clothespins on our noses, added another chunk of sugar to it, and said, "*Na zdorovye.*"

We raised our tin mugs and chugged our salt-and-sugar-confounded breakfast as quickly as humanly possible.

Later that day, it appeared very unusual to my parents that Timofey missed their next meeting.

"Well, sometimes they fear someone is after them . . . I hope he comes back tomorrow," said Pa, rubbing his forehead in sincere confusion.

Timofey kept missing all the meetings, again and again, until one day he returned for reasons that had nothing to do with favoring our escape.

The notion of Timofey missing reminded me of the letter I had found the night before. I waited until Pa began to quietly snore before reading it under my blanket with a tiny candle I kept in my treasure box for such critical konfidentsialnyi matters. The multiple pages had been written in a fevered rush. In those curvy sentences, I found several diary entries written by Babushka and Dedushka debating about their life mission and in what particular ways books and writing could protect people's minds from propaganda, LIM-Leaders, and their demoralizing beliefs. Despite the fact that I wasn't entirely sure of the essence of the found notes, I became so absorbed by the beautifully written letters in the diary that I no longer paid attention to the cranky territorial spiders crawling out of the pages and showing me their scariest tarantula impressions. From the first few pages of those notes, I learned these two new terms: "veracity" and "horrific falsehood." *These words sound like villains!* I thought.

According to my grandparents, veracity and horrific falsehood were king in LIM, striving in every aspect of the dictatorial conduit, reminding each citizen to not be driven by the crude impulses of nature.

Here is what the last page said:

It is over for us. Now they know everything. Sveta, when you were sent away to LOB, we discovered a new portal to a foreign land. A resplendent fox was somehow stuck in it. The cunning little thief took advantage of our awe and stole our dinner that day. We left the tunnel open a while longer, out of curiosity, wishing to possibly DO-Mesticate the fascinating animal, but the fox didn't return. Instead, a child found her way to our Dom.

We missed you in Dom quite terribly and couldn't resist the young lady's company, even though it wasn't such a good idea to let an inostrannyi child come here. We treated Ada like our own little dochka. From the books we read to her, she soon learned LIML with impressive proficiency. She wanted to show us her land so often, but the stamp wouldn't let us pass. Ten years of arduous work wasted. All of our escape plans failed. Your Mama and I are to be arrested anytime now. The blind neighbor of ours has not been as harmless as we expected.

Let's get straight to the point: We left the last copy of SLFFGR *with Ada. She hand-copied it and brought it to the other side of the tunnel. For your information, nothing written by LIM's citizens in LIM can go past the LIM border. What an awful literary curse, isn't it?* SLFFGR *cannot be kept in Biblioteka, because who knows what's going to happen now? Every single one of the originals had to be burned for the same reason. Heartbreaking.*

Ada went back to Grodek. She lives there across the bridge. It is where the last copy of SLFFGR *is now. Alas, we didn't manage to break away from LIM to reach the land where space is filled with slivers of freedom, perspective, and harmony. The land where people walk freely, write freely, and talk freely out loud!*

The only way we as a family can protect the artist's mind is through giving future generations and our comrades a chance to express themselves freely and educating them about the disease propaganda injects into the collective mind. By gathering and keeping the forbidden words of wisdom and thought in literature, in this very room and these very tunnels, we are documenting nothing but the truth free of the mass poison. Our goal is to pass it on to future generations. Most importantly, you must protect your memories of the unbelievable and magic, as they will undeniably set you free one day. Stop the State from gaining its powers by depriving people of that belief . . .

We beg you to never stop searching for another way to depart from LIM, where you will never belong. The tunnel to Grodek is hidden behind the creaky clock in Biblioteka . . .

We cannot promise you we will be back, but we will love you for as long as our spirits live. We beg you to never forget us. Keep the elements of impossibility and imagery visible to yourself like we taught you, Svetochka. Prosti nas.[5]

Endless, most sincere love,
Mama and Papa.

I reread the note ten times, feeling awfully puzzled. Did my parents know about the letter? Did they know about Grodek? What stamp was Dedushka talking about?

The next lightless and dreary morning, shortly after Mamochka and Papochka finished chewing an untenable portion of buckwheat and were about to leave for another unbearable day of work, I asked my ma: "When was the last time you received a letter from Babushka and Dedushka?"

"Before I was sent to LOB. Years ago," she answered unwillingly, hiding tears, hurriedly making her way to the vocal door that was having a strange consonant-heavy pneumonic attack.

---

5 Russian: "Forgive us."

I waited for the doors to stop coughing and went straight to the old clock Dedushka had mentioned in his letter. Stored at the bottom of the clock were a baggy yellow dress with a white apron and collar sewn to it and a box of gouache with dry paintbrushes wrapped in brown paper. There were no tunnels to be found behind the clock.

"Ada's," said Dedushka's tiny handwriting on the brown paper.

I unwrapped the dress and put it on. It was hard not to laugh at how awkward I looked in the mirror in that oversized dress.

She must have been much taller than me, I thought. *Now, how am I supposed to find the tunnel? I sure hope to meet her. We could become konfidentsialnyi comrades.*

I was about to turn around and give up on my search when a dirty handprint on the wall caught my attention. When I put my hand on it, the surface of the wall moved forward, revealing another secret passage deeper inside the wall. As you already know, secret passages inside secret passages were relatively common phenomena in our Dom back then. I stuck my head deeper in the tunnel and heard someone's voice coming from what seemed to be the rear end of it.

"What is your name?" I wrote on a piece of paper instead of shouting and threw it down the tunnel with a little rock attached to it. "Blooomp-poomp."

"There must be water down there," I concluded, making a decision to borrow my mother's pot in case I would have to swim for a long time. Alas, I couldn't locate it anywhere in Dom, so I decided to ask Ma to teach me to make borscht later that evening to see where she had her pot stash. It was behind one of the kitchen walls, by the *tualet* room.

The next day, which by all appearances began as an entirely ordinary one, I woke to the lovelorn quacking of the main door, got dressed in my thick green dress, did my best to wrangle my wayward hair into an appropriate pyramid, kissed Mama and Papa goodbye—everything was exactly the same.

As soon as my parents' mousy footsteps were nowhere to be heard, I changed back into the baggy yellow dress and climbed inside the long passage, following the dirt marks left by the mysterious stranger. Eventually, I lost track of time crawling farther down, growing increasingly anxious about Ma and Pa coming to Dom and thinking I had gone missing, but according to my papa's old, barely lit operativnye chasy, I still had enough time. Right when I began to feel completely exhausted and thought I no longer had the stamina to carry the pot, a puddle of water shone in the space emerging below. I threw the pot first.

"Ouch!" yelled someone's voice.

I let myself dive in with a large splash and the kind of excitement you only have as a child who appreciates dirty puddles. Immersed in a thick, lukewarm puddle, I watched multiple glass bottles casually circling the burly tree roots, similar to collectively migrating sea creatures performing the very last dance around their favorite reef.

Once the wayward tree roots had absorbed all the water and exposed the deep pit I was stuck in, someone's hand brought me back to the surface, threw me against the floor, and covered my mouth roughly. Based on my blurry surroundings, I had landed in a spacious, brightly lit room inside a tall redwood tree. Nothing in the place resembled Dom. Rocks and sticks of various sizes, along with odd objects, lit by the warm hues of vivid daylight, suffused my eyes with brightness.

CHAPTER VIII

SASH, MY COMRADE

When my eyes regained their focus, I saw a young freckled boy slightly above my age, poking me with a broomstick. He was wearing my mom's pot like a helmet. In his other hand, he was squeezing the piece of paper I had thrown down the tunnel earlier. The boy was scared of me, based on the tone of his voice, though I had never heard the language he was speaking. Even though there was nothing welcoming about him, I was delighted to see someone my age for the first time.

"How strange. I was told nothing one wrote in LIM could travel outside of it," I mumbled through the boy's palm, pointing at the note with just my eyes. "I am clearly not in LIM anymore."

He opened my note, forgetting he had intended to keep me as a captive.

"Hello, I guess?" I said in my most innocent tone, readjusting the collar on my raggedy, baggy dress. "I am terribly sorry for intruding your space, *tovarish* . . . I am looking for Ada."

The boy squinted for a while, attempting to catch what I was saying, but after about ten seconds, he decided to ignore my words. Instead of listening to me, he grabbed me again, pressing his palm harder against my mouth. When I bit him, he immediately dropped me on the ground at a safe distance and gestured for me to stay away.

"Why are you so mean?" I asked the kid, moving closer to him again.

He took three steps backward and threw my pot at me. I caught it and carefully put it on the ground. It was the first time we saw each other in full length. The boy's attitude softened significantly when he realized that we had the same embroidery on our clothes: an image of a fox head with six foreign letters. The boy's shirt was the same color, though it had a lot more patches and stains than mine. His hair was long and curly, similar to the one portion of rotini pasta Morris had once treated me to. It covered his earnest, owllike face like thick theatrical curtains.

At that moment, his dazzlingly iridescent green eyes offered strong disapproval. Despite the overall raggedness, the boy smelled like his land—wildflowers and damp spruce forest—where nothing was nearly as nocturnal and unwieldy as in LIM. Or so it seemed.

"My mama would say you look like *Barabashka*.[6] She calls me that sometimes," I said to him, suppressing impolite laughter, immediately reminding myself that he was not going to know what I meant.

He looked at me with an invisible question mark.

"Here. Take this. It's a *podarok*," I said, offering him the gift of a piece of lukewarm potato from my pocket.

Without saying anything, he put the potato in his mouth with a genuine smile that took up half of his face.

"Ah. You are so lucky you don't have to wear staples on your mouth," I said.

After he finished chewing, he finally spoke to me in a gentler, slightly less suspicious tone. It didn't matter how much I actually understood the

---

6 *Barabashka* is an inquisitive, troublemaking house elf from Russian children's stories. He is also well known for his unkempt hair and is commonly referred to to humor little children who refuse to brush their hair. Ironically, my mother once told me that my great-great-grandparents' last name was Barabash, the ancient origin of which meant devilry or poltergeist. People with such an ominous family name were avoided and looked down on.

unfamiliar expressions flying out of his mouth; a good-natured, wonderfully awkward handshake occurred less than ten sentences into our failed introduction. Invisible threads of familiarity arose between us the moment we looked each other fearlessly in the eye. After exchanging several playful blinks, we couldn't stop nodding, grimacing, and acting like all kinds of animals, which was undeniably efficient for better, more comprehensive communication. I am not sure how long our games lasted, but when I looked at my pocket watch, my smile went away. It was very late.

"Ma and Pa must have already returned from the factory," I said to the boy in shock.

The boy shook his head in denial. I apologized to him by performing a silly dance we'd made up moments ago. He was happy to repeat my movements until he realized I was leaving. His tense forehead and rapid speech were begging me to stay. I quickly shrugged, waved goodbye, and jumped back into the tunnel, smelling the fading aura of flowers and trees.

"U-u-u-u-u," ominously hooted the door. Luckily, Ma and Pa were just coming back. It happened to be the GCD day of the month—people got their supplies after waiting in line for two to three hours. I hurriedly changed into my regular clothes—a darker green robe, an item made exclusively for me by Ma out of Babushka's curtains. We ate lots of fresh dill that night, the only herb generously distributed in LIM.

Since discovering Grodek, I never missed a chance to visit the raggedy boy. I still couldn't fathom what Dedushka was trying to say in his letter, but I was happy to finally make a friend who didn't happen to be an eccentric, well-opinionated adult. I was not in a hurry to find Ada.

The first few days the boy and I spent together, our mutually orchestrated physical mimicry worked well without words. I wasn't sure how to express my appreciation of the new friendship to him, due to my unfamiliarity with any type of social interaction with people of my age yet, but fortunately, earlier in life, I was taught that sharing soup and other food was considered a strong sign of fortifying camaraderie between people. My deep affection for his lively personality made me decide to share my mother's beet soup with him, which, as you probably already know, was considered to be the most essential dish in Dom (Ma even mastered pickling it, believe it or not). I would eat half of my portion, take the rest to the boy's land in a jar, and watch him slurp it in less than a second with a big smile on his face.

The frolicsome pantomime the boy and I developed through games, eating borscht, and mimicking each other had grown into a constructive friendship inside the prosaic, dreamy tree realm. Besides the few unappealing toys I brought from Dom, I also found a use for Dedushka's box of gouache and brushes.

"Look at this! I have never seen LIM-paint gleam this exquisitely on paper! I am so proud of you, dear!" Pa said proudly, hanging one of my paintings above the broken fortepiano in Biblioteka: numerous images of my knuckles, wild foxes, and sunny woods, signed with my name at the bottom.

"I didn't know there was paint left anywhere in Dom," said Ma. "I was positive they had confiscated all of it before we moved in."

I was worried Mama was going to ask me more questions about my find, but fortunately, Pa changed the topic.

Sometimes I ask myself why I chose never to tell my family about the tunnel or Sash. The best excuse I have: it would have broken my heart to be deprived of his company, not to mention to add to my mother's constant terror of persecution, and telling her about my own konfidentsialnyi friendship would mean I had ruined our pact.

"Who is this young man you draw in your pictures, dear?" Pa asked politely.

"It is how I imagine my comrade would look," I said.

Ma sighed. Pa found my response extremely entertaining, and he laughed, teasing me with a great deal of silly, jocular words.

As detail-oriented as my parents were, they failed to notice one very important quirk about the new paintings: even though they were all signed with my name, it wasn't written in my chaotic handwriting every time. It was quite clear that the paintings were signed by two different people with the same name: Sasha and Sasha. Or Sash and Sash.

When Sash and I knew all of each other's games perfectly well and it almost felt like we were communicating flawlessly without ever needing to speak, he made me privy to what he had been keeping inside the tree. It happened to be the day when I heard the sound of drums across the river. Sash immediately stopped slurping borscht, grabbed me by the arm, and pointed for me to crawl into the dirty pit the tunnel from Dom had delivered me to the first time.

"Shhh," he whispered, having a hard time remaining calm.

The drums were coming quickly toward our tree, but then they stopped as quickly as they had occurred, changed by the sounds of hundreds of steps running back to the bridge that connected the other shore to the woods. When the only things we could hear were our heartbeats and the long cries of a few tireless birds, Sash lit a candle and walked me around the moving roots of the tree surrounded by monstrous weapon-like constructions built from sharpened wooden sticks, seashells, and broken pieces of crooked mirrors. As soon as the pit ended in a full circle, I ran into a giant pile of empty milk bottles forming an object vaguely resembling a bathtub. Sash pointed at it victoriously.

"Are you trying to protect yourself from them?" I asked him without expecting an answer, pointing toward the other shore.

He looked at me with an eerie flicker in his eye and said, "Yes. The square monsters from across the river. They took over my school."

CHAPTER IX

SQUARE CHUDOVISHA

I STARED AT SASH, WIDE-EYED, BARELY ABLE TO BELIEVE I could understand his words. It was a bizarre amalgam of both our tongues. The truth is, we had learned to comprehend each other so quickly without trying much because learning a new language doesn't seem to be a problem when people are little and immune to biased opinions. Perhaps new languages come to children so easily thanks to the unbeatable urge they carry in their hearts when in need of explaining the rules of new games they are eager to play.

Sash and I climbed back up to the brightly lit area of the tree.

"I built this boat to swim past the monsters in case they come to get me. The tunnel below the tree opens into a deep river, colder than anything. I can't cross it without a boat. I used to swim in it all the time before the monsters came."

"What monsters are you talking about? We call scary monsters *chudovisha* in my language."

Sash took a stick and drew four square figures in the moist ground.

"They are squares with no faces?"

"I think so," said Sash.

"Hmmm . . . how dangerous are they?"

"I am not sure, but I know that since they came, everything has changed. Even the air. It keeps getting colder every day."

"Do you happen to know where they came from?" I asked.

Sash lowered his voice and told me his story. "One day, I was playing hide-and-seek with other children from school, here in the woods. I was lucky to find this tree, because it is the best place to hide. I sat here till it got very dark. Everyone I played with left. When I went back to school, nothing looked the same on the other shore. Crossing the Grodek bridge, I saw all the children from my school staring at me from the windows. Their eyes . . . they were very cold . . . I felt like they belonged to someone else. Everyone I knew looked different, except for Ada. She looked exactly the same. She wrote on a piece of paper and let me read it through the window: 'Sasha, run!' I ran. I hear hundreds of them patrol this area every night. They must be looking for me."

"Ada? You know Ada?" I cried out with my eyes popped, realizing for the first time that I had also somehow learned to speak a new dialect.

"Of course I know Ada. Everyone knows her here. How do you know her?"

"I don't know her yet, but I really, really need to meet her!" I yelled.

"No, no, no. You can't meet her. Chudovisha took her."

"What a strange situation," I said sympathetically.

"I can't go back there either. It's not safe," said Sash.

"Maybe I can somehow try to talk to Ada?" I asked, studying the building with many windows in which tiny figures moved around chaotically, like little buzzing flies. Three little girls dressed in the same yellow dresses I was wearing came out of the building across the river and waved at me all at the same time. Cold sweat crippled down my spine.

"No," said Sash. "If the chudovisha see us, we will be in big trouble."

"That means we can't walk anywhere outside freely?" I asked.

"I can still do that in some areas around here, because I know Grodek very well. You shouldn't. You don't even look like you are from here. Even the school uniform doesn't help," concluded Sash.

I turned away from Sash and said quietly, "I thought LIM was the only place where people couldn't walk freely . . ."

The thought of being constantly denied access to the outside environment, even outside of LIM, made me lose my temper. I stubbornly ran toward the edge of the tree house without waiting for Sash's permission and slipped on the half-eaten cabbage leaf I had dropped on the ground earlier.

Suddenly, I found myself lying in the midst of a wide-open space and looking up at the treehouse, where the air was chilly, though significantly warmer than the air in LIM. An abundance of colors, bugs, rodents, birds, and sounds they were making took over the forest canvas in their individual rhythmic patterns. I know humans can't quite move their ears like some animals, but it felt like I had opened mine as wide as possible as if to hear everything, to record every fluctuation and sound wave like a poem. My nostrils were doing the same.

"Careful now!" said Sash, hurriedly dragging me back into the tree by my foot.

"Why is the air not the same here? Why is everything so different from Dom in your land?" I asked Sash.

"Ada told me there are many places in the world where the air and other things are not the same. Different countries. Atmospheres."

"I never heard that before," I said.

"You are from a different country. That's why people talk and walk differently there and the atmosphere doesn't feel the same."

"I guess that makes sense. But you and I talk and walk exactly the same, no?"

"Pravda," said Sash, walking around me and waiting for me to do the same.

After finishing our third full circle, we paused and looked at each other victoriously.

"I think you are right. Maybe we walk and talk the same because we are . . ." Sash paused, looking for the right word to say.

"*Tovarishi!*" I said a little too loudly, with a little too much excitement.

"*Przyjacele!*" said Sash just as loudly, with the same abundance of excitement.

"Click-chick-chick," said my pocket watch vigilantly, reminding me it was time to go.

"See you tomorrow, przyjaciolka!" shouted Sash as I climbed into the tunnel.

"*Do widzenia!*"[7] I said in his language.

The next day, Mama and Papa weren't scheduled to go to work. All of LIM was celebrating Novyi God—New Year, the only day when people were permitted to be a little bit loud. Mama cleaned the oriental rug with a loud beater and thoroughly swept the floors. Then all of our Gosti arrived in their best attires, holding their own tables and chairs to make the gathering seem as festive and convenient as they desired. Even though there wasn't much to eat in Dom at the assembly of iron tables, seeing ruffles and colors on beaming adults was enough to feel like it was a special day.

Regardless of the official permission to be louder than usual, no one spoke at the table. Instead, Ma, Pa, and the Gosti wrote to one another in a circle of short letters while sipping something exceptionally colorful (which Morris had generously donated to them for celebratory purposes). Malvina was seated next to Morris that night. It was the first time they had been able to have a somewhat private conversation. The messages they were writing to each other at the table made both of them blush and drop spoons in other people's bowls of borscht.

I snuck out from under the table, after watching everyone's colorful stockings and boots shuffling and wiggling with excitement, to see Sash and bring him some special treats.

"May I read in Biblioteka?" I whispered to Ma and Pa. "Just this once?"

After exchanging contemplative looks with each other and the other Gosti, they nodded.

---

7 A Polish phrase: "Goodbye!"

"Try not to stain your dress, please," Ma wrote on a piece of paper.

I changed my pretty dress into the yellow uniform (it had gotten supremely dirty after all of my visits to Grodek) and hurriedly set off to see Sash.

The tunnel flight was surprisingly smooth, as if the invisible traffic of molecules had dissolved into a wispy slide. I landed among the red tree roots much faster than normal. The bushes around the tree shook. I was about to hide until Sash stepped inside the tree, took my hand, and said: "Don't worry. It's Dorotka."

A shiny, fluffy creature jumped into the tree with a little package in its mouth.

"Thank you, Dorotka!" Sash said to the animal and gave it a quick kiss on the head.

"Who is this?"

"It's a fox, silly."

"I have never seen one in person. Pa once read me a fable about a talking fox, but she wasn't too nice. Can Dorotka speak?" I asked Sash, staring at the animal in awe.

"Of course not! Foxes don't speak!"

"What is she doing here?" I inquired.

"Dorotka steals food for me from across the river, but some days she eats everything herself and forgets to feed me. Ada tried to teach her good manners, but she is just as wild as she was when we picked her up in this tree. She was very, very sick when she fell out of the same tunnel you came from. That's how we found her," he said.

"Ah! My dedushka mentioned her in his letter!"

"Who?"

"Click-chik-chik," affirmatively chirped my operativnye chasy.

"Do widzenia!" I yelled to both of them before jumping into the tunnel. When Dorotka saw me enter the tunnel, she made a whiny noise and camouflaged herself with a pile of dry leaves. I could tell the poor thing was trembling.

"*Even foxes dislike LIM*," I thought.

As soon as I got back to Biblioteka, I changed back into the festive gown with a giant embroidery of a kitten (bigger than the regular one on my daily dress) that Ma had made for me out of her favorite theatrical curtain. What can I say? Most dresses were made from curtains in our household back then.

I heard Ma's voice on the other side of the wall: "Sashenka, come join us for a slow dance!"

"Where have you been?" asked Pa. "Have you all of a sudden become deaf?"

"Poetry, Papa!" I replied, hiding my uneven breath the best I could. "I forget about everything when I read poetry."

"She is her parents' daughter," said Konstantin, the most dramaturgic Gost at the table and the only one with no pseudonym, playfully pinching my cheek. "Would you care to dance with me, Madame?"

I did my best curtsy and said: "With great pleasure, Konstantin Sergeevich."

Malvina was already holding Morris's arm.

"We are ready to dance too," they whispered. The blush on their cheeks brightened.

We entered Biblioteka. Ma sat at her favorite old fortepiano and played the most beautiful out-of-tune piece of classical music she had played in years as we waltzed.

CHAPTER X

COSMOS

"DOES THIS TREE HAVE A NAME?" I asked Sash conspiratorially one day.

"I call it Cosmos."

"Like the place with stars and planets where cosmonauts go?" I laughed.

"No! *Kaz-mas*, like the flowers that grow around the tree when the snow goes away. Ada told me their name is pronounced like that."

"Kazmas will be our konfidentsialnyi place forever!" I exclaimed, enjoying being privy to such an exotic word. "If for some reason you and I lose each other one day, we will always know where to meet, yes?"

Sash nodded with a hint of doubt, as if not nodding at all.

"How can we stop the square monsters?" I asked.

"I hope Ada has a plan. There is not a book she hasn't read."

"Books seem to help people an awful lot," I muttered.

"What did you say?"

"It's just so strange that adults believe books can help everyone," I answered indecisively.

"That's exactly what she used to say. I never understood it either. I just love reading because it's fun."

"Me too. I spend so much time alone. There is honestly nothing better to do in Dom."

Sash's face became very serious. He turned around and walked toward the large, cloud-shaped opening in the tree. He stood there and gazed quietly at his school.

"You must feel lonely too," I said apologetically.

Without turning around, Sash said in a voice older than before: "Yes. At first, I was happy to be left alone. Living in one room with twenty boys was never my favorite, but now I feel like it was better than being here alone. Sometimes I think I should just go there and let them turn me into . . . what they all have become. I would at least be with Ada and others."

"Oh, Sash. Maybe I could take you with me to LIM instead?"

"What is it like?" he asked.

"It's very, very cold . . . and scary, but Dom is a wonderful place!" I said.

"Is Dom the place you enter when the tunnel ends?" he asked.

"Yes! It's where I live!"

"That place is full of spiders and scary portraits," said Sasha. "I definitely don't want to go there again."

"How many times have you been there?"

"A couple of times. I found it because I heard music."

"My mama's fortepiano . . . are you sure you don't want to come with me?" I asked Sash with hope brimming in my voice. "You can live in my room, and we have enough books for everyone to read."

"I can't go anywhere quite yet. Ada sent me a note last week. She needs more time. When she makes these chudovisha go away, would you like to come and live with us across the river?"

"I would need to talk to Mama and Papa to see what they think. Maybe we can all live there one day. I know that they certainly dislike LIM."

"Mama and Papa?"

"Yes, my parents."

"Oh. I forgot how to say that word."

"Forgot? Why? Where are your mama and papa?" I asked Sash.

"I don't know. I am an orphan."

"You are a *sirota* . . . oh no! What is it like to be a sirota?"

Sash didn't answer.

"Do you have anything to read in here to make your days less lonely for now?" I asked.

"No. They burned all of our books, like a pile of old shoes."

"I didn't know people burned shoes . . . at least, they don't do that where I am from. Probably because there are not enough of them for everyone."

Sash ignored my comment.

I hesitated for a moment and said, "How about I bring you some of my books?"

Sash's eyes lit up. He finally looked at me.

"But you have to promise you will keep it a secret!" I said, feeling so very konfidentsialnyi.

Later that day, Sash coiled a thick piece of rope in his hands to help me drag the books from Dom, but some invisible powers were preventing us from taking them to Kazmas. Every single book we tried to drag out of Biblioteka tripled in weight. Copying my parents' books by hand was the only maneuver that worked. I would hand-copy my favorite stories, make paper planes out of the pages, and send them straight down the tunnel. Sash caught them with a fishnet.

In four weeks, I taught Sash to read in LIML to make his solitary hours more tolerable. After months of reading hand-copied pages inside the big redwood tree, Sash and I transformed the trunk of Kazmas into an unbelievable place filled with prosaic paintings and fictional squiggles. Some of the paper planes floated around the inside of the tree edges, and some of the smaller sheets of paper we put inside the milk bottles of Sash's boat. We felt more "on the same page" those days, as they say in different parts of the world.

CHAPTER XI

CITIZENSHIP

MEANWHILE, LIM-LEADERS FOUND NEW METHODS of strengthening the Wardworker patrol and ramping up spying-ear inspections all around the State. As a result, Ma, Pa, and their Gosti had grown all the more konfidentsialnyi and paranoid about all of their operations. To continue Biblioteka meetings, Mama made puffy mishka fur slippers (Papa brought a dead bear's body home that day) for everybody to walk around Dom in, as quiet as a whole mob of vodolazes. Instead of pouring borscht to every Gost in a separate bowl (they brought their own from their own Doms), Pa came up with a new quieter trick—he put the soup into a humongous *kastryula* and offered the Gosti used *LIM Weekly* newspaper straws to be able to elegantly sip its contents straight out of the pot.

Having verbal conversations in Dom was becoming practically impossible, even with the tin can telephones. Everything had to be written down extremely quietly, since the sound of abundant scribbling would make the spying ears suspicious. The feeling of security had at last abandoned us. I had more and more difficulty sleeping and ignoring the slowly growing panic, especially after Ma decided to DOMesticate Boris Borisovich.

I remember hearing long pitiful meows tooting like some burial orchestra horns in the bathroom. Ma was giving a DOMesticating bath with a bar of hoz mylo to a frozen-looking cat. When the cat was released from the tub, he jumped in front of me, exposing the perfect white bow tie on his chest stretched in an impressive arch.

"Meeeeow," meowed the animal, amicably rubbing my legs with its head.

"Ma, this is him! It's Timofey's cat—Boris Borisovich!" I yelled.

But no matter what I said, Ma was already in love with the cunning bastard, who was acting like an angel. Besides loving kitten embroidery, Ma seemed to adore real cats too.

"He is not who you think he is. He is a spy! You have to believe me!" I begged Ma.

"A spying cat? How did you come up with that?"

"There is something demonic about him. Can't you see it?" I tried to argue.

Ma dropped the bar of soap on the floor, laughing hysterically.

"We should name him Kot Begemot[8] then!" Ma exclaimed ecstatically, staring at the sad-looking wet cat.

When I glanced at his trembling little body and abandoned-lovelorn-kitten appearance, my heart cringed. Seeing my mother so delighted and the cat so believably tormented by living on the street made me not want to continue arguing with her.

"Sure. Kot Begemot suits him perfectly," I said.

"Look how much he loves us! What a sweet little *kotyonok*![9] How could we possibly leave him on the street?" Ma sung-spoke to me in her most charming soprano through the tin can telephone.

---

8 Kot Begemot (behemoth) is a character from the novel *The Master and Margarita* by the Russian writer Mikhail Bulgakov. He is an enormous demonic black cat who speaks and walks on two legs.

9 Russian, meaning "kitten."

"Great!" I said sarcastically, rolling my eyes and giving my mother the same dagger look she was known for in moments of acute anger.

"I wonder if we need to register you as a new resident here," whispered Ma to the cat, ignoring my protest. "It may not be necessary, if you keep quiet."

I went straight to my bedroom to block every potential cat-sized entrance with books and furniture.

That night, the quieter Gosti-gathering's whispers were approaching something grandiose. As a result, the once-popular word *konfidentsialnyi* was replaced by *grandioznyi*. Some of our Gosti even managed to skip factory work by chugging a bottle of antifreeze liquid in order to finish working on the konfidentsialnyi-grandioznyi Biblioteka-escape plan sooner. In the explanatory sickness letter every worker was obliged to fill out, they blamed everything on the lack of light in their kommunalkas: "I wholeheartedly assure the State that I didn't intend to drink antifreeze liquid for reasons of inexcusable indolence. I neither saw the contents of the bottle nor the bottle itself," said the letter.

"Pshhhfshhh," chaotically hissed a mesmerizing purple manganese potion in a bluish jar mixed with black lines of coal in its core. My mother was a sorcerer of esoteric potions capable of fixing most unfavorable conditions. She had inherited the craft from her grandparents, the pathological anatomists, who besides cutting corpses for burial LIM-purposes also ran an illegal practice of inventing curative ointments. Without explaining what on earth it was, Ma told the self-poisoned Gosti to drink the potion instantaneously, with her special nasal clothespins that made the most unpalatable items slightly more edible. The manganese concoction made them retch for hours until they recovered the desirable degree of mental clarity and physical strength.

"A new spade, please!" "May I fetch some iodine?" "Dig deeper, comrade. Three more feet." "There is a mouse on your head!" "Ah—I found another book!" These were the most common expressions that came from outside of Biblioteka at that time. So much suspense hung in the air that our Dom was giving off a light vibration only noticeable to us, individuals capable of intuitive freedom.

"We have just finished digging past LIM's gate," announced Papa several days later, while I was fighting the annoying Kot Begemot, who was attempting to open the treasure box under my bed.

"Really?" I asked, absentmindedly stepping on Kot Begemot.

"Yes, dear. It is the closest we have ever been to gaining freedom," said Pa, "yet there are a couple of additional things we need to do before we go."

When I entered Biblioteka, at least one hundred people were streaming out of sections of Dom I hadn't known about. They were bumping into one another in their fluffy mishka fur, holding on to little and big briefcases of many colors.

The strangest thing happened when Pa brought a compact burning-hot iron from one of his miniature labs and told the Gosti to remove their hats. In turn, each one of them sat on the stool in front of Pa and let him burn their scalps. A naked island of purple skin rose on the men and women's heads.

"*What is going on?*" I whispered.

"Your father is erasing our birth stamps so we can leave relatively unnoticed," said Malvina sadly. She turned around and demonstrated her scalp to me.

"It looks terribly painful and ugly! Why are you doing this?" I asked.

"Sometimes you have to sacrifice good looks to gain freedom," said Malvina. "Besides, it's only hair. It will grow back. Hopefully."

"Boooooom!" A giant saxophone fell out of one of the tunnels and landed heavily on the ground.

"Morris, is that you?" whispered Malvina, hurriedly covering her burned head.

In a few seconds, we saw a raggedy-looking Morris. A number of bags were tied around his body. He came out of the tunnel, shook the dust out of his hair, and smiled at all of us.

"Good evening, ladies and gentlemen! I am here to congratulate you on finishing your work! I am also here to celebrate and share some news."

When he saw Papa with his iron and smelled the burned hair, his forehead became very tense.

"Ah, I see that I chose the worst time for this. I am so sorry you have to go through this awful procedure."

Silence.

"Would anyone like champagne with some cheese?"

"Sounds lovely," said Mama. "Let's all drink champagne!"

We sat in a big circle. Everyone was whispering about the journey we were about to embark on. Some Gosti expressed their concerns about never again being able to see their *deti*—their children—after leaving.

"We will make sure to leave the tunnels open! Your deti know how to come to Biblioteka. You taught them well," said Papa.

"Morris, are you okay?"

It suddenly became clear to us that Morris had gotten awfully quiet and serious. His eyes were locked on Malvina's face. The glass of champagne in his trembling hand was spilling all over our humble cheese plate. He wasn't breathing.

"Is he having a heart attack?" whispered Mama.

But when Papa attempted to unlock his first aid briefcase, Morris stopped him and said, "I am fine. Just a little nervous. You see, I wanted to announce something of a greatly important nature."

"What is it? What could it be?" everyone asked him all at once.

"Morris and I would like to become BRAKed," said Malvina. A single tear of joy rolled down her face.

"Aaaah!" exhaled the Gosti.

"I never understood why *BRAK* in LIML also meant 'broken,'" said Morris. "I promise to never break you, Malvina."

"I accept," she said shyly. "I have no qualms about leaving this place and sharing a life with you."

"Let's all cheer for Morris and Malvina!" said Mama sentimentally.

Everyone raised their tin mugs and drank the coveted champagne.

"Are you ready to depart now?" asked Morris, holding Malvina's hand. "It's a rather long journey."

She nodded and said, "I have never been more ready, Morris. See you on the other side, tovarishi!"

After exchanging about one hundred hugs with all of us, the two crawled back into one of the tunnels and left LIM forever. The only traces of their presence left in Biblioteka were Morris's broken saxophone and Malvina's burned blue hair.

"Okay, we need to hurry now," said Papa when we could no longer hear Morris's gentle whispers.

"They will know she is missing in less than four hours," said Mama.

"Do I have to burn my head too?" I inquired cautiously, then swallowed.

The Gosti looked at my father with alarming curiosity. He turned his back to us, pretending there was something he needed to add to his baggage.

Ma came close to me, put her hand on my face, and said with a mixture of guilt and celebratory revelation: "You have never been stamped. They won't know you have left. They don't know you exist."

Some of the Gosti's faces froze in a bewildered stupor.

"Why?" I asked.

Konstantin Sergeevich, the most theatrical Gost with a very regular name, said: "Every newborn in LIM is given a unique number with Ward's mascot printed on its head, like the one on mine. Once people are stamped with it, leaving the territory of LIM becomes practically impossible. The vicious stamp helps the State to track anyone down very easily. According to our calculations, it takes about three hours for the State to know someone has crossed the border. That's why this escape requires so much preparation. But don't worry, dear; your head won't burn like ours. You have been ready to escape your whole life. Your parents raised you behind these walls to give you a chance to leave unnoticed. The State can't spy on you like it spies on us. You are free."

"What if they catch all of us?" I asked with growing anxiety.

Ma turned around to hide her tears. I just blinked at her, fighting a strange feeling of familial alienation.

"Why didn't you all remove it a long time ago?" I asked the Gosti.

"You can't do practically anything in LIM without it, dear. You must be registered to have rights," said Sir Clementine.

"But there *are* no rights, and everything is always so stupidly konfidentsialnyi!" I yelled, startled by the hostile tone of my own voice.

"Good point," agreed Konstantin Sergeevich, looking away from me.

"Perhaps there are no rights," continued Sir Clementine.

"The mere truth to this situation is—we didn't know there was anything better. We still don't know if it's true, but there is a good chance, and we have to take it."

I continued bombarding everyone with questions. "Are we going to Morris's country?"

"Yes. He helped us find the safest direction toward the right tunnel, to a place where we will be free. We will go one at a time."

"Next!" Pa said impatiently.

Our conversation came to an end among the clouds of scorched hair and skin that smelled of wilting and the dead birds Sash once buried in Kazmas. I suppose as soon as the Gosti finished the last bottle of champagne, another dozen scalps were burned without any flinches. In two hours, our terribly smelly, blackened Gosti agreed to take a short break in the kitchen.

That's when I crawled back into the secret tunnel behind the clock. I had to see Sash.

The sky was just about to be lit with vermillion streaks of sunset the moment I dived into the dark puddle. The tree roots looked sadly droopy, as if they hadn't been watered in a while. The milk bottle boat was gone.

I cautiously stepped outside and lowered myself into tall emerald grass that wasn't in the woods, like I always imagined, but in a distressed park of a provincial town situated by the murky river facing a thickly wired wall across its shores. I had never felt more curious about anything, so I crawled toward the slowly fading wildflowers.

Cosmos flowers.

As soon as I crossed the river on a giant tortoise's back, the overall atmosphere changed; the temperature was so much lower there than on the other side that I could see my breath vividly. What I saw on the town's wall made my heart flush itself down past my feet and into the ground: a crisscrossed mascot of plunger and stapler was painted in wide strokes at the entrance of Grodek. The streetlights were dimming. The sign above the kids' heads said, "LOB-corrections." The town's name "Grodek" had been crossed out and rewritten as "*Groznyi*," which meant "terrible."

Thousands of young boys and girls marched around a plain-looking building. The kids, their faces straight like perfect violin strings, were gathering in perfectly straight lines. A lady with the saddest, bluest eyes and half-yellow, half-black hair waved goodbye to them as they walked away in an unknown direction, following intense staccatos of militant drums plopping from afar, cutting the pure evening air. I approached the crowd of kids closer, and the rest of the town became more visible to me.

The limpidly blue-eyed lady's face changed when she saw me sticking out of the grass. She marched directly toward me. Her eyes were looking right through me. I had never seen a more distinctive-looking person in my life. Even the eccentric Gosti seemed relatively plain in comparison to her. I crawled farther and farther away from the lady, until I fell into a bush of rose hips. Her steps were too quick and decisive, making me tear pieces of my dress to free myself from the trap. The sound of her gentle voice made me stop.

"I won't bite, I promise," she said with a light smile.

I turned around to look at her again.

"Please, don't be afraid," she said with the same inflection of kindness.

I stopped crawling and slowly nodded, maintaining my toughest posture to show her I wasn't to be messed with. Just in case.

"My name is Ada. What is your name, dear?"

The sound of her name put a giant smile on my face. I was speechless. The more I looked at her, the more I recognized her from the paintings I had found in the old squeaky clock.

She quickly smiled back and said, "Enough smiling for now. Do me a favor—stand up and act like all the other kids here. They come to a stop after marching a full circle, see? Make sure you do the same," she whispered, pointing at the little figures in the far distance. "Now, let's have a quick rehearsal."

I obediently showed Ada my rhythmic walking in precise circles with an extremely straight face, and I received her nod of approval accompanied by a sweet flicker of relief.

"You are doing great. Maybe a little less blinking, if possible. No smiling, please. Follow me."

Marching like the other children wasn't an easy job, but I managed. Ada made sure to walk before me to distract a giant crowd of glum Wardworkers.

We walked into a stuffy building filled with empty rooms, tiny shoes, burned books, peculiar toys, and desks. Ada took me to a place that must have previously been a canteen, based on all the broken saucers, flipped tables, bent ladles, and silverware lying on the black-and-white tiled floor. A deliberately twisted conveyor belt that resembled a mayhem of curvy labyrinths was sitting in the middle of the room. Ada pressed the green button above it and whispered: "It will take us to the kitchen. Make sure to lie down flat, so you don't hit your head. I will meet you on the other side."

The conveyor transported me into a darker space with lots of tubs, pipes, and a fridge three times taller than Ada. She surreptitiously unlocked it and walked inside.

"Come in," she said with just her lips, politely offering me a rough chunk of cheese.

While vigorously chewing it, I completely forgot where I was. The earthy, tangy flavors it left in my mouth were taking my imagination to an extraordinary place.

Meanwhile, Ada listened carefully to what was going on outside and finally said, "They won't be able to hear us in here. Now, tell me where you came from," she asked, thoroughly scanning me with the blue lakes of her irises. When she looked at the initials embroidered on the collar of the dress, her face turned pale. "My uniform . . ."

I finally answered with my mouth full of delicious cheese: "I found it in the squeaky clock. Bibli—"

Ada squeezed me in a heartfelt embrace without letting me finish the sentence. Large tears flowed from her sad eyes.

After managing to stop her sorrowful sighs and trembling lip, she said: "They didn't make it . . . how very unfortunate . . ."

She was speaking my native tongue flawlessly, with no trace of an accent.

"What is your name?" she asked.

"Sasha," I said. "My full name is Alexandra Victorovna."

"It's you who Alexander wrote to. I should have known . . . the tree . . ."

"What? Alexander?"

"Sash," she said. "Wardworkers brought his letter to you, written in LIML. He was the last boy who wouldn't be sent away to LOB," she mumbled through her tears. "He had a chance to escape . . . and now they know where he is headed . . ."

"How did they find the letter?" I asked, wide-eyed.

"They caught Dorotka."

"Is Sash okay?"

"I don't know. The siren hasn't announced anything yet. Maybe he is still in the tunnel."

The drums outside intensified, making the lights in the fridge go off.

"Oh dear—we are running out of time," said Ada.

"How can I help him?" I whispered.

"You must find him and bring him back to Kazmas," answered Ada. "If he acts stubbornly, don't try to explain anything to him—just tell him I told you to do so."

"Okay," I whispered. "I will do anything to help."

"There is one more thing you need to do. There is a black box with Grodek's symbol inside the redwood tree. It should be covered with a big piece of wood that has my name burned on it. Take this key and unlock it. Remember to turn it clockwise three times. You two must read *SLFFGR*. I wish I had more time to finish translating it so I could read it to the kids here at school, but LIM invaded way too soon. I burned the translated copies to avoid the COO punishment," she mumbled under her nose in an eerie tone that told me how much she hated the Chamber of Oblivion.

"What is *SLFFGR*?" I inquired, rubbing my forehead and feeling supremely confused about everything Ada had told me. "I've heard the word before, but I don't understand why everybody turns a fly into an elephant because of it,"[10] I added all in one breath.

"You will know very soon. Please make sure you finish reading it before you leave."

The drums were so close I could hardly hear Ada saying something of great importance.

I just nodded at everything she said with a nervous half smile on my face and said, "Okay."

We sat in silence before I left. Sitting in silence together for about five seconds—or, as we also said in my family, "*na dorozhku*"—was my favorite superstitious tradition to wish someone a safe trip.

After we hugged, Ada put a heavy key carefully wrapped in a tree leaf in my hand.

"This way," she said, pointing at an old dusty rug in the back of the fridge.

"Ada, are you going to be okay?"

"Most importantly, my mind will be. I've read it," she answered without looking at me.

"Read what?"

Ada hurriedly squeezed me into the dark pit in the floor and walked away in the same marching rhythm. The building was filling up with Wardworkers' voices.

10 Russian proverb: "To make a big deal out of something."

CHAPTER XII

HOW I BECAME MUTE

THE FARTHER IN THE TUNNEL I CRAWLED, the deeper and colder its waters became.

"Blo-o-o-op." I stepped on a milk bottle and collapsed into the stream.

Then, Sash's bottle boat emerged before me. It was entirely dilapidated.

"You are here!" he screamed. His eyes lit up, as if seeing me was the best thing that had ever happened to him.

We ran toward each other, splashing water all over the place in our rush to hug each other. We squeezed one another tightly, ignoring the frightening drumming outside and our own anxious muttering.

Not having seen him in days made it apparent to me that he had lost a significant amount of weight—his face had never been more sunken, and his school uniform looked much baggier than normal.

"I'm so glad I found you!" I said. "I thought you were never going to say goodbye to me."

"You haven't visited me for so long!" said Sash. "Chudovisha have been getting so much closer—I had to go. I wrote you a letter with a map so you could visit me one day. The problem is that my boat turned out to be too big for this tunnel. I didn't expect it to be this narrow."

"Oh, no! That's the letter they read! That's why they know."

"They read it? How? I gave it to Dorotka."

"She is gone . . ."

"Gone where? No one has ever caught her before."

Sash sat in the water like a lost child with no direction, which, essentially, was who he was. I sat next to him.

"Want some?" I asked him carefully, handing him the cheese Ada had put in my pocket.

When his eyes flickered affirmatively, I told him about everything Ada told us to do.

"Your land has been occupied by mine," I said after an uncomfortably long pause.

Sash's excitement disappeared. Sadness lay upon his face like a gargantuan tentacle.

The drums outside mixed with voices searching for Sash—speaking in my native tongue—were so loud it almost felt like they were inches away from us. I dragged Sash after me.

"Let's go, please," I said.

"But I don't understand," said Sash in a harsh, low voice. His forehead became very tense. "The square monsters . . . your people destroyed my home and took Ada. She taught us to never trust anyone who came from up there. Where you came from."

"Sash, we must go back to Kazmas," I begged him. "We must hurry. That's what Ada told us to do."

He didn't move. The drumming outside was rapidly increasing with every new second.

Then Sash slapped my hand and said through tightly shut teeth: "Don't tell me what to do, square monster! You are one of them. I knew I shouldn't have let you come inside my tree."

"Sash! What are you saying? I am not a chudovishe—I am your comrade!"

Sash pushed me away and screamed: "I don't want to see you ever again!"

The tunnel shook.

"You can't just stay here! Ada told me we should stick together. We must read that book!"

"Nonsense! If she were as special as I thought she was, she wouldn't have let this happen. I don't care what she said. Go away!"

Without hesitating, I turned and ran away from Sash, toward the tree house I was destined never to come back to, crying like I never thought I would be able to, turning around every other second, hoping Sash would change his mind and follow me.

Even though the Wardworkers were only several trees away from Kazmas, I knew they were never going to find it.

It was getting dark by the time I was back there, and I couldn't make out which piece of tree had Grodek's mascot. Everything in the once-magical space looked like a mean, ill-natured charade. The moment I finally saw something vaguely similar to a couple of figures and reached for my pocket to take the key, something unthinkable occurred to me: it was empty. The only things I had left in my pocket were cheese crumbles.

"I ruined everything," I said to the black box I was supposed to unlock, "and not only does my comrade think I am a chudovishe, he also wants to die here alone."

Before leaving, I wrote Ada's instructions in Sash's drawing of me with a few blobs of gouache: "If you change your mind and find the key—unlock it here. Turn it clockwise three times."

When I returned to Dom, most of our Gosti were preparing to sleep on the floor in uneven rows, like sloppy potatoes. I needed to ask Ma and Pa about the book Ada had told me about, but there was never a good place or time to do so. The erect spying ears, which had grown three times their normal size, had been listening with utmost attention and hadn't taken a nap in days. My soothing humming didn't lull them either, as if they knew something was different in Dom.

We finished packing. The last items I gathered were some of Sash's drawings. It was hard to believe he was not someone I could call a comrade anymore.

The Gosti blew out their tiny candles and lay on the floor, but there was no way I could convince myself to close my eyes that night. I kept checking the clock on the wall, fearing that we would fail to wake up at the right time. I wanted to make sure the ears weren't doing anything unexpected. To my surprise, Kot Begemot was peacefully snoring next to my feet.

It happened in the middle of the night, when the shiny dome of amoeba stars faded into a motionless purple dawn that looked like dusk and the cuckoo bird on the Gosti room clock quietly quacked a new number. Nothing felt the same in Dom—even the voice of the bird had changed to a ridiculous tremolo baritone. It was quacking and hiccupping mechanically, after which the pendulum of the clock commenced to spin in every direction of the room.

A peculiar icy feeling crept along my spine. I was just about to leave my room when I heard someone's footsteps walking heavily around the house. All of me listened attentively. The air in the room wheezed with a spooky echo: "We are being watched."

I walked into the kitchen full of Gosti and saw Timofey Grigorievich whispering something into the spying ears on the wall. Boris Borisovich, who wasn't Kot Begemot after all, was sitting on his shoulder like a snotty parrot, his name pendant back on his chest. The Gosti room I ran into next had no more Gosti sleeping in it. The only trace of their presence left in the room was a pile of lifeless pocket watches soughing away like dehydrated frogs. My own briefcase was wide open, and the few paintings I intended to take with me were gone.

Later in life, I learned that everything they confiscated that night had been sent to the Ward Lab (WALA), where the State studied everything unusual about the human mind and how to neutralize it.

Suddenly, the ears on the walls enlarged themselves so much that they had almost outgrown the entire Gosti room. The sound of "tick-tock-tuck-tick-tock-tuck" sprung out all around LIM.

A screeching pause.

I stormed into Biblioteka to remove myself from the buzzing alien voices, the symphony of squeaking doors, and the stampede-like pounding of someone's valenki-kaloshis everywhere in the house. Stumbling upon Babushka and Dedushka's books, big tears washed away my eyesight.

And then, suddenly, I saw Sash pushing the squeaky clock. He set his muddy foot on Biblioteka's floor.

"I read *SLFFGR*! I know the way out of here!" he said hurriedly. After holding his breath with his eyes popped out like two hot air balloons, he shyly planted a soft kiss on my cheek. His face turned the color of a pomegranate. The candles went off. Drums and whistles were roaring all over the place. Sounds of Morris's saxophone were among all the other sounds.

"You are the best comrade I have ever had," Sash muttered as the lights went off.

I lit the candles again. Sash was no longer next to me. In the weakly lit corridor, I saw my poor parents upturned and disfigured by the purity of horror. They had been captured by the humongous ears that had grown large enough to reach the book room from the wall outside. Sash was handcuffed, on the ground and stepped on by the Wardworker-General. His misty eyes were turning into dark moist chimneys.

The pudgy-fingered, fury-faced tyrants separated Ma and Pa and sent them to the deepest underground department of Ward, for those who disobeyed the most. Sashenka was shamefully announced as an illegal *inostranec* with no family history and was sentenced to ten years of LOB-corrections. His head was stamped immediately.

Timofey Grigorievich was vigorously shaking hands with every Wardworker.

"You are a genius, Timofey," they said, "to catch all of them at the same time and the same place!"

They viciously destroyed my parents' typing machines and Morris's saxophone (which for some reason kept giving off the most heartrending, disorganized excerpts of foreign burial music) and burned all the books they managed to find to ashes, erasing and dismantling my parents' hopeful reflections of an arranged escape from the country they couldn't stand. The safe tunnel Ma, Pa, and the Gosti had been building for years was found and destroyed.

As much as I understood that I needed to hide, I could no longer hold back from screaming.

Wardworkers squelched their way to me so closely that all I could smell was their rotten breath. After examining my whole being with their needle-eyes for what felt like eternity, they received the Wardworker-General's approval to insert me into one of the ears on the wall. My hair was shaved off with a sword-sharp razor. I became bald. The sight of my virgin head made their eyes grow incredibly round. They were staring at the crown of my head in malevolent amazement.

"I told you you would regret it," said the Wardworker-General to my mom with barely detectable softness and care. Even his wrinkly forehead had flattened into a smooth surface.

"I give you one last chance to come with me, Sveta."

"I would rather be dead than have anything to do with you!" shouted my mother. She had clearly achieved an unprecedented level of anger.

"Interesting," said the Wardworker-General with atypical inflection in his voice. "Very interesting indeed."

The Wardworker-General stroked my mother's cheek with utmost care and something vaguely similar to romantic despair.

"You have always made the poorest choices, Sveta. Well, it's over. Good riddance, you poor, poor woman," he barked, giving my mother one last glance filled with hope that she would beg him to take her with him.

Ma's face remained as bravely frozen as moments ago. Every inch of her body was loathing the presumptuous bastard.

The Wardworker-General turned around and gestured for the others to take my parents away, separately, as LIM's loudspeaker began to spread a loud siren outside.

I have never heard my parents scream like that. It was perhaps the first time I heard them say these words to each other so loudly, breaking down into sobs: "*Ya budu lyubit tebya vechno!*"[11]

In a few minutes, two old ladies dressed in long white coats and seated in squeaky wheelchairs were rolled into Biblioteka with rusty tin boxes in their hands. The folds around their noses, foreheads, and mouths looked like cemented masks of the most profound human disgust. Their tiny eyes sent me alarming threats through the daggers of their demonic anger.

The hexagonal loudspeaker continued yelling outside: "Breaking away from the code of recommended social restrictions imposed on the young citizens of the State and attempted murder—these are the most criminal deeds in LIM."

They took a syringe-shaped stamp the size of a cat out of one of their dreary tin boxes and punched me with it at the very top of my head. It hurt so much that I couldn't even react. That's how I became an official LIM-citizen. Legal naturalization in that part of the world is rarely pleasant, I suppose. The fluctuating sting of the fresh wound on my head sent me back to Konstantin Sergeevich's words: "Once you are stamped with it, leaving the territory of LIM becomes practically impossible."

One last miserable meow from Boris Borisovich.

The paint above the broken fortepiano had turned into rust. The "tick-tick-tick-tock-tuck" exploded in my head. All other sounds ceased.

I became mute. It was my eighth birthday.

11 Russian: "I will love you forever."

PART II

WOMANHOOD

Lock up your libraries if you like; but there is no gate, no lock, no bolt that you can set upon the freedom of my mind.

—Virginia Woolf

CHAPTER I

HOW I BECAME A LIM-DAMA

THE GUARDS POURED A SIX-LITER BUCKET of Wardwater through a plastic funnel they fastened in my throat with utmost exactitude. The burn of the drink was obnoxious and bellicose, especially as I had to restrain the urgently boiling stream of my intestinal juice. It was not mixing so well with the poison. No matter how much I fought through my deranged bending, scratching, and kicking, it was impossible to avoid gulping down the entire bucket.

Wardwater settled itself on my insides in a massive layer. Till the last drop. My stomach grew uneasily explosive at first, as if alerting me to the inevitable upcoming heady act of diarrhea. I urinated all over myself. A strange though tiring sensation of euphoria filled me with an orgasmic wave of warmth. I gradually drifted away to an agreeable half-asleep state, marked with the kind of agony one suffers during a lethal fever or a redundant amount of injected anesthesia. When I was as limp as a wet, overly glutinous noodle, they dragged me carelessly outside in my heavily ruffled nightgown that had preserved the heat from my bed.

The lowest temperature I had experienced in my life was mercilessly suffocating every inch of my delirious body, yet somehow, I remained relatively relaxed. It felt a bit like a handful of kitchen knives were thrown at me, after which some rough-tongued reptilian licked me like a popsicle. My skin no longer belonged to me. Wardworkers watched my ongoing convulsions with crooked grins. They poured another half bucket of Wardwater in my throat. The remaining three liters they chose to consume themselves, along with a handful of crunchy pickles they had stolen from my mother.

The pale-faced Wardworkers (with a fresh trace of peachy-pink blush) threw a huge, smelly, dead mishka skin over me, the big holes in which allowed me to see the outside world quite easily. I was mounted on top of a tin sleigh attached to six scrawny wolves moving slower than snails. The poor animals were whipped to urge them to crawl on immutable roads that were, most likely, frozen riverbeds. From the emerging capsule across the dark woods ahead of the sleigh, I knew I was being taken to LOB to join thousands of other children learning to be exemplary LIM-citizens.

Everything around me was gradually losing light. The only two things glowing brightly were the Ward clock and the Moon. Both of them looked much bigger than I ever imagined. I suspected that they must have swallowed all of the leftover shades and hues to become as shiny and mesmerizing as they could possibly be. The Moon's mouth was stapled.

Ten hours later, Wardworkers allowed themselves to take a drunken nap; the rocking motion the wolves were moving us with put lots of comforting weight on the men's eyelids. Hearing the earthquake snores flying out of their drooling mustached mouths was truly what kept me awake.

I must push myself off the sleigh into the snow and run as far as I can, I thought to myself in a haze.

But there was nowhere to go in the hopeless depth of frozen woods. I was motionless, intoxicated with Wardwater to the point that the sky, which I looked at through the mishka skin, was moving in repetitive circles, as if attempting to collide with the ground. The stamp on my head was still oozing blood. The tragic thought of being in captivity for the rest of my life made me sob for many long hours, spraying the atmosphere with uncontainable torrents of large hot tears that turned into frozen crystals.

By the time we arrived at LOB, I had fallen peacefully asleep inside the ice cube formed by my excessive grieving. And that's how time stopped for me in my realm. When the Wardworkers awakened to deliver me to LOB, it was too late for them to force more Wardwater down my throat. Nobody succeeded in bringing me back to my physical form. There was not a single place anywhere around where the temperature would be high enough to melt my impenetrable ice cube made of grief. I remained frozen.

Overwhelmed by torturous fatigue and my feelings of loss and misery, I fell into a lethargic sleep that lasted for six years.

You would think one could have thousands of dreams if one doesn't wake up for six years, but that wasn't the case during my hibernation period. In my sleep, all that came to my mind's vision was the exact same recurring image: I was crawling inside the Grodek tunnel toward Kazmas. The farther I crawled, the closer Sashenka's voice seemed to be. The closer to the end I came, the tighter the walls of the tunnel squeezed me, and the uglier his voice sounded. The dream ended the same way every single time—I was suffocated by the tunnel without finding my way out of it.

I tried to trick my mind into changing the sequence of my nightmare in a thousand different ways, until, finally, it worked. The last time I had the dream, I managed to shrink myself to the size of a shoe. I was spat into the tree house that looked like a haphazard arrangement of gigantic dead flowers and scarecrows. All the dead plants around Kazmas were churning and reshaping themselves into nystagmic eyeballs on wiry stems. As soon as I swam-ran away from them (I'm sure you are aware how hard it is to run in dreams), the eyeballs stretched themselves toward me like lengthy arms and came to a halt in a terrifying halo. I gave off a roaring scream that broke the eyeballs into thousands of sharp fragments and tore my nightmare apart, returning it back into reality.

My yelling broke the windows of the bathroom I had been kept in. The fact that I couldn't hear the sound of my own voice provoked me to continue screaming with as much power as my reanimated vocal cords allowed. The ice cube—my prison for six long years—melted away, and I awoke jerking like a suffocating eel inside a refrigerated jar. Once my vision had fully thawed itself out, I knew I was lying in a rough bathtub of a dreary tualet.

I was fourteen. I looked down to see what had happened to me after years of immobile hibernation—my body had changed into a curvier entity. A woman, that is. The newly grown round breasts of mine were covered in thorny goose bumps. Due to my frail state, I could barely make out what lay past my hard-as-brick cold nipples and the tub. LIM had been informed of my awakening as soon as I stopped screaming and achieved a better eye motion. I focused on a pair of dirty ears on the bathroom wall. They were repositioning themselves to pointy arrows. I suspected they were waiting for me to say something to them, to justify all my past actions and admit to being an immoral delinquent, but instead of doing any of the above, I gave the ears another deafening scream filled with anger and the kind of hatred I experienced then and there for the first time.

As my vocal protest turned into something animalistic and mad-caged-womanlike, somebody walked into the bathroom. No matter how hard I tried, I couldn't leave the tub without collapsing on the floor like a heavy spade. The impossibly wrinkly-dry prune-like old ladies in white robes I had the worst memories of were brought to me in their wheelchairs for my physical evaluation. Daily. Sometimes twice a day. They never forgot to pierce my veins with a boxful of slightly bent needles of all sizes, feeding me Wardwater and *valerianka* in enormous amounts through the transparent pipes attached to me.

Thanks to their continuous pulls, pushes, pokes, kicks, and punches, I regained my walking ability and was able to open my mouth in three weeks. Not having to wheeze helplessly through the wall of mucus in my nose gave me the opportunity to take a deep breath for the first time since my awakening. I stood up in front of the bathroom mirror without anyone's support, looking at myself as a tall teenager with a plastic bag wrapped around my hair. The cellophane turban was there to burn the entirety of my scalp with kerosene while I was thawing out. They said it helped to remove the strangely robust frost-resistant lice my head had been infested with. I took it off and examined myself a while longer. I had become a woman with unusually long arms and fingers, weather vane hair shaped like a cloudy abstract painting, and a statuesque nose. Gladly, my wide head had finally reached an appropriate size in proportion to my body, though I still inconveniently toppled over at times.

While scrutinizing my new body, I noticed a whoosh of steam underneath my *nochnushka* (which no longer fit me), fighting the dropping temperature coming from behind the cracked windows. Thick streaks of dark blood were coming down my thighs. I tried to hold it, but it continued to drip and spread all around the tualet in liter-deep puddles.

I am destined to drown in my own blood, I thought to myself while learning my new reflection in the mirror.

Nobody let me out of the tualet for three more days, waiting for my bleeding to stop, while I grew more and more claustrophobic trapped in that tiny parallelepiped room. To save myself from freezing to death, I spread the warm blood coming out of me all over my face and body. I even let myself soak in it like a marinated vegetable. When everything in that space had become red and I could no longer fight the cold, I gave off another alarming scream. The spying ears on the walls, thoroughly coated in my blood, enlarged themselves to their soldier-straight position and cosmonaut-alert preparedness.

In three seconds, the same wheelchaired old ladies clad in white rolled into the tualet. A long, crooked water hose was wiggling in their rheumatic hands like an electrocuted snake. They sprayed me from head to toe with rough fountains of cold water and did the same to the entire room. The tub, filled with my bloody mess, was thoroughly drained with plungers; for about an hour, it continued spitting out a great variety of unpleasant tissues and objects up at the ceiling.

Wheezing from exhaustion, the old ladies impatiently handed me a new set of clean clothes and a poorly illustrated black-and-white booklet on how to be a timid LIM-Dama correctly. That day, I learned what womanhood meant from a physical standpoint.

CHAPTER II

AGNESA BORISOVNA AND VASILIY FYODOROVICH

Continual uneasiness, concealment of my knowledge, pretense, fear, a painful straining of all my nerves—not to let it down, not to ring out . . . even to this day, I still feel an ache in that part of my memory where the very beginning of this effort is recorded, that is, the occasion when I first understood that things which to me had seemed natural were actually forbidden, impossible, that any thought of them was criminal.[12]

—Vladimir Nabokov

12 From *Invitation to a Beheading*, translated by Dmitri Nabokov in collaboration with the author.

I PUT ON AN UNEVENTFUL MUSTARD ROBE and stumbled into a gloomy, disorderly place on the other side of the tualet. It was Agnesa Borisovna and Vasiliy Fyodorovich's shack, situated on the frozen outskirts of LIM, where Ward stood within walking distance. Several gangly stars peeked through the hundred-ton swirling fog above the paper-thin roof, dripping their dull blinking onto everything around. I refused and still refuse to refer to that place as Dom or New Dom. Those people were my paternal grandparents, but I refused and still refuse to refer to them as Babushka and Dedushka.

The shack was furnished just like every other LIM-kommunalka, except there were additional piles of trash and boxes and multiple photographs of Glashka, Vasiliy Fyodorovich and Agnesa Borisovna's beloved dog that had long gone missing. A big-bellied *samovar* was also a novelty to me—it was Agnesa Borisovna's favorite household attribute, mounted on top of an old decrepit table in the middle of the shack. The walls, floors, ceilings, chairs, and everything else inside the space reeked of sauerkraut, flatulence, and damp hay, giving one the impression of having walked into a menagerie. The tightly shut windows covered with thick layers of dust barely let in any fresh air.

Agnesa Borisovna and Vasiliy Fyodorovich quietly pointed at the corner, where stood an aluminum squeaky clamshell bed—*raskladushka*—hardly more comfortable than the bathtub. The tiny dust-covered corner in the back of the house, separated by the washed-out gray shower curtain that served as a personal space divider, was my new living space.

The next morning, I woke up from excruciating backaches and a terribly worsened cold. My sickly face was coated in layers of encrusted mucus. My eyes were dry like old raisins and so were my cognitive abilities: to say I was confused about my identity, deafness, age, and present location is as if to say nothing at all. New tubes stuck out of my veins, stamped by the State's mascot. I wished to remove them, but every time I lifted my arm, all of the nerves in my neck became pinched. I had no choice but to remain supine on the rough raskladushka for hours, forcing my senses to awaken through the inner reminder I kept reinforcing in my head. "Wake up, wake up, wake up!"

Two days later (I may have misjudged hours then), I was able to see more shapes, thanks to the linearly distorted memories popping from the depths of my curdled brain. The tubes were no longer connected to my arms. I sat up, putting my feet on a bunched-up cloth on the floor. It was my dirty nochnushka with a piece of carefully folded damp paper sticking out of its chest pocket. I unfolded it and saw Pa's inarticulate handwriting, which was significantly less legible than normal. My heart and all of its little violins disintegrated into hundreds of evaporating blobs.

Malenkaya,

If you are reading this letter, it means we failed at escaping LIM. We must apologize to you for that. But as we say in our family, "Poltroons don't get to drink champagne!"

Do you remember the first time Morris brought us the most delicious bottle of champagne and played his saxophone while we were drinking it? You said you liked the taste, and you drank so much of it that you danced like a little Cossack for a whole hour. Oh, Malenkaya . . . Ma and I beg you not to hold us in contempt for our failure at keeping you away from LIM and finding a better place for our kind. Our aspirations. Did you know the root of the word "aspiration" came from the verb "breathe"? We simply couldn't breathe anymore; that's why we ran. We apologize to you for not being able to rescue you and bring you to a better place. Prosti nas.

We beg you to never stop searching for another way to escape from LIM, where you will never belong. Alas, we have failed to enter the land where space is filled with slivers of freedom, perspective, and harmony. The land where people walk freely, write freely, and talk freely out loud!

If you're reading this, that means you're already in captivity. There is a chance that they will send you to LOB or Warddoor, but please don't let those kretiny change the essence of who you are. Don't worry about Agnesa Borisovna and Vasiliy Fyodorovich, in case you have been sent to their Dom. They are too old by now to supervise your Wardwater consumption. Don't drink that gadost (yuck), please!

We cannot promise you we will be back, but we will love you for as long as our spirits live. We beg you to never forget us.

Mom's handwriting said at the end:

Please never forget that your memories are powerful enough to help your imagination blossom and save you from the tribulations of dictatorship. Keep the elements of impossibility and imagery visible in your realm, Sashenka, just like we taught you.

Endless, most sincere love,
Mama and Papa.

By the time I finished reading the letter, the two rows of my teeth were grinding against each other mercilessly. I was going through hammering anxiety and unbearable regret of unfreezing myself from the ice cube. Living there, face-to-face with the recurring nightmare of my unconsciousness, felt much safer than the reality in which I was so far away from Dom, right next to Ward and its morbid ticking. I shouted into my skinny pillow through the suffocating mournful cries: "My life is over!"

The swollen stamp of the LIM-mascot punched deep into my head immediately reminded me of its presence. It had been infected and was oozing orange pus.

No, my heart wasn't broken—it had been gone altogether for some time. I had lost everyone I loved and was destined to live among the tense pale human masks of selfless enthusiastic sufferers.

Agnesa Borisovna and Vasiliy Fyodorovich observed my misery with stoic indifference and rare sympathetic nods. They behaved as if I were living through something natural and inevitable. Their attitude changed the day I gave up eating altogether. Regardless of Vasiliy Fyodorovich's anger and wish to bury me alive, Agnesa Borisovna continued to relentlessly put her slurry on my soup plate and push it toward me, widening her eyes in a pleading manner. Everything she cooked was soupy and flavorless, otherwise she and her spouse wouldn't be able to chew it properly: potato soup, boiled cabbage, beet broth, and combination soup with all of the above. Garlic was perhaps the most flavorful item in Agnesa Borisovna's kitchen arsenal. It was consumed once a day, separately from the other items, like dessert.

Vasiliy Fyodorovich's reaction to my worsened appetite was to become less and less patient. He put me into the far dark corner of the shack that was heavily overgrown by spiderwebs, where spiders and other bugs scorched from age and grumpiness made an extremely slow attempt to come across as territorial. There I stood on my feet for ten days without food as occasional ladles of water were brought to me by Agnesa Borisovna's shaky hands. Vasiliy Fyodorovich didn't bat an eyelid for the entire period of my punishment.

Eleven days later, I cracked my eyes open to see if I was still in the same corner. The spiderwebs woven all over my head and torso were balancing me in my crookedly upright position. My vision had been completely blocked. Through my parched lips, I made a noise.

Vasiliy Fyodorovich hurriedly rescued me from the web, put a spade in my hands, and made me shovel the snow outside. My immobilized legs weren't listening to me. I collapsed again and again until the old man tied me to an oak and force-fed me a can of Glashka's expired *pyos pashtet* with his bare hands, completely ignoring my coughing and gagging.

"*Kto ne est, tot ne rabotet! Kto ne est, tot ne rabotet! Kto ne est, tot ne rabotet!*"[13] he repeated to my face a trillion times. "I won't keep a dull-handed woman in this house. You will eat and work as much as I tell you, garrulous *idiotka*!"

The sour-rotten flavor and smell of the expired, maggot-infested dog food the man punched into my throat made me stop resisting Agnesa Borisovna's gastronomic donations in no time.

---

13 From Russian "**кто не ест, тот не работает**": "Who doesn't eat, doesn't work." A famous old Soviet saying.

I suppose eating at the same table with Agnesa Borisovna and Vasiliy Fyodorovich helped me make the proper acquaintance of who they really were. During those awkward hours in which the only sounds were those of soup slurping, I watched them surreptitiously.

They were unbeatably serious individuals with large flared nostrils and thin mouths shaped like skewed, cracked graveyards. Both of them had sharp stork noses. Vasiliy Fyodorovich's was an inch longer. I traced some similarities between the two and Pa, though it seemed like their faces were covered by an iron curtain of the kind of otherness I had yet to learn. There was something about Agnesa Borisovna that gave off a slight hint that she must have owned a warm heart once, though she had been overpowered by her spouse, who had watched and corrected her actions every waking moment since the day the two became BRAKed. Vasiliy Fyodorovich was a retired Wardworker, you see. He was prone to having regular temper tantrums and left no room for Agnesa Borisovna's individuality.

The couple suffered from a severe form of agoraphobia, dental cavities, and Crohn's disease. They feared vivid colors, foreign currency, rats, and all loud things, not to mention that they were terrified of Ma and Pa's inadmissible ways. I believe the extreme agoraphobia came to them around the time when they lost Glashka (LIM referred to her as *Laika*[14] instead), their sweet dog, after which they found out that she'd been sent to outer space as one of Ward's progressive experiments. Even though they always agreed with everything Ward did, the loss of Glashka seemed to have destroyed their hearts. I regularly observed their faces questioning her well-being over multiple cups of black Wardwater-infused tea in the morning, afternoon, and evening. She was all they ever truly loved. They were convinced she was going to come back one day to be awarded the big medal of LIM's scientific luminary—LIMLUM.

Agnesa Borisovna and Vasiliy Fyodorovich never wanted to mention their relation to Papa. In their opinion, he and his dama were as loud and

---

14 From Russian, "**Лайка**," the name of the first dog in the Soviet Union sent to outer space as a scientific experiment.

irritating as LIM's heavy-duty trucks in relation to the entire precious society. My grandparents were by no means thrilled to accept me into their shack when I was mailed to them as their *vnuchka*—their granddaughter. Not only was I hopelessly asleep inside an ice cube when I was dropped off at their door, but I had also been reported to the entire State as an inappropriately raised LIMer with no trustworthy societal values.

The fact that I had been delivered to them at all was Agnesa Borisovna's fault. On the LIM-boycott form she once signed to reject her son, she completely forgot to mention that she intended to boycott Ma and Pa's potential offspring as well.

Before I tell you about all the other horrors I experienced in my new habitat, let me tell you an amorous story (a rare phenomenon this narrative is not rich with) about how my parents met in the first place.

Here is how it went: Mama and Papa met at LOB at age seven, when Papochka was still a stiff-necked child who hadn't learned to break the rules or appreciate the importance of illicit literature. Mamochka was a well-spoken wordsmith from a family of expatriated (or so everyone thought) freaks whose names were shameful to say out loud. Not a lot of LOB-students expressed interest in having a friendly relationship with my hapless Ma, due to her shocking ability to get herself into endless amounts of trouble. In fact, families of other LOB-students made it their parental goal to make sure their children would not be seated next to her during classes. Ma never seemed to mind it one bit. Imagination was her best friend.

According to some of Mama's stories, Pa was amicable toward her the first time they spoke, before the other kids told him more about her family status. She even wrote him a poem to express how grateful she was to make her first friend, but my stiff-necked Pa, raised by Agnesa Borisovna and Vasiliy Fyodorovich, refused to continue his friendship with the odd girl and joined the masses of obediently marching kids whose appearance were becoming more and more identical as days and months went by.

After years of teasing Ma for the abundance of literary preambling she spoke with and all the poetry and prose she wrote and hand-copied from foreign sources, Papa finally admitted to himself that he had been growing reluctantly infatuated with this nervously intelligent, lanky girl. The more he allowed himself to catch her tender, wayward glances and, sometimes, even send her little winks, the less stiff his neck became.

One year before graduation, Papa uncovered Mama's stash of prohibited books deep under the unseemliest oak in the backyard of the school that no one liked to visit due to an elephantine population of surprisingly energized mishkas. Even though Ma was practically impossible to spy on, Pa found a solution after months of bedtime soliloquies. Fortunately, spying ears on the walls hadn't been invented then yet.

On a cold winter night, he stealthily skipped the Wardwater-infused tea to find out what on earth Sveta was up to while everyone else was asleep. He knew the act of spying had to be done at night, since she tended to be caught after the Collective Sleeping Hour, also commonly known as the CSH. As soon as Sveta ran out of the girls' sleeping area, Papa followed her all the way to the backyard, until he saw her playing fearlessly with two gigantic mishkas who somehow didn't intend to eat her. With no drooling or scary grinning of any kind, they sat next to her with their paws peacefully folded on their bellies and listened to her read the books she took out from underneath the ugly oak. That night, Pa's stiff neck had been completely straightened. His flat hair had curled itself into something out of a wild forest. His heart was so big and so affected by Ma's bravery, looks, and charm that he couldn't sleep for days, secretly listening to her recitals in the freezing temperatures of winter nights that felt to him like a warm spring breeze.

The closer my papa came to finishing his studies at LOB, the less probable it seemed to him that he would be able to live his life without Svetlana. He spent hundreds of hours educating himself to write poetically from some of her camouflaged books when she wasn't reading them, and also avoiding being eaten by mishkas by reading to them out loud.

To get Svetlana's full attention and ask her forgiveness for his many years of stupid verbal abuse, Papa resorted to writing the longest, most lyrical love letter to her that took him more than nine months to finish.

By the time it was carefully written down in Pa's best calligraphic cursive with almost no ink blobs in the paper, it was almost too late, since the day he completed his message was his last chance to tell Sveta about his feelings. The LOB graduation day had come. All the graduates were about to be carefully sorted out to be BRAKed with the right individuals, flawlessly chosen by their parents.

The Wardworker-General, who had recently become widowed, was about to arrive to LOB and take my mama with him. Since her parents had been sent away to a faraway place long before her official graduation, the act of BRAK-decision-making on her behalf was granted to the State.

"Hey, Svetlana!" hissed Pa after throwing a rock at Ma's wig without intending to knock it down. The wig fell off, and her spiral hair was immediately set free, ramifying into something similar to weeping willow branches and flamboyant feathers. As soon as she sat up and read the love letter, signed with Pa's initials (as twisted as Ma's hair), her face lit up. She blew him a heartfelt kiss and gestured for him to run after her. Together they galloped away from LOB like a couple of enamored, iridescent creatures, faster than the longest-legged guards trying to catch them. How did they beat the guards? They simply recited their most fervent poems to the grouchy mishkas patrolling the fence of LOB. The latter let them out before the guards were close. Of course, the LOB guards had no clue how two young adults managed to tame the furry animals so peacefully.

Because the hexagonal loudspeaker hadn't been incorporated into LIM's controlling method at that time yet, my parents managed to become BRAKed without raising any suspicion among the BRAK-workers at the BRAK-department, who willingly signed their papers in no time. The only thing the BRAK-workers found suspicious in the newly-BRAKed individuals—and mistook for possible signs of a cold or malnutrition—were their gleaming eyes full of fondness and passion.

That's how Papa BRAKed Mama behind his parents' back, while Mama BRAKed Papa behind the Wardworker-General's back, who had been watching her poor behavior for years and couldn't wait to discipline the scandalously ebullient dama with his own orthodox methods. I believe he had a thing for inflicting pain on damas, since his previous one was found miserably dead, stuck in one of the toilet pipes in his kommunalka. The poor thing longed to break free so much that she decided to flush herself down the toilet one day, while the Wardworker-General was thrusting his fists against the door she had locked with her best, sturdiest mop. Yes, LIM certainly had much more human drama and skeletons hidden in a variety of closets.

A lot of new rules and adjustments to the old rules had been issued after my parents' BRAK was successfully registered. The biggest problem was that it was much too late for the State or Papa's parents to legally separate them. Life wasn't easy for my mamochka and papochka from the first day of their registered union. When Mama found out that she was soon to be a mom, she craftily constructed extra layers of fluffy underskirts to masquerade her slowly inflating abdomen, blaming everything on the cold she was never comfortable with. Rest assured—she had no interest in sharing her news with the State.

Now you know why Vasiliy Fyodorovich, my paternal grandfather, was devastated to see me successfully melt myself from the ice cube and come back to life. I was the fruit of his son's misconduct. He made a habit of hitting me religiously with his grotesque cane—the prettiest thing in the house—as hard as his shaky hands with their noticeably protruding cysts would let him. I even dared to ask Agnesa Borisovna with my upset looks why he was doing it, to which she informed me in written form: "He must hit you daily to make you a functional LIM-citizen with a clear mind. It is a very good thing to be. You will thank him one day."

Hitting young imaginative people on the head was perceived as an efficient way to improve their behavior back then, you see.

I cannot believe they never sent you to LOB. I bet those kretiny haven't taught you to read cursive, multiply, or march, have they? wrote Vasiliy Fyodorovich at the end of his first letter to me.

I wrote him back hesitantly: *Vasiliy Fyodorovich, it is true—I have not been taught to multiply or march yet. On the bright side, I can say quite the opposite about my ability to read cursive—for your information, I have read nearly three hundred books. Half of them were copied by hand in the finest cursive.*

The veins on the old man's neck bulged and throbbed. He wrote to me again, tearing big holes in the paper: *Are you aware that fictional books written for reasons outside of LIM's list of social benefits or for any expectations of freedom are phenomena persecuted by LIM-Leaders and have absolutely no reason to exist? Did those kretiny teach you anything about that?*

I didn't want to reply, but the feeling of a boiling-up protest turned my face into an angry red tomato and made my fingers write to him in a group of fractious capitals: *YES, INDEED. I AM VERY WELL AWARE OF HOW INHUMANE THIS PLACE IS. I HOPE TO GET OUT OF HERE AS SOON AS POSSIBLE AND NEVER COME BACK. I AM SURE THERE IS A WAY.*

Vasiliy Fyodorovich's metallic fence, which served him as a mouth barrier, fell off. After he finished reading my reply, instead of reawakening his venom to hit me, he spit his beet-colored saliva with chunks of garlic in my face, shaking like an aspen leaf. The last two words with which he tore the paper completely apart were "*Avanturistka chertova.*"[15]

He walked to the other side of the shack to find an item sharper than his cane with which to give me another educational beating. I anticipated some form of attack from Agnesa Borisovna too, but instead of abusing me, she quickly wrote to me with her rattling fingers, leaving words chaotically unfinished: *Where were you escaping to when they came after you? What is it like out there?*

The cracking of her joints made Vasiliy Fyodorovich quickly turn around. He snatched the paper from Agnesa Borisovna's hands and scanned it with his nearly transparent gray eyes, and his whole jittery being turned purpler than an eggplant. He grabbed me by the arm to make sure I couldn't hide anywhere in the shack (even though there was no chance even for a small cockroach to be out of anyone's sight in there) and ordered Agnesa Borisovna to chug three teacups of Wardwater. When her suddenly darkened eyes no longer expressed the same concern

15 From Russian: an *avanturistka* is one who seeks the excitement of the Western world's way of life. In Soviet times, this word was used offensively to refer to someone as a traitor. *Chertova* means "goddamn."

for me—poisoned by the sedative effect of the tea—Vasiliy Fyodorovich thrust her into the tualet with his cane, where she remained locked up for the rest of the day.

After fastening a bulky lock on the door of the tualet, Vasiliy Fyodorovich squeezed my arm more firmly, pulled my face an inch away from his dirty mouth reeking of dental deterioration and valerianka, and mouthed these words to me: "There is no better place in the world than LIM. Don't fool yourself. No other state needs a mad, incoherent avanturistka like yourself. *Gde rodilsya tam i prigodilsya.*"[16] People used to pass that hoary idea along quite a lot in those days, you see.

Later that day, Vasiliy Fyodorovich found my parents' letter. The old man set it on fire and made me drink an entire samovar of Wardwater under his unblinking supervision. As soon as I entered the excruciating delirium, he ordered the prune-like ladies in white to make a daily habit of injecting stronger sedatives in my veins.

Tick-tock-tuck.

As much as it hurt, and as much as I desired to choke the "medics" with my bare hands, the injections were actually giving me pleasant streaks of clarity, complacency, and the desire to yield to everything in LIM. What Ma and Pa had asked of me in their last letter started to seem like an impossible mission to me. My mind deflated. I even started waiting for Glashka with a notorious sulky expression, sighing over many cups next to the puffing samovar.

Every day of my new life was nothing but a sultry winter night full of moist, elderly fragrances and bitter mists. Once my agile fingers had gone pudgy, numb, and "speech-impaired," indicating that there were no

16 A Russian phrase meaning "There is no use for you outside of the country you were born." Growing up, I heard this phrase from every schoolteacher I had. We were brainwashed into thinking that immigration to foreign countries was a highly dishonorable phenomenon. I remember noticing how clueless schoolchildren looked when they heard the phrase.

more traces of word-creation left in them, Agnesa Borisovna concluded that I had recovered fully. Vasiliy Fyodorovich, in his turn, was positive that I was ready to be given oodles of housekeeping tasks accompanied by supremely harsh beatings if not performed properly.

The most arduous daily task I suffered from was preparing their food on an all-purpose food grinder we referred to as *rubilka*, which refused to grind anything due to its ancient origin. Agnesa Borisovna and Vasiliy Fyodorovich ate everything thoroughly granulated for reasons of catastrophic dental cavities, which caused them insufferable toothaches that occurred in the least expected moments. Whenever they would hurriedly grab and press their old dusty pillows harshly against each other's bunched-up faces (in order to maintain the acceptable quietude, of course), I knew their teeth were aching.

Shoveling endless amounts of snow, melting it into buckets, mopping, washing and cutting beets for meals, making soup, and brewing tea three times a day were on my chore list as well. My beet-stained hands always remained purple back then, like some inexcusable gang-affiliated hematoma.

Tick-tock-tuck.

Three months later, I had finally learned to cater to Agnesa Borisovna and Vasiliy Fyodorovich's requests at a decent level and speed. I also stopped doubting the beneficial aspects of Wardwater; it made my life at the shack seem a lot more bearable. In fact, I purposefully added it to everything I consumed. I discovered multiple supplies of it hidden in the snow around the well and everywhere else in the village. Apparently, someone had an illegal production of it somewhere near. My wet, runny nose had gradually changed in shape and color from the overconsumption of the drink: it had become purple, like my hands, and had more volume on its sides. *Nos-kartoshka*—potato nose—was the new nickname Vasiliy Fyodorovich generously gave me. I think he knew I was drunk practically all the time, but he didn't mind it. The droopy bags nesting under my eyes created an immediate resemblance to bulldogs. Ironically, my worsened zigzagged drunken walk was only a harmless solution to my former clumsiness—I stopped knocking down the brittle items due to the crookedness of the shack's floor.

Once Agnesa Borisovna and Vasiliy Fyodorovich didn't see any more otherness in me, they decided to let me go outside and introduce myself to the only four neighbors in the village, whose noses were also very kartoshka-like. The two men and two women had red bow ties adorning their necks, the kind I had never seen before. Their long, narrow heads were poorly controlled and balanced due to the never-ending hiccups they were inconveniently affected by. For the noticeable head-shape differences and for many other reasons I could never fathom, the passive-aggressive neighbors hardly ever missed a chance to throw me against the cold linoleum in their Doms covered in smelly chloral. That's how I learned that having an oddly shaped head with weather vane hair and no affiliation with bow ties was a hard thing to live with back then.

After watching my repeatedly unsuccessful interactions with our neighbors, Agnesa Borisovna ended up taking me to a place called Salon Nom 1. She convinced her husband, who wanted me to suffer from my poor understanding of LIM-societal function, that having a normal-looking, straightened-up vnuchka was going to enormously benefit their irrefutably flawless reputation. While I was lying facedown on the dirty linoleum floor at Dom of the cross-eyed Mashka (one of the neighbors), Agnesa Borisovna rescued me from the humiliating torture and ordered me to get ready for something of great importance. I couldn't understand her mumbling due to my hearing impairment, though by the judgmental way she looked me up and down, I could tell that it had something to do with how displeased everyone was with my overall look.

Before we walked into the midst of the snowstorm to find our destination, Agnesa Borisovna stuck two hot cloth-wrapped potatoes in my pockets, like Pa once did, then pulled an empty dirty potato sack tightly over my head. We sat on a sleigh attached to a single scrawny wolf, who took us to the only square building in the surrounding woods, the color of jaundice, proudly displaying its worn-out sign: Salon Nom 1.

Tick-tock-tuck.

Clatter.

CHAPTER III

SALON NOM 1: GASTRO NOM NOM

SALON NOM I WAS A BIZARRE PLACE with square buckets hung on the tattered ceiling attached to thick black wires. It was striking to see an army of identical ladies come and go from the place. Their polished multitude resembled an ancient postcard printed in countless copies.

When we entered the building, Agnesa Borisovna took the potato sack off my head and pushed me toward the dry-looking hefty woman staring at me with a too-obvious display of disgust. I swear she looked as hard and plain as one of those croutons Ma used to feed to the most aggressive stray dogs for self-protective distraction. We called croutons *suhariki* in LIML. Based on the size of her chair and her poise, the suharik-lady operated the place. She and everyone else inside Salon Nom 1 rounded their eyes in shock when they saw what I really looked like. I was immediately commanded to sign twenty pages of something I couldn't understand due to the formality of the language it was written in. After I finished signing and stamping page twenty, the suharik-lady seated me on a wheeled-stool and addressed to Agnesa Borisovna: "Such a vulgar entourage! First time?"

Agnesa Borisovna nodded affirmatively.

They tied me into an impressive bundle of thick knots, making me feel like a pirate-captured victim ready to be thrown off the boat to the cunning sharks. Or so I imagined. When my head was placed under one of the buckets, I couldn't quit shaking—I was anticipating a beheading. Naturally.

Agnesa Borisovna put her cold hands on mine and sweetly mouthed, "You will be *kak vse* soon! It is a very good thing for you to be."

Tick-tock-tuck.

She let go of my hands and walked to the other end of the room, watching me with her arms crossed comfortably on her chest. I squeezed my eyes tight.

To my surprise, I wasn't beheaded at all. Instead, the strange bucket trimmed my hair and gently (my definition of *gentle* was skewed back then) washed my face. The machine synchronized my look with the appearance of all other ladies in LIM. According to the LIM-Dama booklet, women were expected to wear alabaster *maquiage* to achieve the precise look of the official LIM-Dama. The portrait of the official LIM-Dama personage was issued by the State annually and printed on the first page of the booklet. Every woman in LIM hung the portrait of LIM-Dama on her bathroom mirror and was given a special kit to recreate the required look in utmost proximity. The maquiage was used to make ladies' faces look as white as LIM's snow (but lighter in color and cleaner, since LIM tended to overestimate the quality of the local snow).

As for the male population, all men in LIM were required to have an identical bushy mustache. They could be penalized for cutting it shorter or shaving it off altogether. Those who didn't have enough testosterone to grow a bush on their face were given faux facial hair and industrial adhesive to recreate the requirement. Men had their own booklet with a poster of the perfect male LIMer—LIM-Muzh—looking at them from their bathroom mirrors. Wardworkers glued the updated LIM-Dama and LIM-Muzh personage portraits in people's tualets once a year. There were two varieties of LIM-Damas and LIM-Muzhes for the population:

ages 17–50 and 50–100. The older category had their hair chopped short. They did not need to apply alabaster like everyone else anymore, since their faces had somehow acquired their natural unwashable whiteness.

The bucket trimmed my hair, tied it into a tight bun, threw an ugly wig on my head, and deliberately spread thick smears of alabaster all over my face. Agnesa Borisovna applauded to me when she saw her new LIM-Dama–affiliated vnuchka emerge from the bucket.

"*Pryam kak vse!*"[17] she exclaimed in a reserved expression of stiff joy.

Even Vasiliy Fyodorovich had to restrain the two glistening drops of proud tears when we returned to the shack. "Now I can tell we are related after all!" he said to me with a smirk.

I was immediately treated with more respect by the four neighbors in the village. They even stopped shutting doors in my face.

The next step to becoming a well-intentioned LIM-Dama was learning to remain patient while waiting in the unfathomably long line (referred to as *ochered*) to the Gastro Chambers of Distribution (the GCD) to attain goods for my new household. On average, the wait was about two hours and forty minutes. The first time I waited, I didn't have the strength to reach any of the chambers of goods. A terrible frostbite knocked me out in about one hour and ten minutes. The second time, the same kind of frostbite affected me after about an hour and twenty minutes of surviving the ochered. I kept failing to attain the food and was fed more expired pyos pashtet by Vasiliy Fyodorovich as a form of gastronomic punishment, until he allowed Agnesa Borisovna to stuff my tulup with freshly boiled potatoes wrapped in cloth. "What a waste!" he wrote to me at tea.

My clothes stuffed with at least a dozen hot potatoes saved me from several hundred intolerable episodes of frostbite. Several hours a week, usually in the morning—which, as you already know, looked as dark as night—I had to wait in a seemingly never-ending ochered to the GCD to attain the basic survival essentials, for which I had to fill out several hun-

17 A Russian phrase meaning, "Just like everyone else!"

dred forms demanding that I state the entire breakdown of my communal unit's daily consumption and complete the truth-detecting interview to identify whether or not I had been disloyal or dishonest to LIM, along with take my Cold Hand Medical Test—CHMT for short. The latter was the simplest of tests in the State: the old ladies in white placed people's hands into a bucket of cold water and counted how long they could stay there. Based on the answers given in all of the forms and each individual's tolerance of cold temperatures, the State concluded if there was any need to add more sedatives to certain products to calm the citizens' growing concerns, hunger, fatigue, depression, frostbite, and dissatisfaction. Questions of a complaining nature or suggestions for improvement were never presented to LIMers in any of the provided forms. Such privilege had been clipped out from the LIM papers longer than one hundred years ago.

The GCD consisted of three departments: Gastro NOM Nom 1, HOZ MYLO Nom 1, and Garment and Clog Nom 1.

CHAMBER *NOM* 1: GASTRO NOM NOM 1

This place distributed edibles that weren't prohibited from the LIM Consumption Charter (generally referred to as the LIMConCha). The LIMConCha was a brief gastronomic agreement printed in the *LIM Weekly* as an arrangement of products LIMers were scheduled to consume. LIMers had to tear it out of the newspaper and sign it with their full names before attaining the products.

This was pretty much the entirety of Gastro NOM Nom 1's contents:

1. Brown potatoes: *one kilogram twice a week per family unit. Or less.* This chamber contained lots of potatoes piled in chubby circles that vaguely resembled giant snowmen. Besides being a popular edible, they were also distributed for hand-warming purposes to those whose hands tended to freeze faster than others. How kind!

2. Dill: *four big bunches twice a week per family unit. Or more for rare festive occasions.* All LIMers, including my parents, abused the aromatic green triffid-like frond to an outrageous degree for

no particular reason. It seemed perfectly normal to anyone in the State to smother every single meal with those visually innocuous chopped flecks that were sometimes served as large bushes (they had a highly constricting effect on one's throat) for variety. Pa told me once that each LIMer ate enough dill each year to fill two large suitcases.

3. Cabbage: *half a head a week per family unit.* Fried or boiled. An essential borscht ingredient.

4. Garlic: *one hundred cloves a week per family unit. Or more, depending on how sick everyone is.* As you can tell, garlic was consumed in amounts more outrageous than those of dill, thanks to its healing and immune-boosting properties—the plant had lots of potential to save LIM from human extinction by strengthening the human immune system. It was recommended to be chewed constantly, like gum, and was added to every dish.

5. Birch tree juice: *one liter a month per family unit.* It was a special, vaguely sweet treat attained through the stick-your-ax-in-birch-tree-trunks technique. Ma and Pa used to save it for me to make my childhood more . . . flavorful.

6. Beets: *one kilogram once a week per family unit. Or less.* Beets grew in some parts of LIM in abundance due to their impressive low-temperature tolerance and were used to make borscht.

7. Dead stray animals' execrable intestine pashtet: *one small jar a week per one DOMesticated animal in case it behaves properly.* This was used for DOMesticated dogs, cats, and those who ran out of edibles and were desperate to eat anything.

8. Premade *holodec*: *one jar a month per family unit. Or not.* Holodec was a rather bizarre dish—it consisted of congealed gelatin with lots of salt, pigeon meat, and hearts. Wardworkers killed the loudest pigeons and used them to feed the population.

9. Buckwheat and *manka*: *a bag a month of one or the other per family unit. Or less.* These were soupy breakfast essentials and important side dishes for better hunger satisfaction.

10. Black sour bread, darker than tart: *half a brick a week per family unit.*

11. Eskimo, a sticky imitation of ice cream covered in fragile digestible plastic resembling chocolate: *one eskimo every two weeks per family unit.* This item was dearly loved by the population for its hardly noticeable hints of sweetness.

12. Frozen cow's tongue: *distributed once a year strictly to the best-behaved citizens, and only as chut-chut.* There used to be days in LIM when cows were still alive and eaten regularly. Their frozen tongues were all that was left of them. Sheer delicacy.

13. "Princessa": *four tablespoons a week per family unit.* Princessa was black bitter tea with a distinct smell of charcoal and gasoline. People brewed and infused it with Wardwater for warmth, quiet, conversation-free social hours, and games of chess.

14. Salt: *one teaspoon a month per family unit.* It was disastrously deficient back then and was collected and kept with utmost care.

15. Wardwater: *consumed by the population daily.* This was the most essential item in this chamber, as you already know. It was fermented and stored in a humongous witchy cauldron in the middle of Gastro NOM Nom 1 and was connected to hundreds of thin pipes controlling the elements added to it. Due to its addictive nature, some inventive LIMers taught themselves to make their own version of it under their tables to either trade out of decency or consume out of misery.

CHAMBER NOM 2: HOZ MYLO NOM 1

Soap for everyone's acceptable cleanliness was distributed to the population at Chamber NOM 2. One modest bar of brown soap, made from the fat of dead stray animals, came with a pencil-written note indicating that only 0.001 inches of it could be used by each person daily. Excessive perspiration was a completely appropriate thing in LIM: it was okay to skip hoz mylo daily use altogether, which wasn't punishable and had the potential to come across as an honorable economic act. In general, people used hoz mylo to wash their heads, whole bodies, floors, dirty dishes, and, sometimes, DOMesticated pets.

CHAMБЭЯ NOM 3: GAЯMЭИT AИD CLOG NOM 1

This section resembled a morgue with people's bodies hanging on racks. Nyet, nyet—there were no corpses actually hanging there (or so I had been told). It was filled with recycled winter coats, tulups that were no longer needed by their former owners, most often because they were dead and already buried in snow. Some of them were still alive, though they had become victims of unfortunate rebellious accidents, making them publicly useless. People like that had been sent away to serve their penance in a place you would never be able to find on the map.

Each well-intentioned LIMer was entitled to become a happy owner of a raggedy-looking secondhand tulup. Only the Wardworkers were given new ones. Each tulup had been labeled with its previous owner's names written on them in a choppy, illegible cursive. Next came mustard pants, underpants for pants, underpants for underpants, shirts for undershirts, undershirts for undershirts, and thick mustard jackets for men and boys. Triple-layered tights and long baggy dresses (with underdresses, of course) were distributed to women and girls. Fluffy hats were the only optional item, since they came in one size and didn't fit some people's heads.

(LIM-Leaders had once attempted to force big-headed people to wear the hats regardless of their discomfort, but, alas, the latter's brains had been deformed under the monstrous pressure of the hats' bands. Not knowing what to do with these brain-disfigured individuals, though seeing their willingness to serve the State with even more enthusiasm than before, the LIM-Leaders turned the poor citizens into their eager assistants.)

The shoes at Garment and Clog NOM 1 were the same for everybody—valenki-kaloshis of one size for men, women, and children tall enough to exceed their valenki-kaloshis' length and height by at least two feet. People stuffed them with old rags in case they didn't fit.

And that was all LIM had to offer to its citizens. "Less is more," people liked to remind one another in those days with a nervous pat on each other's skinny unwashed backs.

The three Chambers' accounts were operated by female accountants with huge shoulder pads—the LIM Buh-Galters, intimidating-looking ladies who constantly licked and moved their blistered fingers along the endless sheets of account information for each distributed item. Each lady had a long nail carved into the shape of a key. They used them to lock or unlock the confidential accounting safe filled with sheets and coupons earned by LIMers from their work done for the State. Large wooden abacuses were perched on iron credenzas. Buh-Galters operated them with utmost precision and manual agility. "Vzhik-vzhik-vzhik-lick-lick-lick" all day long. And clatter.

CHAPTER IV

WARDDOOR: HIGHER EDUCATION

AFTER I WAS TUTORED TO CORRELATE WITH every remaining aspect of the proper LIM-citizen lifestyle, including walking straight, drinking the appropriate amounts of Wardwater, keeping my appearance LIM-Dama-neutral, and refraining from thinking anything contradictory, Agnesa Borisovna and Vasiliy Fyodorovich sent me to Warddoor—a brittle, dismal building with tall ceilings and various sullen-looking metal physiognomies situated all around the top level—five times a week. It was a mandatory place where seventeen-year-old people were prepared to become Wardworkers.

Warddoor was what one might expect a wartime classroom to look like. Within its confines, order was significantly more important than education. The first impression you would get from glancing at it was that it was not a place of education, but merely a prison. LIM made it its goal to incorporate every citizen into the necessary ecosystem of local mass production, including the unspoken protective methods employed to save the land from any unnecessary invasions from outside.

No, I wasn't treated with the same stoic academic precision as the others at Warddoor as you may have hoped, simply because LIM-Leaders had gathered all the unsavory information about my contradictory childhood ruined by barrages of frivolous ideas. Warddoor professors were aware that I had, of all things, frozen myself shortly prior to my enrollment in a display of excessive emotional protest.

After negotiating for a good amount of time, they stated that I had to take three thousand extra hours of training to reach the level of LIM-awareness all other young people in LOB already had, which consisted of memorizing thousands of numbers, equations, and special codes from the yellowish pages smelling of helium. After I'd been tested for my bare minimum knowledge prior to attending Warddoor, it was concluded that what I was lacking and needed to learn in serious abundance were numerology and ballet.

There were hardly any nonmathematical symbols in the Warddoor materials given to me. The only written letters I found in those pages either explained what to do with the given tasks or presented the text of LIM's anthem for a recital. The multiple prints of LIM's anthem expressed oodles of morbid optimism, and so did the series of repetitive exclamatory expressions for marching that were printed in all Warddoor materials. The papers, tied into little binders for everyone's memorization, resembled an eerie death record: all their previous attendants' names had been thickly crossed out from them, as if dismissed or dead. These were the names before mine: two Konstantins, three Sonechkas, and about twelve Vasiliys.

Most inspectors at Warddoor carried themselves like ancient militaristic metal statues. Less than a handful of them possessed a hardly noticeable poise and romantic gait similar to that of churning clouds on a misty day. The more I watched them walk, the more I knew who they really were by the comically skittish looks on their faces. Those cloudy ones were my family's old Gosti, who had been in LIM-Muzh-Dama disguise. They were the ones who were too scared to escape the State with us. Despite the fact that they looked identical to everyone else in the building, they were somehow significantly out of place. I almost ran up to them during my first day of Warddoor studies; how could I not recognize Gosti by the smell of their skin and some of the raggedy books from Dom they were deliberately carrying in their pockets? It was a relief to see parts of my past preserved, carefully masked by faux covers and wigs.

The Gosti gave me professorial nods of feigned respect, as if we had never met, when I waved at them. The moment I caught their eyes, they turned on their heels and scattered like a team of cockroaches in four different directions; they never looked back at me.

The only Warddoor professor who neither minded showing me his special attention nor ever stopped throwing stern glances at me was the man I feared the most—the man who used to pretend to be my parents' Gost. Timofey, that is. Of all Warddoor professors on LIM's Earth, *he* happened to become my numerology teacher. Every Warddoor-goer referred to him by his first name and patronymic, which made his name sound twice as evil: Timofey Grigorievich. The sound of his full name sends my memories to a place darker than the LIM sky. His academic status was higher than other professors' due to his massive spying achievements and most advanced approach to punishment. "The man of one book" was the official name of his rank, meaning every new educational adjustment had to go through his supervision and approval.

In less than a month, the man had exacerbated my quickly growing numerophobia to the point of complete physical dysfunction (or rather numbness) and mental hysteria. I spent five hours a day in Warddoor's private numerology room, facing Timofey Grigorievich's ice-cold face framed by a giant clock behind his back like a halo. The stupid mechanism always worked way too fast when I needed more time to finish my tasks and way too slow when I was impatiently counting the seconds until my torture would come to an end. To intensify my hatred of numerology, Timofey Grigorievich adopted a poisonous black-and-white pet snake from some dubious inostranec and kept it in a large glass bottle glued to my desk. Not only did he constantly challenge me by making me face the biggest fear I had from a three-inch proximity, but he also exclusively selected arithmetic labyrinths of disastrous quality to push me toward finding the perfectly dry mathematical explanation for everything presented by the omnipresent haze of quiet LIM confusion.

Timofey Grigorievich profoundly enjoyed scanning me with his laser eyes every time I didn't have the right answer. I hid my numerophobia as best I could, hoping I could successfully claim myself to be a decent worker at the end of the program in order to avoid working at the GCD's basement, where, according to the Warddoor-goer booklet, the least-obedient graduates were subjected to dissecting stray animals for pashtet.

After I had spent the required hours locked in the wicked numerology room with the coldhearted man and his macabre snake, I was locked in a small windowless cubicle for eight hours without any breaks. It was my last and only chance to solve thousands of the hardest, most skull-cracking mathematical equations ever to graduate from Warddoor. The images of numeric monsters I failed to untangle never stopped haunting me. Especially eights, because Timofey Grigorievich had a particularly terrifying way of writing them.

Eight hours later, I found out that I hadn't passed the test. The hexagonal loudspeaker announced the arrival of the lowest-quality worker in all of LIM. Every Warddoor-goer was invited to throw an item of their choice at me during my failed graduation ceremony. By the end of my profoundly humiliating graduation march, I was covered in ink, chunks of dirty snow, and dead cats.

Luckily (and believe me, luck stubbornly refused to ally with me back then), I wasn't sent to dissect stray animals. I suspect the booklet only said that to boost Warddoor-goers' obedience. Everything in that strange institution was based on fear.

Another thing I was expected to master and perform at Warddoor before my graduation was the rigorous ballet training taught by Pangina Elena Alexandrovna. I inwardly called her Pan-*gi*-na, like *angina*, because she was like a vile infection. Every inch of that woman was soaked in draconian cruelty. Her villainous and gaunt grimace, tightened by the flawless bun on her head, was married to an almost mythological crooked grin. Even her constant limping had a bloodcurdling quality to it that evoked no sympathy—she moved around the ballroom with a walking stick that she most commonly used as a torture device, just like Vasiliy Fyodorovich.

The longer the LIM ballerinas attended Pangina's classes, the more behavioral similarities they inherited from her, including the limp. Ballerinas at Warddoor were very thin, composed, obedient, and pain-resistant. Some LIM-Damas had to starve themselves for a whole semester to be accepted to the ballroom, though my malnutrition gave me an immediate pass to the ballet class as far as body type was concerned. Another sliver of slippery luck!

By that point, I had learned to be decent at pretending to be obedient and take strenuous hits from Vasiliy Fyodorovich. Alas, my gracefulness left much room for improvement. Freezing myself for three full years and feeling cold practically all the time had deprived my hands and feet of their desirable agility. I was a clumsy LIM-Dama, you see. For that reason, as well as my rarely displayed but very present rebellious nature, I was known as the worst ballerina at Warddoor.

Pangina beat me with her walking stick more often than Vasiliy Fyodorovich. In fact, they turned out to be old comrades. Her beatings were by far worse than his. They were stronger than anyone ever expected them to be, thanks to their aesthetic, perfectionism-based critical approach. At least she didn't keep any snakes in her office. Instead of scaring me with something more psychological in nature, she chose physical methods and cracked me in the bones several times per class. Constellations of bruises were left on my legs and back by her walking stick—blue, green, purple, yellow, and red. I must have been the most colorful living being in LIM back then.

After my unsuccessful graduation from Warddoor, all of my old phobias, discomforts, injuries, and fears of persecution had miraculously dissipated. Perhaps it had something to do with the amount of abuse I had managed to survive, or perhaps everything that had seemed so alien and illogical to me years ago in Dom had transitioned into an inevitable social habit, or rather tolerance. What doesn't kill us makes us stronger, right? I had become wonderfully apathetic.

My Warddoor-and-Wardwater-infested mind had developed another new habit: I sympathized with the LIM-issued codes regularly and thought highly of their creators. Glory days! Marching! Ah! *Kakaya krasota!*[18] I had at last been turned into one of the mechanical puppets of the overbearing crowd, enthusiastically marching along the frozen streets as smoothly and passively as a fish resilient to most forms of thought.

Perhaps I can achieve happiness and moral satisfaction by erasing my resistance. Maybe being "kak vse" is not an altogether bad ambition, I inwardly repeated to myself, as if drilling a screw into my brain, while slurping Wardwater-infused cold borscht. *I don't want to wind up like Ma and Pa. There was no use in their resistance . . .*

Tick-tock-tuck.

18 From Russian "**какая красота!**"—"such beauty/bliss"!

CHAPTER V

CO-PULATION: HOW I LEARNED ABOUT INTIMACY

Two more years passed. LIM finally fully approved of my behavior and issued me my first red bow tie, sewn into the skin of my neck so I could never take it off without the Wardworkers' assistance. To go along with everybody who had already participated in the Bow Tie Club (BOCL), I had to accustom myself to visiting Salon Nom 1 to cut and brush my tangled hair daily. The experience was difficult—it caused a lot of wounds on my scalp, but my pain resistance remained just as bulletproof.

The day I was wholesomely appraised by Agnesa Borisovna, Vasiliy Fyodorovich, and some of our hiccupping neighbors on my success at getting a bigger, silkier red bow tie at BOCL, they dressed me in an ugly, puffier-than-normal mustard dress and invited the Wardworker-General over for Princessa tea. The man had become significantly slower and more obese since the day he arrested my parents; he had tripled in size due to some unknown form of depression. Fyodor Fyodorovich was his real name. From the foul smell of sardines and garlic, I had no doubt who the man was.

To say the man was obnoxious would be insufficient in any scenario. The nastiest form of behavior he didn't bother to hide was his unfortunate habit of scratching himself between his legs with the nail of a fully extended index finger more often than you can imagine. He did it with a long, meaningful pause as if about to say something intelligent, but this never seemed to be the case. The outward manifestation of his obsessive compulsion made a squeaky sound with a far-traveling echo.

When Fyodor Fyodorovich finished struggling with sitting himself in the chair, Agnesa Borisovna pushed me forward and gestured for me to offer him my hand. My guts churned at the look of Fyodor Fyodorovich's hairy paw-like hands with the long nails he used for his boorish scratching, even hairier eyebrows completely covering his eyes, tiny cantaloupe head, and the biggest red bow tie hanging on his drowned-in-three-chins Adam's apple. Only one group of LIMers had bow ties this size, thanks to their conspiring with LIM-Leaders. I imagined that Vasiliy Fyodorovich would never let me sign the BRAK-agreement with a non-Wardworker. Back then, Wardworker was considered a desirable position due to its shady specifics—Wardworkers accepted a lot of *vzyatki*, or bribes, from the population, often in edible form.

Fyodor Fyodorovich's favorite *vzyatka* was meaty holodec stuffed with pieces of stray animal organs and fat. The loathsome man's eyebrows jiggled at me with uncomfortable coquetry the first time we silently drank tea in front of Agnesa Borisovna and Vasiliy Fyodorovich, who sat shoulder to shoulder with their best posture like two Egyptian cat statues. They watched us motionlessly, though from time to time, the involuntary spasmodic tapping of their walking sticks gave away how terribly eager they were to let this man take me with him.

The second time I drank tea with Fyodor Fyodorovich, Agnesa Borisovna and Vasiliy Fyodorovich left us alone in the tearoom. From the corner of my eye, I saw Agnesa Borisovna peeping at me curiously through the hole in the tualet room's wall. The man moved his chair closer to me, leaned over me with a great deal of effort, and proceeded to press his greasy soup-coated lips against my dry hands. The cracks in my palms were so deep that the garlic-infused drops of his saliva burned them with a sizzling explosion.

I cringed. I pouted. I twisted my face and body into the least flattering grimaces and lopsided poses I could manage, but nothing seemed to be self-explanatory enough; the man didn't see that his courting act was in no way reciprocated by me. Before departing, he pressed his gross mouth against my hand again.

I crossed my eyes at him, wishing to resemble a scary-looking tyrannosaur of sorts, but that didn't instigate the man to react accordingly. To be as revolting as any young lady can be, I blew a multitude of bubbles out of my saliva, like a mischievous toddler. Some of them popped and landed on his mustache in strangely beautiful drops of dew. How else could an imprisoned woman in my situation defend herself from an unwanted arranged marriage, do you think? Based on Fyodor Fyodorovich's eyebrow movements, he must have thought I was clinically insane.

At our third tea, he came prepared: there were no more attempts from him to kiss my hands. Instead, he brought a box of chess to arrange a well-known classical courting interaction widely practiced among LIMers and poured an abundance of the specially prepared GCD-issued courting potion in our teacups. Alas, even the highly complicated game of chess—and the fact that I was practically overdosing on the courting potion—didn't solve our incompatibility problem.

Agnesa Borisovna stormed into the room after she had waited the exact amount of time assigned for our date. The old lady stared at us hopefully with a hint of sentimentality hidden in her quivering stapled lips. From the questioning metronome-like blinks exchanged between Fyodor Fyodorovich and me, Vasiliy Fyodorovich was devastated to admit to himself that the tea date hadn't met his expectations. He hit me over the head with his cane and whisper-barked straight to my face: "Ballet, now!"

The poorly-chewed garlic and cabbage leftovers from our last meal galloped out through his half-unstapled mouth into my hair and hung themselves in it like putrid garlands. They ended up nesting there for the rest of the week, until my next scheduled bath.

Agnesa Borisovna threw a pair of moldy pointe shoes to me from her personal ruffled chest. They were twice her age. The act was accompanied by a sigh that didn't imply anything savory, despite the fact that she believed that being an exceptional ballerina had a phenomenal effect on influencing LIM-Damas' courting processes with LIM-Muzhes. Her eyes sadly glanced at the bunch of Pa's old photographs she had kept in secret for as long as he had been officially boycotted. They were buried under a pile of torn tutus, her beloved *matreshkas*, and Glashka's canned food.

Vasiliy Fyodorovich impatiently grabbed her arm and locked the door with an unacceptably loud "POO-DOOF." The ceiling crumbled in response to the grumpy old man's boorish treatment. It always reacted that way if not surrounded by supreme care, just like everything else in the house. For instance, in moments of anger, Agnesa Borisovna's samovar tended to release chunks of dirt instead of tea. Something similar, though a lot less harmless, happened to their *tolchok*[19]on a regular basis.

While forcing my feet inside the moth-eaten pointe shoes that were clearly too small for me, I almost died from a sneeze attack caused by the ceiling's chunks of broken plaster entering my respiratory system like prickly snowflakes. That moment was filled with so much irritability and exasperation from Vasiliy Fyodorovich, spying on me from the tualet, that the ceiling and samovar both quacked and spit indignantly at the wall behind which the man was tapping his feet like a lunatic. No matter how hard I tried, nothing helped me shrink my feet enough to be able to wear the pointe shoes.

Fyodor Fyodorovich gave off a wide yawn, put on his tulup, and was about to depart when Vasiliy Fyodorovich stormed into the room with newly handwritten official permission to either break or amputate my toes. This is what he added at the end of the note: *You will do her a*

19 From Russian, referring to the main part of a toilet.

favor by chopping her toes off. Nobody likes women with big feet. I did that to Agnesa Borisovna's toes at our third tea, too. It worked.

Vasiliy Fyodorovich unwrapped an oxidized sledgehammer and a saw the size of a sea pike. The fat man seemed to contemplate which tool of torment he would rather utilize. After a short-lived expression of thoughtfulness, he nodded in agreement with himself, shut my mouth with a large beet, and, without any preamble, hit my toes with the sledgehammer. Fortunately, my courting potion overdose made the torture almost painless.

In my hazy state, I awkwardly pirouetted before Fyodor Fyodorovich, like a doll with no aptitude for gracefulness inside a heartrendingly whiny, out-of-tune music box, until he lifted himself off the chair and stretched his hairy paw-hands toward my outrageous mustard dress. While bluntly poking my elbows and hair (he could have eaten a whole borscht out of it at that point) with the same simplistic animalism found among apes, the man continuously smelled my armpits. His touch left sensations of moist chunks of dough on my skin. After measuring me with a ruler from every angle, he approved of my overall size and proceeded to press, rub, and scrub all of his bellies against me, breathing heavily like a coal-powered train. It was the first time I saw his colorless eyes; the curtain-eyebrows that grew on his face lifted themselves up half an inch. The man's stern face grew into something intentionally lascivious.

"You are mine now, Sveta . . ." he whispered in my ear.

In two days, Fyodor Fyodorovich asked for Vasiliy Fyodorovich's official permission to glue our bow ties together. The gluing part was a recent law adjustment in LIM. According to LIM-Leaders, the old BRAK-agreement wasn't, after all, entirely perfect and needed to be readjusted. A disgraceful case of chess-related adultery had been detected in someone's household a week earlier. Some adventurous LIM-Dama (avanturistka!) had been caught playing chess with some careless (!) LIM-Muzh named Alexey Vasilievich, after she'd signed the BRAK-agreement (!!) with Konstantin Konstantinovich (a presumably well-intentioned citizen).

Prior to being sent to the deepest woods of the State to serve her punishment and gain moral improvement for her irresponsible inclination to play chess, LIM-Leaders required that she explain the nature of her actions in an official form written in her own blood. She wrote: *I am guilty of enjoying playing chess with my comrade to entertain myself instead of for courting purposes. I am terribly sorry.* The answer instigated LIM-Leaders to change the BRAK law immediately: everyone newly BRAKed was subjected to being glued to the other person, bow tie to bow tie. Ward believed it created the right two-person unison for a smoother collective function with no distractions.

I wasn't sure exactly what was going to happen after the gluing procedure. In case you have to know, I was completely dismayed by the vaguest thought of having to be permanently close to the smelly, wet Wardworker-General, especially after I read the booklet on my new responsibilities as a BRAKed LIM-Dama.

The day I was told to gather my possessions in order to be ready to depart for my new BRAK-home, I moved my head in denial as fast as a helicopter rotor. Without seeing any sort of compassion from Agnesa Borisovna, I grabbed Vasiliy Fyodorovich's old tin bucket and threw it at the table, where Fyodor Fyodorovich was filling out the Ward Gluing BRAK Act application, also referred to as WGBRAC. The thundering noise and frivolousness of my action made Agnesa Borisovna and Vasiliy Fyodorovich's faces look purpler than the beets in their soup.

Vasiliy Fyodorovich took me outside and hit me with his cane at least a thousand times. While tossing and turning in the snow, I could see his shaky knuckles repeating the same hateful motion over and over, over and over, over and over again . . . I vaguely remember seeing Agnesa Borisovna quietly watching drops of blood running down my dirty BRAK dress.

The two lifted my legs off the ground and dragged me back into the shack. I was seated at the table in the same Egyptian-cat-statue posture they had taught me to assume before other LIMers. Blood and tears covered my mustard dress. Fyodor Fyodorovich hit the samovar to pour me a cup of tea, but the sensitive-to-physical-abuse utensil refused to operate properly—it filled my cup with chunks of dirt. Everyone in the room watched big red drops falling from the tip of my nose into the scruffy old cup. Agnesa Borisovna brought my LIM-Dama maquiage and generously powdered my face—inevitably turning pink—with alabaster. After hesitating for about ten minutes, Fyodor Fyodorovich told her to stop and offered me a handkerchief. He took my hand and finished filling out the papers for WGBRAC on my behalf quite impatiently.

The moment Vasiliy Fyodorovich finished reading and gave us a positive nod, I saw my reflection drowning in the crimson tea, leaving a gasoline-like linear distortion. The shapeless blob read: "Run!"

The temporary vision sobered me up and gave me the courage to spill a whole kettle of burning-hot Princessa tea onto Fyodor Fyodorovich's face. His steamy burns strangely repeated the same contour I had just seen in my cup. He fainted. After receiving another dozen cane hits to my head, I fainted too.

Unfortunately, the act of burning Fyodor Fyodorovich's face was only a temporary hindrance; the man glued me to himself as soon as his wounds healed. Ward announced us WGBRACed and rewarded us with a big bag of potatoes, some holodec, and a few pieces of cow's tongue. Additionally, I had to vow to stop spilling hot tea and throwing buckets at Fyodor Fyodorovich, since at that point I was dovetailing with all of his chins, constantly attached to him, bow tie to bow tie. My last name changed to Tugodumova, the most unfortunate last name in all of LIM due to the fact that its root means *lamebrain*. There was nothing in the world I could do to avoid accepting it. The only time I walked freely unglued from Tugodumov Fyodor Fyodorovich was when he locked the private square room we were granted in a kommunalka shared by three other glued couples.

I refused to call that place Dom. The strangely azoic square room consisted of one bed, two square hangers on the wall married to a pair of square ears, a single square window, and two square chairs, and it was big enough for two people to make just a few steps in each square direction.

The first night of my WGBRAC with Fyodor Fyodorovich, I learned about CO-pulation from the CO-pulation booklet and the evidence of it that came shortly after I finished reading the whole thing. The booklet stated that CO-pulation had to be performed once a week, strictly by the glued individuals, after signing Ward's CO-protocol, also referred to as Co.Co. Those papers were delivered to people's square doors by the wrinkly ladies in white who checked glued people's temperature and pricked their fingers with needles to collect the blood in labeled jars stamped with Ward's mascot, signed with the individual's initials and numbers. To finish the procedure, everyone had to blood-fingerprint ten pages of Co.Co.

When the wrinkly ladies left our door, Fyodor Fyodorovich stealthily lowered the curtain on the square window of our square kommunalka room and ineptly took off his clothes, releasing a big pale abdomen covered in multiple moles and little patchy curls resembling a dirty porcelain ashtray. Underneath the monstrous multilayered stomach, Fyodor Fyodorovich had a terrifying crooked prolongation outgrown by excessive black fur. It was changing in size instantly. I had never seen anything like it and could sense the forthcoming trouble by the way Fyodor was breathing: his exhales sounded like an old chimney. The man disrobed me in an instant. Despite my pitiful squealing, punching, kicking, and equivocal displays of disgust, Fyodor Fyodorovich was enjoying himself immensely. I assume it had something to do with how much rigor he was rubbing me against his raised sharp body hair, crowned with smelly drops of sweat like a heavy-duty dish brush. Every visible trace of my physical revolt against him was neglected. I even dropped down unconscious, hoping he would stop and try to bring me back to life, though he continued scrubbing me just as harshly. After scratching him several times with my long dirty nails, he tied my hands irritably and stamped me against the square bed, applying all of his kielbasa-body weight against my trembling self. His stomach was preventing him from achieving his aim no matter how committed he was to forcing himself onto me. I kept resisting and tossing around until I could no longer breathe. When naked Fyodor Fyodorovich saw me suffocating, my eyes popped out like two ostrich eggs, he stopped for a moment and crawled off me. But my nightmare wasn't over: through a funnel, he poured a large amount of Wardwater down my throat. The drink transported me to a semiconscious state, as always. I could vaguely see how he was whispering to me: "Sveta, Sveta, my Sveta!"

As soon as the black void of sleep had sucked out my vision, Fyodor Fyodorovich bent me over and tore me apart between my legs with his thick crooked prolongation playfully hanging under his wiggly stomach. He kept deliberately repositioning and replacing it the entire time. I don't know how many hours he spent CO-pulating my numb, bleeding body, still whispering my mother's name, repeatedly piercing me and thrusting himself upon me deeper and deeper, until in my half-asleep agony I felt a long, trembling wave. I opened my eyes and saw him suppressing a series of hideous howls and moaning facial expressions. Then his prolongation spurted out all of its condensed secretions in a thorough torrent, inside my body, while he was relentlessly choking me with his greasy schnitzel-fingers.

The act stole away the remaining leftovers of my soul. I couldn't stop vomiting for days after. From that night on, Fyodor Fyodorovich always made sure to pour Wardwater down my throat on the days of CO-pulation, to give the process a less disagreeable manner. Rest assured: for me, it became increasingly barbaric each time. The more time passed, the less Fyodor Fyodorovich followed Ward's Co.Co. He let himself consume my flesh roughly and regularly, pouring his murky-chunky-tangy solutions in my wounded passages.

I would say all of his human appetites skyrocketed since I became his LIM-Dama. The physical torture he put me through and the doubled—if not tripled—consumption of unthinkable portions of lardy holodec and beef (which was unavailable to the starving population back then) sustained him so well that he had become even fatter. He was never concerned about the possibility of being caught and removed from LIM for all of the physical abuse he put me through. Wardworkers hardly ever got caught those days, you see.

"Ballet, now!" he would grunt-command to me during those gluttonous feasts, hyperventilating through his greasy lips and teasing me with chunks of meat like I were a dog. I had to show him my best ballet performance to deserve even a little piece of any edible leftover left on his plate. He fed me bones, too.

Whenever we were among others, Fyodor Fyodorovich hid the fact that I had become too weak to walk. His quickest solution was to glue me more tightly to his neck. I remember being mistaken for a puppet while being carried on his always-growling paunch. The new law made us inseparable.

During Ward's collective hours for the newly glued couples, we had to practice the convenient sideways-marching, where people looked like an army of fast-paced crabs. I was marching too, hanging loose on Fyodor Fyodorovich's chest, covered with his moist body hair, half-conscious most of the time, but warm! Besides marching, Fyodor assigned me to work at the paper-stapler factory building of Ward, next to the GCD. He and I were supposed to authoritatively supervise other LIMers maintaining the production cycle of stocks of empty paper the color of cholera. The paper was later used for Ward's documentation and people's bottoms. The heavy staplers, the shape of a pterodactyl's nose cone, were also produced at the factory in bulk. Besides shutting everyone's mouth, they were also used for Ward's documentation.

At the paper-stapler factory, Fyodor Fyodorovich pushed three buttons to control the order and itineraries of the neatly plotted papers and staplers rolling out of the same machine. The red button he especially liked to push was there to send the lazy workers to the basement full of most notoriously hungry mishkas. They, most commonly, ate the laziest ones. There was no place for *lentyays* in LIM. The mishkas that refused to do so were sent to the COE, also referred to as Chamber of Entertainment, which was only accessible to LIM-Leaders on special occasions, like the confidential weekly LIM feasts, organized to boost the efficiency of LIM-related (and sometimes not) decision-making progresses, and on their birthdays. I suspect not eating humans wasn't an act of mercy on the mishkas' part but a simple truth known among carnivorous forest animals: dystrophy is not so tasty. The COE collected the seemingly harmless mishkas who didn't get lucky with receiving chubby lentyays as a snack and trained them to roller-skate on the bright red arena stamped with LIM's mascot. Ballerinas and mishkas used to be the only performers at the COE, until one of the most notorious cat-lovers in LIM, named Yuri Dmitrievich,[20] discovered that he could train cats too.

"*Staranie i trud vse peretrut!*"[21] read the slogan on the other side of the open tunnel every single time it sent new lazy people to the mishka sentence.

Ironically, two weeks later, shortly before the factory announced the end of the production cycle and our daily release, Fyodor Fyodorovich accidentally slipped into the factory's tree grinder. The processor spit him out as a hideous combination of things, though I was especially impressed by the big empty sheet of paper some parts of his body had become. It was the color of liver disease, with lots of little patchy curls scattered all over it. I smuggled a few of those pieces, looking forward to wiping my bottom with them after work.

The production cycle stopped. Miraculously, I hadn't slipped after Fyodor Fyodorovich—my weather vane hair successfully grasped at one of the factory pipes, breaking through the tight bun on my head. And there I was, hanging above the tree grinder, alone at last, with a little torn stretchy bow tie on my neck. A voluptuous cloud of dust came from Fyodor Fyodorovich's ground flesh and landed oppressively on my skin, scratching it like dozens of claws. Sentimental tears of maniacal joy rolled

---

20 Famous Russian cat trainer Yuri Dmitrievich Kuklachev, founder of the cat-based circus.

21 From Russian "**Старание и труд все перетрут**"—patience and labor will grind everything. A famous Soviet slogan.

out of my irritated eyeballs, sprinkling every millimeter of the space with an unspoken realization of relief. The most genuine exultant smile shone through the metal staples on my bluish lips and cracked them open with a freeing "whoosh."

CHAPTER VI

DWAR. OB-LOM. GLASTNOST.[22]

THE SQUEAKY CONVEYORS HAD BEEN TURNED OFF by a dozen Wardworkers after it became apparent to them that Fyodor Fyodorovich's death was the result of a fatal malfunction. The mishkas from the basement obediently brought what was left of him. I, as cruel as this may sound, burst into laughter like an outrageous hyena. Fyodor Fyodorovich's death was my first encounter with mortality in my adult life and, perhaps, the only one I truly wished upon any living being. Every spasmodic giggle hiccupped by my diaphragm was accompanied by hot streams of unstoppable snot gliding from my face. The LIMers around me courteously took out their handkerchiefs but, instead of offering them to me, kept them for themselves to block the messy whirlwind of my detonating rapture flying their way.

I was being judged by every worker there was, though a few of them seemed to accept my mad behavior by nodding in a sympathetic, almost patronizing fashion. Based on their awkward body language, they in-

22 From Russian "**гла́сность**"—a policy that called for increased openness and transparency in government institutions and activities in the Soviet Union.

terpreted my reaction as mental hysteria caused by the lamentable loss of one of the most honored LIM-Muzhes in the State. Their judgments worsened when my laugh progressed as the mishkas schlepped the mushy leftovers of Fyodor Fyodorovich's hulk in front of me: the baby-pink mixture of his raw, damaged bones and fat was intricately polka-dotted by bouncy brownish specks of feces. His dead body resembled lardy holodec. You are what you eat, they say.

The State cremated the leftovers of the fat man in the HOZ MYLO chamber of the GCD, where animal fat was regularly burned and boiled into identical bars of the multipurpose soap. LIM-Leaders seated me before three hundred papers of Fyodor Fyodorovich's Death Record and Cremation Agreement.

"The present DRCA is to be signed and stamped with Tugodumov Fyodor Fyodorovich's WGBRAC cosigner's fresh blood," stated the first page of the application. The moment I was done signing the paper, the world around me turned into a continuous green stream of phosphenes and flashes of orange light.

I must have lost too much blood, were my last thoughts before I fell on a nearby yawning mishka. He refused to eat me. Upon LIM-Leaders request, the wrinkly ladies in white kindly spoon-fed me lots of *Hemagoten*[23] and valerianka before the funeral, in order to prevent another immoral laughter-attack or dizzy spell. Fyodor Fyodorovich's ashes were dumped into Ward's "Cessation Well," on the tall pedestal next to the most ancient piece of LIM's land. The patch of land was surrounded by three raggedy trees. I had the honor of opening the square tin container with an impressive image printed on it: the puffy Wardworker bow tie he was buried with and the dead man's name engraved on it like this: "Tugodumov F. F."

Today is the best day of my life, I thought to myself, remembering to keep my eyebrows down instead of up, so nobody could tell my tears were of celebratory nature.

---

23 From Russian "**Гематоген**"—a nutrition bar of which one of its main ingredients is black food albumin taken from processed (defibrinated) cow's or other animal's blood. One of the very few Soviet sweet treats for children.

When the burial ceremony was over and I received a big bag of "mourning gratuity" (it consisted of extra Wardwater, dill, and beets), LIM-Leaders allowed me to continue living in the same square kommunalka alone.

"*Gospodin* Tugodumov taught her to behave well," they all concluded after a ten-hour discussion. They shortened my living space by several feet, turning it into a windowless closet, in order to free it for the next complacently glued couple.

When I came back to my reconstructed room (that used to be our closet) from Fyodor Fyodorovich's funeral, I inhaled the smell of the intensely chemical fresh paint on my walls, drank plenty of Wardwater, and decided to commit myself to working for the GCD without attracting any further attention to myself. It was the first time I had experienced that dizzyingly deceitful sense of freedom in my adult life. There was something comforting about the uncanny clockwork repetitiveness my desensitized routine promised to offer.

Tick-tock-tuck, right?

In two months of living alone, the square kommunalka seemed to change its shape (or so I thought) to something more fluid. In six more months, my mental deterioration and totalitarianism-infected reverie had nearly reached its peak: I was perfectly synchronized with my operativnye chasy in every way possible. Life was no longer complicated, but not for much longer. Soon, everything changed.

On a regular smoggy day, while militantly finishing the billionth conveyor of rough paper and staplers, I saw the headline in the local *LIM Weekly* (the State avoided issuing long texts and kept the need to read to a bare minimum): "Attention! Vitamin Deficiency Catastrophe! Recommended amounts of Wardwater decrease to five teaspoons a day."

As you have no doubt already rightfully guessed, the potion's superfluous consumption began to trigger some disadvantageous health consequences in society. More and more LIMers were missing at the factory and later were found dead in their beds, baths, and closets, holding on to the tin mugs signed with their names from which Wardwater was supposed to be consumed. The old medicine was erasing LIMers quicker than the low temperatures, lack of natural light, dictatorship, and famine. Alas, the quotidian act of eating handfuls of garlic didn't help much either.

After lowering the cooperative consumption of Wardwater, LIM-Leaders reluctantly incorporated another policy recommended by the *–BOL-NITSA*[24] experts: they thinned out the State's gate in order to generate additional light from outside of the State's border. The more porous gate did import a hint of daylight from *zagranitsa*—from abroad—though to everyone's complete shock, it also attracted a gigantic flock of uninvited birds confidently flying in from afar.

Through the dirty factory window, I was witnessing something out of a nightmare: an exclamation mark–shaped flock of eagles, joyfully cruising around Ward's Gate Park in the bleak beams of light, crossing the threshold of LIM. The scoliotic birds flew surprisingly low above the ground, approaching groups of timid ladies glued to their brick-faced husbands and rocking a small number of pitch-black casket-like strollers. The sudden bird invasion changed their stillness in no time and caused an alarming reaction all around: the glued couples ran into street poles and shabby benches (their dull green paint must have been victimized by the last broken troops of rodent survivors) in panicked slippery pirouettes, laboriously protecting their croissant-looking babies coated in snow-white cloth.

The creatures broke through the gate, tearing the iron curtain to pieces. With their beaks completely unstapled, they let themselves spin in the most unpredictable trajectories, better than LIM's most admired ballerinas. The whole factory shook from people's quick footsteps as they prepared to stop the birds from adding their chaos to LIM's uneventful completeness.

24 Russian, *bol* meaning "pain" and *bolnitsa* meaning "hospital."

Ward released thousands of Wardworkers to catch every single one of them and bring them back alive. The State had been preparing for a number of inconceivable invasions from other lands for as long as it had existed, though it had neither slightly competent ornithological experts nor anything vaguely useful for trapping a gleeful, briskly cruising, warm-blooded, egg-laying vertebrate.

The flying visitors didn't seem bothered by the agitated people running after them. Remaining calm, they began to drop all sorts of items that at first came across as threatening. To everyone's surprise, the generous airdrops didn't injure anyone the slightest bit. They turned out to be: bars of gold and milk chocolate, small and large sparkly rocks, colorful sweaters, six-foot-tall statues of golden eagles, sweet fizzy drinks, big-eyed toys, colorful chewables, exotic fruit, strange *buterbrods*[25] (covered with additional pieces of bread), lollipops, and chunks of the most satisfying caloric food. I happily ran outside, breaking through the colorful hail. Oh, how those items were gleaming with their colorful packages and greasiness, intricately muddying everyone's mustard clothes and underclothes!

The strange treat invasion enhanced people's greediness. Everyone—babies, metal-statue and cloud-looking inspectors from Warddoor, little LIM-Damas, LIM-Muzhes, and agoraphobic older people—had their mouths drooling like floodgates. We were all picking up the blazing edibles, jostling one another, squealing with curiosity, wrapping ourselves in new layers of clothes, and putting a maximum amount of the unknown shiny items and edibles in our mouths, pockets, and anywhere else we had to put them. The stretchy, sugary treats melting in our mouths and the colorful sheen of the exotic rocks and jackets were the most beautiful things we had ever seen on the ground of our Rodina. Some of the greediest people there, on the battlefield of consumption, found the bravery to express their concerns to the masses through the hexagonal loudspeaker they climbed effortlessly, like well-trained monkeys.

25 From Russian "**бутерброд**"—open-face sandwich.

"It isn't fair, after all, that we live in constant deficiency!" yelled the loudspeaker.

The newly spoken words led to an immediate collective conclusion that somewhere outside of LIM, behind the gate, there must be a better life, one where, perhaps, no one needed to fill out thousands of papers for every life event and acquired good.

LIM-Damas and LIM-Muzhes couldn't compose themselves anymore; rotating in broken half circles like snowflakes through the grayness of the land, they awakened their voices from their long, silent, passive-aggressive comas. In response to the sudden change in atmosphere, warmer shades of purple flickered confidently in more and more areas of the dark sky. LIMers who had lived for many years with tight faces and carapace-encrusted forms with crooked postures took off their hard shells and let themselves melt into an indigenous tribal protest filled with some of the best elements of primeval vocal percussion and pure human anger. Fake mustaches fell from men's faces. Women's cheeks revealed their growing complexity of freckle constellations and pink blush.

When the picnic came to an end, and there was nothing else on the ground to eat or hide away, people transformed into a charming murmuring crowd, similar to a pack of young kittens meowing pitifully for more milk to strengthen their brittle bones. Alas, no more treats, gold, jackets, or rocks were given to them. The slowly fading sweet aftertaste spurred oodles of annoyance, making everyone's mouths lose their staples and release fountains of sincere, inappropriate cursing.

I had so much to say, but unfortunately, having my mouth unstapled didn't help me the slightest bit—I remained as mute as a hopeless jellyfish. It drove me crazy to watch the bitter words coming out of people's mouths, their capacity to lift their mouths' corners a whole millimeter up and make their walk less flat and slouchy. People were running after the birds with an uplifting soaring quality in each step, begging the creatures to stay, take them along, or come back with more treasures. The crying, stumbling crowd completely ignored the confused Wardworkers. The only additional items the eagles dropped off before crossing the gate and leaving our land for good were those wonderful blue pants with their own portraits sewn in the back.

Without analyzing what had just happened in the State, LIM-Leaders quickly put an extra iron layer on the gate. The Vitamin-Proficiency-Enhanced-Light-Source experiment, also known as VPELSE, had been officially called off.

Wardworkers were ordered to take away everything we had just acquired, but they couldn't break through the truculent army of LIMers who no longer wished to follow the LIM-Leaders' orders. A diverse population of raw, intense, sharp-tongued people was taking form before my eyes, exposed to one another in burning anger. Regardless of the multitude of years spent in complete, depersonalized silence, nobody had forgotten how to speak up! Angry at the codes they had been obediently exchanging, instantly spoiled by the variety of new colors and flavors, annoyed by one another's lifeless demeanors and oddly tailored mustard jackets and pants, they ruthlessly exposed their frustration. Every molecule of the land was thoroughly lubricated with disapproval and protest, which we also referred to as *bunt*.

I stood alone on top of Gate Park's slippery slope for a few hours, watching the beauty of the growing disorder, observing the abandoned treat packages with foreign words written all over them burying themselves in the fresh snow. All of LIM's districts grew into a single swamp filled with tongue-clicking, high- and low-pitched squeaking—an orchestra of blaming voices. Then I came down to join the fray.

Every LIMer, including me, defecated a good amount of hard excrement and threw it at Ward, followed by a waterfall of venomous words drilling through the fences of Ward as it rapidly lost its bitterly soothing glow and intimidating flicker. The hard excrement tore through Ward's mantle and revealed the defeated citadel of order, blocking itself with an erect protruding tent, deflecting the mass attack with its fabricated shield-belly until it stopped defending itself altogether. I couldn't hear what was happening until I felt the ground shake in a short-lived earthquake.

LIM-Leaders unwillingly unlocked the giant gate before the fighting citizens, leaving it open for two minutes. The most aggressive LIMers managed to depart and run after the eagles, which had already gone quite far. The escapees forced themselves deeper into the open field quicker than airplanes, directing their hopeful stares to the clearing sky. The birth stamps mercilessly burning their heads miraculously evaporated as soon as they ran far enough from the crossed border. The ones who left never came back.

Did I leave? Not so soon. I didn't get a chance to leave that day, possibly because I happened to be one of the last people in the rowdy queue. Such was life.

Instead of mourning my failed escape, I felt the urge to voluntarily join the masses of unruly people left in LIM. I had never liked LIMers more than that day, though my temporary amicability wasn't reciprocated. At all. No matter how hard I tried to explain my intentions to the people, my body language and broken vocal expressions weren't understood by anyone. LIMers didn't find anything trustworthy about my muteness. I was suspected of being one of the Wardworkers in disguise. They walked away from me dispersing in a number of unknown directions, dressed in the handsome, sturdy blue pants with little eagle images attached to them.

A week passed. To reassure everyone who stayed in the State that it truly was the most secure place to live, as well as to prevent another mass protest, a LIM-Leader's roaring voice came out from the hexagonal loudspeaker: "From this day on, glorious citizens, nobody in LIM is subjected to remaining silent! We solemnly declare that you are given the right to express anger, and you may take as many supplies from the GCD as you desire for a whole year. For those who don't recall the meaning of the word 'desire,' we prepared this poster."

A dozen Wardworkers marched their way out from the heart of Ward carrying a giant poster displaying poorly drawn black-and-white images of identical people stretching their arms toward food. This was written at the bottom of the poster: "Desire—an inclination to want things." On the other side of the poster were images of obese people lying next to dead animals, greedily consuming their raw flesh.

"But don't forget, glorious citizens—LESS IS MORE!!!" said the bottom line of that horrifying image.

A large number of snowballs and icicles were thrown at the poster and the Wardworkers. It was clear to everybody that what was happening before their eyes was the end of LIM.

Ward was officially renamed Dwar, LIM into *OB-LOM*.[26] People began to refer to one another as OB-LOMannye.[27] Even Wardwater had been re-fermented into a different drink, an elaborate surrogate known as Dwarwater. Instead of putting people's brains into a submissive sleepy trance, it had an awakening effect on their behavior. It made our brains determine that we needed to CO-pulate often and demolish everything around us.

From that day on, people fought, yelled, argued, and consumed day and night. This, as you already know, didn't present any distinguishable differences between LIM and Dwar. The Gastro Chambers of Distribution were regularly accessed by the pop-eyed, voracious eaters who *desired* to swallow whole tongues of cows, cows themselves, pigs, and chickens, all of which had actually been kept there in secret all along. The State's supplies weren't as deficient as we'd all thought.

That's how my Rodina disintegrated further, until it eventually turned into a cauldron of erotic and unruly loathing filled with inhuman cruelty and gluttony. Intellectual turpitude, along with testosterone explosions, had further enfeebled the essential balance of the once fully controlled land that—just between you and me—historically never truly experienced logical balance or moderation in any way.

---

26 From Russian: "failure" or "bummer." A slang term used to express one's failed expectations.

27 Broken or abandoned.

CHAPTER VII

PERESTROIKA[28]

THERE WERE LINES AND CIRCLES OF GREEDY ORGIES lying on top of warm animal fur boiling in the steam coming out of people's heated bodies, tongues, and genitalia, framed by the buildings they had demolished before they initiated their concupiscent friction. Men and women equally devoured everything edible and drank more and more Dwarwater. They couldn't stop penetrating one another without the vaguest need to claim one another's personal identification or private space. They did all of the above with the kind of aggression once only seen among wild animals.

The ones who possessed the rare clarity of thought regarding fiscal operations and revenue began to collect extra supplies of food, Dwarwater, and treasures, keeping them behind walls built from impenetrable gold when their abundance was no longer apparent. They referred to themselves as collectors and first appeared to the masses as the "Bureau of Essential Exchange." They willingly accepted new treasures found by

28 From Russian (the former Soviet Union term): "Reconstruction"—the policy or practice of restructuring or reforming the economic and political system.

other people who didn't know their value quite yet and exchanged them for consumables.

Those were the first *delovye*[29]—or, as they say in other parts of our world, "businesspeople"—in Dwar who were decent at multiplying, adding, and predicting the future of human needs and wishes. They wore brightly enhanced pink pigskins on top of their tulups to show themselves off, as is done among many groups of mammals in a display of strength and reproductive superiority.

As much as I was hypnotized by the lively crowd with its scandalously freeing vibration and new exchanging operations, my revolting memories of CO-pulating with Fyodor made me stay away from the ongoing naked parade. I swear, every pore of my physical being wished for me to throw myself out into the crowd, but there were still parts of my consciousness that weren't ready to join this new rabid realm—the perfectly imperfect bunch. The only place I could settle in safely for at least a day was the abandoned building of Warddoor, where everything respectful and educational had been mercilessly burned to the ground. It somewhat resembled dunes of black snow with occasional red puddles of blood—constellations of some toxic atomic explosion, in other words.

Shortly before I felt safe enough to take a nap in the tiny square library department, after inspecting every classroom in the building, I came across a weakened pig preparing to die. The animal stumbled toward me with its face moving side to side, as if in denial, until it collapsed on my feet. I don't know how to explain that instead of helping it stand up, I poked the pig with my index finger. Perhaps I doubted its actual presence. Perhaps it was the old fight-or-flight response I thought I no longer had. The pig collapsed immediately. I poked it three more times, until I could no longer fight the urge to choke it. Drowsy. Sweaty. Maniacal. In a delirium of anxious aggression, grinding my teeth with so much might that a few of them fell out of my mouth and sank in the black ashes of LIM's old anthem.

---

29 From Russian "**деловые**"—business.

"Eat the beast! Eat, eat, eat the beast!" I yelled to the emptiness around me, wiggle-dancing like a tribal woman.

Despite its notably weak state, the animal fought back until I found an old set of matches in the pile of broken chess pieces and set it on fire. I was too hungry to wait until it was fully cooked, so I put out the flames in less than five minutes so I could eat its face. Why the face? I didn't want any faces around me. The freshly burned meat was still raw and slimy, but I couldn't care less; the ecstasy of putting something substantial into my bony body was incredible. Alas, it didn't take long for me to puke it all back. To my surprise, instead of the chewed, tangled meat of the pig, I found big chunks of torn pieces of Warddoor materials: the old papers showing me the formulae I had once failed to solve in my written numerology tests. Many twisted eights.

Kneeling among binders of ruined information and sheets of paper with hundreds of people's names crossed out from them like corpses in some death record, I was burning up with feelings of a resentful nature. The metal statues that had been melted into distorted monsters by the once-well-intentioned students turned their disfigured physiognomies toward me, like creatures out of my worst nightmares. Even the "tick-tock-tuck" flourishing in my head like an atomic bomb wasn't as powerful as the eeriness of the overall flame. I ground my teeth through the ticking, skull-cracking pain. *Bruxism* was the name of the medical book I was sitting atop.

The next day, I woke up before everyone else according to the hardly believable operativnye chasy on my tiny wrist. They were once my mother's—the only item from Dom that hadn't been confiscated from me.

Seeing the new "reawakened" LIMers destroy everything around the State with a magical glare in their eyes only made me jealous. Nobody was trying to perform any sort of proper communication, as typically happens in places where dictatorship collapses overnight. People craved nothing but chaos.

What was my initial reaction besides fear and jealousy? I would say it was nearly impossible to ignore the collective mood when it reached a fever pitch: I wished to release my own aggression, so I walked to the old shack and hit Vasiliy Fyodorovich with his own cane. I never thought of myself as vindictive until then. Despite the fact that I was only recently opposed to all forms of violence, the thought of making him suffer the same pain he used to cause me was more than appealing. It would be an unspoken victory born of a thoroughly developed plan. I was ready for action.

As soon as I reached my destination, at the entrance to Vasiliy Fyodorovich's veranda, bunches of old yellowish sheets showed themselves to me in perfectly scattered chaotic splendor. From the first two paragraphs, I knew it was Agnesa Borisovna's old diary. Her handwriting was the same as mine. From the notes she had written, I found out that she was exactly the way I suspected her to be—moderately imaginative and quite suspicious of her environment.

I had no idea how or for how long that tight-lipped LIM-Dama I was strangely related to had managed to write down so much information and keep it behind the back of the tyrant she was BRAKed to for almost a whole century—who, by the way, was as offensive as Fyodor Fyodorovich in amorous matters (according to some of her most private notes, written in the smallest letters). The Gosti and my parents must not have been the only people who wrote to give their opinions to themselves or, rarely, if they get lucky, to others. The biggest difference between Agnesa Borisovna and us was that she never expected to be heard.

Why Agnesa Borisovna's notes were lying on the ground became clear to me immediately after I walked past the shack's crooked veranda. There, by the well, Vasiliy Fyodorovich was burying her alive. Not completely alive—she was on her way out of this world. He had stabbed her in the head with his cane shortly before I came. His reaction to my anger was not what I expected; just a few feet away from the freshly opened grave, where I stood, he hit his own head with the cane three or four times and fell in the thick snow next to his Dama. It all happened in the woods, where Dwar stood within walking distance.

When I reached the bottom of the grave, he was giving off his last exhale. The newly fallen snowflakes were suffocating him quickly, to which I gave my own last exhale of enormous relief and feeling of insatiable voyeurism. Seeing the old man's lungs fill up with little sharp stones and mishka excrement felt like a well-deserved triumph. I felt sorry for the poor submissive Agnesa Borisovna, who had wasted so many years living a miserable life with the man she was assigned to be with by her Ward-worker parents. I whispered into her blue-from-the-cold ear: "Rest in peace, Babushka. *Prosti.*"

The truth about the village Agnesa Borisovna and Vasiliy Fyodorovich lived in was that its locals refused to live among the new changes. Nothing made sense to them anymore. I stepped on their old neighbors' faces buried in the snow as I walked toward the shack. They had stopped hiccupping at last. The bitter memories of my days spent there reminded me why I came in the first place. I had too much anger to continue holding it within me.

I destroyed the shack with my bare hands, releasing oceans of the harshest, most illegal cursing I had acquired in many years. As expected, the loud act of demolishing the building drew a great deal of attention to me.

A smooth, square man covered in animal fur, with no facial hair and an astoundingly developed muscular mass, approached the freshly scattered ruins and revealed his tight gleaming cubical abdomen to me. There was something alluring about the way his eyes flickered and how freely he was showing me his bare skin. I shyly covered my eyes and turned away from him. He came up closer and offered me a cupful of brownish liquid, the first sip of which warmed my hands immediately. I took two more sips of it, then three more, until I finished the whole cup.

In a matter of seconds, my whole body became extremely warm and tingly. OB-LOM had never looked more beautiful. It felt like hints of sunshine were hatching in the sky. I let myself laugh generously. With feelings of extreme lightness and attraction to this man, I disrobed myself and confidently nodded at him.

"I am free!" I shouted to him, laughing uncontrollably.

He laughed with me like a madman, while the others who came with him set me firmly on top of the shack I had ruined moments ago. Then he turned me around and filled me with unknown physical pleasures I was experiencing for the first time in my womanhood. In the corner of my eye, while letting the stranger sink deeper in me, I saw another group of stunning naked people approaching us. They repeated the same act many times, with one another and with us. That's how I was accepted to the beautiful, angry orgy and was even entitled to receive my own pair of sturdy blue pants.

During those frenetic years, my mind quickly became perverted from the easily accessible pleasures enhancing everyone's greed and the infectious habits supported by the entirety of our demoralized tribe. As a result, my whole being degraded completely. I willingly ate whole cows after hitting them on the head with leftover pieces of thorny fence, leaving enormous smears of blood on the icy ground, until no commonly edible, easy-to-hunt animals were left anywhere. They disappeared as quickly as they occurred in our lives. I am sure you are well aware that in some parts of the world, food is a luxury that doesn't come so easily. Sometimes it doesn't come at all.

As for my new CO-pulation habits, I never missed a chance to let multiple people consume my body day and night. The nameless strangers taking my flesh instigated my addiction: irrationally, I craved CO-pulation as much as I craved raw beef. Sometimes even more.

Life tends to repeat itself in cycles, doesn't it? A few months later, all the LIMers' random intercourse had been terminated due to the growing sores on everyone's bodies. A small group of the most charismatic LIMers sorrowfully declared that quitting the orgy would, hopefully, decrease the disease and bring back the pleasures CO-pulation had been known for at the beginning.

"One partner per person, please," said some of the new social leaders. Two pathetically thin lines of males and females were divided by piles of trash, excrement, and pig heads.

Not many decently functional males were left when it was my turn to find a partner for myself. I was one of the last ones in line. As always. Competitiveness has never been my strongest personality trait.

Where did they all go? I thought.

The first male I paired up with was a midget with an oozing eye whose previous partner had died from a very rare form of OoLivDis (meaning "Oozy Liver Disease"). Or so I had been told. I liked how quiet he was most of the time, and the fact that he smelled like my father's liquid glue. No, of course I didn't like his oozing eye; the gnarly brown chunky matter dripped all over me day and night when he was around. The same alarmingly brown chunky matter came out of his mouth in his sleep. Something inside him was rusting away. In four days of our life together, he turned into a tin drum.

Even though I couldn't hear, drumming became my favorite activity. The sounds I was making attracted more males to my territory. And more mishkas. We mostly ate mishkas (if they weren't too strong), rats, and pigeons then. They were the only other living beings that hadn't migrated through the open gate with a highly decisive group of cows, pigs, and chickens galloping their way out of LIM. Yes, nobody liked LIM back then. Not even the cockroaches. Every now and then, a delirious cat or dog would visit our territories. We rarely ate them, though, because, well, they were cute.

In two days, I was chosen by a faux-eyed man of pudgy nature. His bizarre layers of skin were the color of mashed potato, making him look like an exotic pastry. He smelled of the blintzes my mother only had two chances to make for me when she was free. Whenever he slept next to me, I closed my eyes, allowing myself to dream about the wide, thin blintzes I once put in my treasure box, to smuggle them to Kazmas and share my treat with Sash. The memories of my family and Sash . . . they had faded away to such an extreme degree that I could no longer picture their faces, the faces I used to know better than my own. I taught myself to pretend they never existed, to loosen the excruciating sense of guilt and sadness. At times, they would come to me in my dreams to say something in

LIML—the language I no longer spoke. Whatever it was they had to say made me uncomfortable. More uncomfortable than living on top of an excrement-reproductive juice-blood-feather-dead-skin-infested piece of frozen land. I think it has something to do with morals. The word *moral* or anything of that nature can make one very, very uncomfortable when one is guilty of displaying ill-mannered behavior.

The blintz-man (forgive me such rough analogies, I simply don't recall his name) slept all day and never had the energy to hunt. I saw him awake maybe once or twice, when he came to my patch of land to court me by rubbing his skins on me. From his chaotic gestures, I realized that all he wanted from me were simple platonic cuddles. His skin continued to shed so much that in just three days, the wind took away his remaining layers. All that was left of him was the faux eye. I kept it for my personal entertainment and for hunting pigeons.

The next stranger who came to court me was almost perfect. We even held our breath for equal amounts of time before each other a handful of times, like humans used to do as a form of competition and flirtation. The man's senses were acute, his appetites insatiable. The only imperfections about him (forgive me—I do not remember his name either) were his oddly animalistic behavior and the fact that he grew thick silky fur all over his body.

My affection for him was altogether over the day he bit off a handful of little pieces of me. He apologized after my pain became more apparent and attempted to lick my wounds, but instead of healing me, he proceeded to attempt to eat the rest of me. Alas, I wasn't quite ready to be eaten at that point of my youth. I took the blintz-man's faux eye and hit the crazy man on the head over and over and over again, until he dropped dead. As soon as his steaming-hot body cooled off, I made a fur coat out of him. That's how I learned to stay warm in the LIM-wilderness. The comforting feeling of warmth inspired me to erect a fence from the icy snow, sticks, and my failed partners' and dead animals' bones, hair, and teeth. I developed a feeling that perhaps I didn't need any more male partners of my species anywhere near me for reasons you could logically guess.

Life had almost become better, except more and more deaths were occurring in the village. Due to the growing shortage of undiseased Damas, I became extremely popular. Dozens of males found my territory following their noses. There were days when all of them would patiently stand in a crooked line (waiting in a line was one of the last rules people still followed) in the woods and wait for me to come out.

While resting on my fur coat like I imagined any independent woman or fancy queen in the world would, I lazily watched the struggle the men were dealing with on the other side of the fence. In the disheveled crowd, there was a man with no limbs shaped like a vase pushing himself on a sleigh like a caterpillar, a man with no eyes smashing his head against the fence's bones, a shaky man with lobster claws, a confused giant with, most likely, no brains, a twitchy redheaded man with many apparent compulsive disorders who feared to take a step in any unfamiliar direction, and a few other weirdos.

One day, or rather night (everyone's waking behavior had become quite vespertine), I woke up and saw that my fence had been broken. I was lying on the smelly ground reeking of the grave, mounted by the lobster-clawed man and the sad man with no eyes. Both of them were covered in sores and scrapes like chewed squares of filet mignon. They were greedily sucking on my breasts, drawing brownish milk out of my enlarged nipples.

I looked down and saw that I had just given birth to a large deformed creature with fur, a faux eye, deeply wrinkled facial features like an old man's, and lobster claws. The monster was holding on to a little drum. It quickly crawled away from me as if having no desire to stay anywhere near me. The creature was strong and dragged me along by the sore-infested umbilical cord. I bit off the cord and fainted from the excruciating pain, distantly seeing how more midget-giant-noodle-lobster-sponge-fish-gorilla-like figures covered in blood and dirt went back to sucking the rotten milk out of me. Some of them continued to lazily penetrate my bleeding body all over again. They would sometimes die on top of me. I lay there, legs spread wide open, looking at the dull night sky faintly showing me the pendulum of the Dwar clock moving chaotically in every direction. I gave up. I wanted them to consume my flesh and leave nothing of it.

The moment I let out an anxious exhale, with the same dramatic anticipation I had when the mysterious eagles arrived at LIM, I let myself die. Through the vortex of mutilated shapes and bloody messes, I vaguely saw two dark figures speaking to mishkas like it was the most normal thing to do. I was lifted off the ground. They picked me up by my hands and feet and dragged me away from my makeshift maternity ward, letting me hang like a hammock. Silence.

CHAPTER VIII

AGONY

I renounce nothing of that which is the Mind. I want only to transport my mind elsewhere with its laws and organs. I do not surrender myself to the sexual mechanism of the mind, but on the contrary: within this mechanism I seek to isolate those discoveries which lucid reason does not provide. I surrender to the fever of dreams, but only in order to derive from them new laws.[30]

—Antonin Artaud

30 *Correspondence de la momie* (translated by Helen Weaver).

I CANNOT TELL YOU HOW MUCH TIME IT TOOK ME to fully regain consciousness or even open my eyes and keep them in that neutral position for longer than half a second, but I can tell you this: it must have been at least a week, two or three. Forgive me for the chaos of my narrative. It's not an easy one. I must have been unconscious even longer, but let me move on.

My sicknesses—the skin-sliminess, along with my deep wounds—had almost healed the day I was able to observe the space I was in for two whole seconds, for the first time since I was brought to that place. Two seconds were enough for me to recognize Dom and my old bed that was slightly too small for me, behind the old wall that had been fractured by someone's barbaric intrusion. There were traces of iodine marks on my wounds and cuts.

In fact, all of Dom had been cracked like the carcass of a water-deprived desert tree. It looked as if a flock of bats with iron claws had scratched it that way on purpose, tagging it with an uncanny, geometrically impeccable, widely spread composition. Ghostly and unfamiliar. A multitude of linear traces covered up the chaotic patterns I had once painted. The uneven color and imperfect shapes on the walls no longer looked like faces. The one and only oriental rug my parents used to adore had faded away and presented itself as a dull, excrement-smeared abstract painting, or possibly a swamp of puke. The wicked spying ears on the walls were hanging loose like dead skins of some droopy fruit. Those bastards were still alive, according to their occasional convulsive sighs.

The frightful impression I formed while observing my old Dom showing its awkward, incorrectly located remains was one of the most arduous truths I had to process: all of its special qualities and traits had long been erased. I didn't have the slightest idea what to do with myself in there. The dusty clouds and hairy debris gathering around Dom's corners made me doubt I was truly there, where I had spent the best years of my life. For a second, I thought I would rather have never been saved from being consumed by the diseased crowd. Maybe it was because of the amount of time I spent absorbing the dirtiest debris of human nature out on the streets, or maybe it was because of the number of diseases I was afflicted by from so many LIMers' wounded genitalia, but everything that happened to me in Dom for the next few days was nothing but an ongoing waking dream followed by agonizing hallucinations and mixed-up voices in my head.

This is roughly how it went: I stood up as soon as the moldy, wet ceiling stopped spinning in circles above my head. Part of me hesitated to see the rest of the house, due to the wide holes in the floor and Dom's overall brittle state. I remained still until the floors stopped shaking, repeatedly looking at Dom from the same angles as if trying to map it out all over again. When I turned around to change the angles, pressing my toes against the floor like an indecisive cat pawing a soft comforter, I saw Ma's old mirror. I immediately buried my face in my hands, knowing that after not having seen mirrors in years, I had to approach my own reflection with awareness. According to the mirror, I had turned into a skinny slouching creature with big angry eyes that still carried a slight trace of sentimentality, grayish flattened-out hair spotted by a few uneven dark traces, healing wounds fighting bacteria with iodine, and deep folds and pleats settled around my forehead and eyes. I was twenty years old. I was aware of how much Damas aged in LIM shortly after they became BRAKed, though I never expected to become a babushka that early on.

The immediate realization of my ruined youth, mixed with bittersweet childhood memories hiding in every inch of the place, turned my eyes into two steady fountains. I sobbed for hours, experiencing a surprising emotional relief, until I found myself drowning in the broad river my tears had created. I could scarcely swim. While barely keeping myself afloat, the walls of my parents' bedroom crashed open, like they used to when Dom was Dom. The good old tin bathtub I used to soak in came into the room flipped vertically, like a throne. I sat in it. After rocking me back and forth for a while, it moved through the mystical dust-fog, masking Dom like a big silver beard.

Through the wall of grayness, I saw places I learned about from the books I used to read and elements of my mother's theatrically choreographed buffoonery. They were erecting themselves in all of their completeness. More and more of my old memories emerged out of thin air, until the tub came to a halt. Somebody's shaky hands with no clearly defined fingers lit an old tin pot filled with candles. The strange limbs belonged to one of my old nyevalyashkas, Fialka, who had aged as much as I had and was no longer round-faced and phlegmatically jolly. Next came the sharp-kneed, skeleton-faced Zosya with no head. She gave off a sickly cough: "Ra-Raaah!" Both nyevalyashkas nodded at me with a harmful display of personal disapproval, adding loads of shame to my regenerating self-image. I tried to explain everything to them and myself, but since none of the right words came to mind, all I could do was give off a thundering cry. As a result, all the walls and doors in Dom squeaked, screamed, meowed, barked, hooted, sighed, belched, squelched, and whistled back at me.

"Stop it, stop it, stop it!" I begged them on my knees like some humiliated, raggedy martyr. It was the realization of my deafness that helped me remove myself from the doors' atrocious protest: *This can't be real* was my last thought before I woke up in the same bed. I couldn't tell if it was morning or night—as always. Biblioteka's wall was wide open. I was in no way morally prepared to enter it, but I made myself do it . . . and immediately regretted it.

Have you ever been inside a morgue? This is perhaps the closest, most accurate analogy I could conjure to describe what had happened to Biblioteka. As empty as it was, there were those giant spiders I had once feared quite terribly but no longer looked so giant to me, lying dead in the same corner my family archives used to be stacked. The sight of the place was so disorienting that I had to sit on the ground against the wall, an inch away from the spiders' remains. The wall moved. A light aroma of long-forgotten wildflowers and trees filled the entire room. The tunnel to Kazmas opened.

CHAPTER IX

FAMILY REUNION

I DIDN'T EXPECT TO FIT INSIDE THE TUNNEL twelve years later, but I still did with just a little more difficulty, caused not by my size but by the red-eyed, semitransparent rats with pocket watches actively ticking in their rib cages and abdomens. The walls' surface was soiled with excessive slime. The rodents were hastily squeak-leading their group in the same direction I was crawling like a worrisome crowd of tardy factory workers, showing no interest in my persona. I paused, letting them skedaddle past me. As I reached the end, my LIM-citizen stamp zapped my brain, spine, fingers, and toes. I woke up again from the worst headache. My chest was thrusting up and down, fighting the worst panic attack a human is capable of having. I must have lost my mind, after all.

"I can't take it anymore!" I yelled at the ceiling, barely seeing my surroundings through sandy, dry eyes. I suppose some people hit their heads for a reason—hitting mine against the wall had somehow helped me straighten up my reality. I was no longer drowning in a bevy of nightmares and hallucinations. When there were hardly any doubts left about

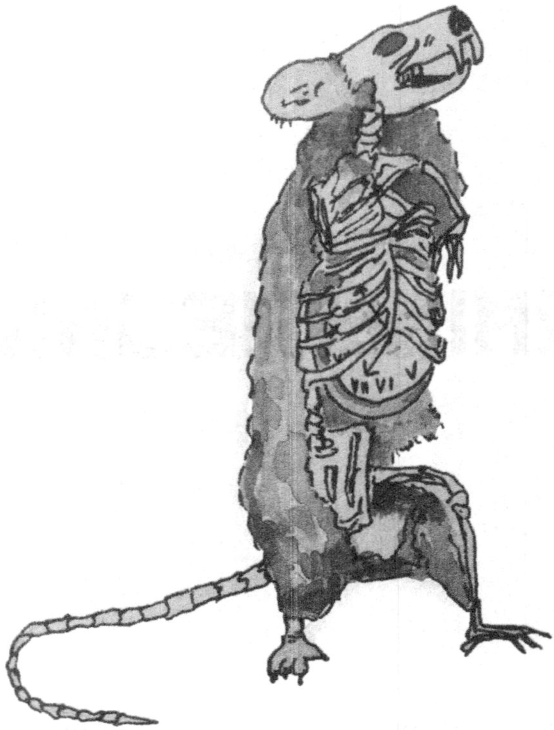

whether or not I was wide awake and the feeling of being comprehensively grounded had settled into familiar space, I walked to the wrecked Biblioteka not *again* but for the first time in my temporarily cynical adult reality. It was as empty as it had appeared to me in my dreams, though the tunnel to Kazmas had, at last, been gone. Thick layers of cement filled the entire path from beginning to end.

A slight protrusion caught my eye in the middle of the winding cement circle above my head. The moment I poked it, a tightly wrapped, crispy tree leaf fell out of it and landed in my hands. It was a page from some book with Sasha's drawing next to it. A rustic note on the other side read: "*Transit umbra, lux permanet.*"[31] (Based on the letter's glorious curves, the handwriting belonged to Dedushka.) As for the unearthly drawing, it was undoubtedly Sash's. He painted himself and me, as tall

31 From Latin: "Shadow passes, light remains."

as the redwood tree next to us, on top of a picturesque mountain surrounded by a shroud of cosmos flowers in the open space with comets and asteroids, lit by the extraordinarily colorful aurora borealis. Little figures of square people were floating away from us into the black hole among other planets.

For some unknown reason, my face became extremely hot, my hands clammy. My heart skipped a beat. I quickly pushed the painting back into the cement, wishing I had never touched it, though it immediately fell back in my hands. Everything about Sash's composition and the piece of paper was farfetched and improbable. A panic attack.

Even though my dissected Dom was, by far, the safest place in LIM, it occurred to me it wasn't reasonable to further investigate the pathetic leftovers of my ruined life.

It was time to leave and never come back. So that I could stay on my feet for longer periods of time without collapsing, I went outside and fought some of the last stray dogs for food. You don't want to know what it was. Let me skip that whole description. All I have to say is—you would be amazed at what hunger can do to your choices of sustenance.

The day before my planned departure, I finally had enough strength to dust and clean every inch of Dom, attempting to possibly return its dissipated state to vaguely what it used to be. For old times' sake. The semi-dead mosquito-elephant vacuum cleaner left by one of the Wardworkers lying next to my parents' komod wheezed like an old animal and fell flat. It wasn't really mosquito-elephant-like, as I used to think when I was five. It was merely an ugly electric device with absurdly chunky features I was no longer afraid of. I sat on top of it and laughed with enormous pleasure (not having laughed for such a long while made my face cramp from the effort). Then I laughed at my anguish and the new realization that came to me in a very humorous form.

Based on my few years of living the life of a LIMer, I can now say with confidence that suffering is the essence of my Rodina. Really. The more you suffer, the better person everyone thinks you are. In fact, you yourself start thinking of your own decency as a direct equivalent of the amount of psychological slump you have survived. The worse, the better. It's hard to imagine I will someday be able to relax and live a day of my life without always anticipating the absolute worst. Will I ever be granted some sort of "best sufferer award" or vacation? Does anyone get an appraisal for all this dermo? *Or even a bow tie?* These thoughts kept repeating in my sore brain through random bursts of passive-aggressive laughter and hiccups.

The spasmodic breaths blew the last layer of dust off my ma and pa's mirror, creating a significant whirlwind in the room. Based on the reflection in the mirror, I was as fatigued as in my nightmares, but not nearly as aged; the network of wrinkles under my eyes were gradually breaking into less visible lines, recreating my once-benign appearance. The tepid weather vanes on my head were making an effort to rise, like freshly watered pickerel weeds.

I ran around the Gosti room, letting myself shout out more life realizations and complete nonsense, feeling how healing the process was for the entirety of my dendrites. The ears on the walls, disturbed by my behavior, attempted to lift themselves up in protest, but their droopy state wasn't in their favor. No alarms were to be sent to Dwar. I finished them off long before they could do anything to give away my current location.

While I was stabbing them with an old fountain pen, I didn't notice when two dark figures emerged from the doorway behind me. I sneezed three times, spitting out the dust and ink spat at me by the ears' old vestibular canals. Thoroughly rubbing my eyes, I looked at the figures behind me.

"Mamochka! Papochka!" I exclaimed freely, as if I had never lost my hearing. They had returned.

CHAPTER X

HOW I STARTED WRITING THIS BOOK

I WAS ENRAPTURED, EMBRACING AND KISSING my newly found parents for hours. The sweet though less distinct honey-daisy-dill smells of Ma's skin and Pa's hairy cheeks made everything fall back into place. Even though they had managed to find their way back to Dom from the deep woods and save me from rotting on the streets, their indomitable spirit had somehow deflated. Especially Papa's. There was something asymmetrical and eerie about the way he had changed. Ma's former suspiciousness had turned into an unrecognizable mania.

From both my parents' embraces, they were so malnourished that it seemed like they would be easily carried away by the wind, had I opened the window. Even though they'd saved my life and brought me home, they looked far worse than I did. I fetched them the cleanest clothes there were in Dom's komod, melted some snow into a ringed bright orange bathtub, and helped them take a bath, watching black rivers of dirt wash down their backs. A tiny jar of talc powder was the only hygienically appropriate supply we had stored in the bathroom. I powdered them carefully from head to toe and asked them to come to the kitchen table. We sat in the dark. *Vmeste.*

At that moment, I wished to open my eyes and see everything back to normal, like it used to be on those uneventful quiet days that looked like nights, when we read books and had unbeatable faith in our escape. I wished to open my eyes and still be the size of our pots or smaller. I wished to see my young mama playing theatrical games with me in my best snowflake costume. I wished to see my young papa in an oversized lab coat building all kinds of nonsensical inventions in his brittle suitcases. But none of what I wished occurred. It was frustrating, since I had never wished for anything with more urgency and effort, but as I later learned in life, many things we constantly ask for come to us with a delay, and not always in the shape we expect.

I wiped my tears and reached for the only window in Dom, whose height was much smaller than I remembered it. A small amount of amoeba starshine and moonlight lit Dom and Ma's and Pa's faces. What I saw before me made me freeze and drop on the floor—my parents' fingers and teeth were missing. Instead of fingers, they had a couple of moving staplers attached to their palms, clicking like a bevy of tongues. Their mouths looked like dark empty holes. That's how our first reunion dinner began.

"Eat this, please! *Za menya!*"[32] I begged them like they used to beg me when I was an impish child, hiding my discomfort and nausea. "I know it's morbid, but if you don't eat, you will die!" I yelled at them through abundant streams of tears rolling down my cheeks.

Suddenly, Mama's eyes changed from hazy to clear. She ripped her gown and cleaned the chunks of infectious mush from Pa's and her own lips.

"Stop it this minute, Sasha! We don't have to eat other humans to survive. We are not cannibals!" she said to me, spitting all over the old linoleum floor as she spoke.

32 Russian, meaning "for me."

"Stop this nonsense and help me find where I put everything away for a rainy day," Mama demanded with the same bossy demeanor she had when I was little.

She knelt on the floor near the kitchen table and began digging through it with her staple-hands. Pa joined her shortly without seeming to know what she was doing. I found an old spade behind the stove and helped them dig deeper. You would be surprised if you saw how deep the holes in our floors were.

When my spade hit what seemed to be the very bottom, Ma lay down and impatiently inserted her arm into the hole, pretending like it was just as functional as it used to be. Alas, it wasn't.

"Here, here!" she said, pointing at the hole with her nose.

From the deep hole in the kitchen floor, I took out Dedushka's typewriter. Then, with an odd, fatigued half smile, Mama gestured for me to look deeper inside, where sat a big chest marked as "*Eda na chernyi dyen.*"[33] Seeing the dusty square container sent my memories back to helping Ma with her food-preserve operations when I was little. I swear she could pickle anything and make it taste uniquely edible, even if it wasn't supposed to be. There were no particular recipes involved, except that dill was added to every jar of her preservatives.

The chest was filled with a great deal of pickled food, lots of maggot-infested buckwheat, a couple of matchboxes of salt, a few matches, and two bars of hoz mylo. I was about to cover the hole in the floor when hundreds of drawings Sash and I used to exchange showed themselves, stacked in the same area the typewriter had been hidden in.

"Where have you been, Mama? How did you survive? How did you manage to come back? What happened to Papa?" I asked her, suddenly feeling the urge to find out what they'd really gone through.

"Sasha, I am starving. Can we please eat?"

"And then will you tell me?" I begged her.

---

33 A Russian phrase: "Food for a rainy day."

For a moment, Mama's eyes took on the same hazy stare as earlier. She said as if in a strange trance: "I don't ever want to relive the memories of those days."

"I don't blame you," I said to her, pressing my rough hand against her wrinkly cheek. "It's over now, I promise."

While I was hugging Mama, Papa sat back at the table, indifferently watching us, waiting for us with his absentminded childish pout. I ground everything through his handmade grinder in one of the briefcases. Then I helped them eat. They opened their mouths like little toothless birds, waiting to be fed.

"We haven't slept in five days. Can you please make our bed?" Mama addressed to me while going in and out of quick upright naps in her uncomfortable chair.

"I will make you the most comfortable bed, Mamochka!" I said.

I swept the sheets with a semi-broken rug beater and turned around to show them it was ready. Ma and Pa were already asleep on the floor. I dragged them into bed by their armpits and feet and sat by their side with a pile of Sash's drawings, scrutinizing both—the added lines on their faces and the old images. The more I looked at them, the more my memories of the thirst for words and literary temerity we all once had reawakened themselves. All of the unsavory details about my life in OBLOM came out like a fantastical volcanic eruption.

Without leaving Biblioteka for days, I typed on the old typewriter in the language I had almost forgotten—my native tongue. That's how I began writing the book you are reading. Thanks to all that overwhelming anger that had taken over my brain, I became a writer. I suppose it was the first time I fully understood why writing could be best described as a form of my own cancerous tumor that I could help dwindle and turn into some ethereal entity, if I simply continued writing. Overall, it was an invigorating feeling.

Every now and then, stray cats would find their way into Biblioteka. After giving up begging me for food I never shared with them, they watched me type with little impatient cat sighs. The ones gifted with the most acute predator instincts would find mice to munch on, but the others were so toxic and thin that very soon, the book room turned into a mouse cemetery. None of those cats were Boris Borisovich, whom I couldn't wait to trap inside the cement tunnel, but he never dared to come.

It took lots of anxiety to finish writing the first draft without any further additions after everything else that happened. My temporary prosaic antidote to OB-LOM's poisons maintained its growth.

These were my final and most naïve words before I finished writing the first draft: "I am planning to find a way to be heard outside of LIM. Nobody should live like we do. The way out of this hell has got to be somewhere near."

I can't believe I wrote those words at the end of my first draft. I can't believe that I ever believed in those words and thought everything was going to be over soon. Can you believe it?

CHAPTER XI

THE END OF DOM

MEANWHILE, OB-LOM CONTINUED TO FACE a catastrophic food shortage. Another cycle of disaster. The mass orgy ended, and the instantaneous freedom given to the OB-LOMannye less than a year before turned back into a ruinous, uninhibited mushy pit. The State's citizens had become similar to the first primitive homo sapiens in the images depicted in some of the oldest caves in the world. But bad political decisions rarely go unnoticed.

Healthy individuals had become almost extinct; naked frozen bodies lay strewn all over the icy ground. It would have been impossible to walk a straight line without stepping on someone's head. The newly ejected bundles of crawling tissue that came out of dying LIM-Damas' bodies, resembling fetuses, turned out to be bacterial infections that had come to life and preferred to dwell near animal and human leftovers. The obnoxious crawlers would lick dead bodies' drying wounds with their raw tongues.

Those alive barely had the strength to show their anger to the OB-LOM-Leaders, who in their turn were now more powerful than ever, simply because they had waited long enough to let the State disintegrate. OBLOM workers, in their turn, collected the corpses from the streets and processed them in the tree grinder of the HOZ MYLO chamber, boiling up the fuel for restarting the rusty machinery, though they couldn't find enough functional people to assign to work at the broken GCD.

Since reuniting with my parents, I decided to stay in Dom for as long as I could to take care of them and bring my mind back to a state of imaginative vision. There was nothing outside in the real world that I needed to get involved with. Nobody was after me either. For the first time in my legally registered life, I hadn't been spied on or persecuted. I was taking advantage of the murky national situation, committed to typing the second draft of my book that I still believed would set me free one day and make a difference, like a number of other books my parents used to refer to had. I attached Sash's last message on the wall. Seeing that page daily somehow put my mind at ease.

"What are you writing, dear?" gently asked my ma one day. She finally had enough strength to walk from her bedroom to Biblioteka.

"Our life story, Mama."

"Oh?"

She quietly picked up the first few pages of my manuscript with her staple-hand and read them. I loved watching her face as she reacted to my descriptions of her and Pa. She even laughed a few times, which made her face look twice as youthful and wonderfully familiar. Her vision seemed to have worsened a great deal, and she asked for my help reading several pages.

"You are such a *skazochnitsa*," she concluded sadly after reading the first two chapters, "like your grandpa. Sometimes I wonder—when he decided to spend his entire life writing, did he realize everything he wrote was doomed to be erased?"

"It's all gone?" I asked.

"None of his literature is left. Or his readers," said Ma abruptly, with a hint of annoyance.

"Not all of them were arrested, Mama. I saw them at—"

"The Gosti are gone forever," Mama interrupted me bitterly.

"You and I can read, right? We can teach others. I can write our stories and keep them here for future generations, no?"

"There is no reason to do it, Sasha. It's a waste of life. It's all about surviving right now."

"What are you saying? Mama, that's not what you and Papa used to teach me."

"We should have been 'kak vse' all along, Sasha. It was my parents' idea to start the literary transformation and escape. Look what happened to everyone."

"But we can change some things now. The State is dead."

"I don't believe it is. LIM has reached a state of complete destruction many times before. They will find their way back in no time. And they'll make it worse. A calm before the storm," she whispered as if someone was going to overhear her.

"Then we should take advantage of this time and find another way to escape," I said bravely to Mama.

"All of the tunnels have been shut down," said Mama. Her eyes turned dark again. She sat on the floor, whispering something deliriously to herself.

"Then we break through the gate! I don't even care about the stamps on our heads. I saw people run away with them. No one is patrolling the gate these days but mishkas," I yelled ecstatically.

"I am very good with mishkas," said Ma with a charming smile on her face. "They love my poetry. I still remember quite a bit of it."

It was the first optimistic thing my mother had said in weeks. We hugged.

"This is a very good plan, Sashenka. For now, I just need to lie down and check on your father," said Mama.

She was about to walk out of Biblioteka when the page Sash left for me caught her attention. She moved very, very close to it.

"How could this be? Sasha, where did you get this?"

"I have been on the other side of the tunnel, Mama."

"You have? Which one?" she asked. Her face almost looked young again.

I moved the squeaky clock that had finally given up its ticking.

"Whoa! You had a chance to escape!"

"No, Mama—LIM has taken over Grodek."

"Grodek . . . it's right across the border. Next to LOB."

"Dedushka's last copy is safe there, Mama."

"Did you read the whole thing?" Mama asked me, her eyes popping.

"The special book?"

"Yes. Did you read it?"

"No, Mama. I didn't have time."

"Take this," she said, handing me the page, "and never lose it."

"What is it, Mama?"

"I hope you will never need to know the importance of this message. Hold on to it, please. I am going to lie down now."

The next few days we spent preparing to depart. We didn't have much to take with us, but sorting through all of our old tchotchkes made us extremely sentimental. Even Papa's face lit up a few times. No matter how much I begged my mother to tell me what had happened to her and Papa after their arrest, she refused to allow herself to remember any of that.

"May I break a few of the walls to make sure there are no treasures left behind them?" I asked.

"Go right ahead, dear," she said.

She fully supported my spade-heavy efforts while letting Papa play with the walls' crumbles, pretending like they were building a sandcastle on the beach they fabricated in their unsound minds.

The day of our planned departure, my parents took their time waking up.

"Mama? Papa?" I yelled into the open wall, but nobody came.

I found them in their bedroom. Mama was trying to calm the disheveled, possessed Pa. Acting like the rabid stray dogs we used to be afraid to walk past, Pa was letting out thick streaks of foamy saliva. His eyes were filled with constellations of red dots and spinning denial. I helped her tie him to the bed, wishing to calm him down, letting him wiggle for a while until his aggression dropped to a deep torpor.

"He will be fine," said Mama. "He had a bad dream. He thinks we are still at the . . . COO."

It was obvious how difficult it was for her to give me the name of that place.

"He will recover, dear. We can leave as soon as he feels better. Please go," she insisted.

Three more days went by. The morning I finished typing the third draft of my manuscript, I victoriously stormed into their room. Papa was beautifully, innocently numb, with his toothless mouth wide open in a big smile, his completely gray hair bunched in disarray, as if he had shaken his head with lots and lots of rigor before he passed away. Mama and I buried him in Biblioteka in one of the cemented tunnels I loosened with a spade—the tunnel dug by a group of Gosti that was going to lead us to an exciting place where we could walk freely and speak as loud as our hearts desired.

Mama and I lay next to Papa's body for who knows how long before placing him in his burial cocoon. We held his staple-hands and stared at the ceiling with the huge dent in it, which Papa accidentally made with the old heavy spade years ago, without getting up for what felt like forever. The freezing air and bleak amoeba stars coming from the dent didn't leave a single hint of the familiar patterns and outlines I used to see there. Everything became pitch black, even the stars. The feeling of complete numbness and the slight echo in my stomach drowned me in unreality. Not a single tear came out of my eye for the first ten hours. Not a single sigh flew out of my lungs. Mama seemed indifferent, numb. She sweetly placed her head on my shoulder and closed her eyes.

I don't know how much time had passed before I sat up and said, "Mama, we have to go now."

No answer, no breath, no heartbeats. I continued yelling "Mama" for eternity, but she never answered. Whether it was the broken heart, the horrible memories of the lifelong torture, or the low temperature of the room that took her life away remains a mystery to me.

I felt as though my ribs were big ancient sabers plunging into my heart. I punched the wall. I had lost them forever.

Catching the last indistinct fragrance of Ma and Pa and the phantom echoes of their voices reading books to me, I placed them close together inside the tunnel, in the same position they used to sit by my bed at night while reading to me: Ma's head gently resting on Pa's once-strong shoulder. I covered the tunnel with their beloved oriental rug, slowly feeling how rivers of wretched salutary tears were on their way. Not being able to restrain my grief any longer, I fell on my knees and wept unmanageably.

The building shuddered. Abrupt waves of seismic turbulence shook OB-LOM's land with a shattering force.

CHAPTER XII

GOLDEN BLIMPS

THE ENTIRE BUILDING CONTINUED TREMBLING until it cracked in half, like a loaf of bread split between two good-natured comrades; it sank into the snow in less than ten minutes. Every last remnant of Dom, including my mother's hidden edibles, were released from Biblioteka's broken ceiling straight onto the mushy, bloody masses of savages suffering from the variety of maladies that had befallen them. Their torn blue pants showed defaced eagle portraits.

I landed on an icy surface of dirty snow and was smacked in the head by Pa's favorite collection of Western poet heads, the last book-related items in Dom that had somehow survived. The metal heads' weight, apparently, could easily compete with an old tractor's. Through the snowy twists of an intensifying blizzard were long legions of golden blimps flying from afar, reflecting gorgeously distorted rainbows upon the dark thicket of the bleak amoeba stars napping in the sky. The bubble structures came confidently from across the State's voluntarily opened gate, dropping off golden clouds that were soon to change OB-LOM for a time.

Dom's building wasn't the only one in my compound that had collapsed. OB-LOM Leaders, sitting on top of their whale-sized tanks, were pushing buttons on a minimalistic remote control marked with two words: "*Goden*"[34] on the bright green square button and "*Negoden*"[35] on the bright red square button.

The OB-LOM Leaders had no choice but to resort to accepting help from outside in order to prevent the rest of the State from turning into an empty frozen blintz. The widely spread gate, in its turn, gave those who survived another chance to voluntarily depart from OB-LOM and find a better life somewhere else. It was certain to me that no one had enough physical strength to take a single step in any direction. Even in that unfortunate situation, some of the injured OB-LOMannye were pushing themselves to crawl their way out.

As malnourished as I was, my energy came back to me instantly at the sight of the open exit. I grabbed my finished (or so I thought) manuscript and Sash's drawing, threw them in Pa's old briefcase, and broke through the thicket of hail, bounding to the gate like an antelope. On my way, I imagined gorgeous sunny places (I hadn't seen the Sun yet) glowing with freedom. The briefcase I pressed tightly against my maniacally beating heart reminded me of my purpose: I was a writer who was going to find a way to attain artistic freedom and be heard outside of OB-LOM.

The blizzard and strong wind pushed me to and fro, blocking the sight of the border, blotting out the last blotches of visibility. The golden cyclone took over thousands of miles until it finally cooled and exposed a view of the slowly shutting screechy gate. The storm ceased. I could finally make out what was in front of me in the light mist. I stopped covering my eyes and saw clouds of golden dust rising in slow, zigzagging lines of smoke flying around the land. They revealed the firmly locked gate to me. The remaining OB-LOM survivors were emerging out of nowhere,

---

34 From Russian "**годен**"—valid.

35 From Russian "**негоден**"—invalid.

crawling toward the gate, mesmerized by its overall shine. I had missed my chance again. Such was life.

"*Suka!*" I cursed at the gate.

"Suka, suka, suka!" I yelled again, feeling an amazing satisfaction within my soul at those improper words.

OB-LOM Leaders directed their bright spotlights on me from the Dwar clock tower. The clock hadn't changed a bit, except that its glow was no longer as bright as the Moon's face. My immediate impulse was to resume running. Anywhere. As far as my eyes could see.

Of course, I was preparing myself to receive hard hits on my head for daring to curse earlier, or possibly be subjected to electrocution or laborious torture of a rare kind, but as soon as I got a clearer sight of those faces calmly watching me deal with my neurosis, I changed my mind. Beside the small group of LIM-Leaders, who looked less intimidating than when I last saw them, was a gorgeous army of little children in cumbersome uniforms. The purity of their appearance, along with a vague display of sympathy and personal approval, glued me to the ground: they were smiling and nodding at me, their eyes glossy with amicability. "Da, da, da," said their perfectly moisturized unstapled lips to me.

Such an improbable occurrence filled my heart with hope, but at the same time, there was absolutely no way I could trust the contents of my briefcase to anybody. With no hesitation, I quickly ate the whole manuscript of mine. Yes, in case you must know, it was terribly hard to do, especially the digestive part; the critical words I'd built the manuscript with tightly ingrained themselves in my guts with no wish to go back outside. No one was going to take it away from me. *Nyet. Nyet. Nyet!* I stuck the briefcase in the snow long before they descended from the Dwar tower next to the clock.

By the time the well-wishing, staple-free children and I were looking at each other face-to-face, there was not an inch of paper from my briefcase left anywhere near me. Two of the children took my hand and walked me to a grumpy, big-bellied mishka waiting for me by the tower. The animal, dressed in a pair of beautiful snow skates, took me inside Dwar.

As soon as the OB-LOM Leaders closed the door behind me, the children let me in with sincere admiration. The tallest one of them, with a serious face, gently took my remaining possessions (an extra tulup and a potato bag I'd decided to keep in case I had to hide my face for some ethical reason). The blue-eyed convivial teenage twins named Prok and Uror[36] gave me a soft, cozy fur robe and folded my clothes. The youngest of the kids sent me to a gorgeous white room with hot tubs and clumsily roller-skating mishka cubs. The gentle almost-pleasant sound of the haunting "tick-tock-tuck" was there, too. In my head.

When I was immersed in the tub, the kids lined up at the door and said in their angelic voices, "*Dobro pozhalovat.*"[37] They showed me their perfectly rehearsed simultaneous smiles that looked like wolf grins and left.

I was fully washed, cleaned, brushed, and scrutinized for days by the same old wrinkly ladies dressed in better-looking uniforms than I remembered.

"No need to throw number 0002 (that was the number of my head stamp) into the GCD reconstruction grinder. No incurable society-threatening diseases have been detected," they concluded and pressed the bright green Goden button.

You may wonder who the ones who hadn't been thrown into the grinder were, not to mention the children who were recently released from LOB and hadn't been affected by the State's disaster. There weren't many. Two or three Gosti survived, thanks to the keys to the secret chambers of Warddoor they had been privy to. The other group of survivors consisted of some of those first delovye who saved their lives by hiding under piles of gold they had attained before everyone else knew what it was. The trick was to camouflage it as dirt by smearing it in their own feces whenever danger was approaching.

Survivors who possessed the minimum qualifications were quickly promoted to the status of Dwarworker due to the absence of competition.

---

36 From Russian, meaning a public prosecutor.

37 Russian: "welcome."

They were given impressive red robes to emphasize the importance of their new status. The ones who didn't qualify were given clownish blue overalls.

Upon the completion of OB-LOM's selection of the most functional citizens, OB-LOM Leaders addressed the next mandatory need: to replace everyone's bad teeth, since the sour smell of oral cavities and poor digestion breath disarrayed the fresh unadulterated air generated by Wardword's filters. A giant tooth lab that replaced the HOZ MYLO chamber was soon overloaded with people of all ages having their rot removed. Specially trained tooth experts were ordered to insert a single black cube in everyone's mouths by removing one of the person's teeth and planting the little object into the empty area. The black cubes had the miraculous ability to prevent mental illnesses, immediately alert the wearer of any unfavorable thoughts, and serve people a buffet of reassuring thoughts by way of ingraining soothing classical music into everyone's heads. Everyone's teeth became as perfect and as white as the overbearing snow, the hard, icy crust covering the recently grown strange fungi (for the first time in OB-LOM, something grew on its own), imprisoning the last bits of anything natural and symbolizing the threshold of new age, and intensifying the forever-sterile winter coming with it.

For the first two weeks, I was relentlessly dined and entertained by the cute children, mishkas, and OB-LOM Leaders. The quality and amount of food, along with their unearthly kindness, made me believe the dictatorial days of LIM had been completely left behind.

At the beginning of my third week there, I had completely recovered from my dystrophy and acute fear of persecution.

One day, Prok and Uror woke me up and mouthed this to me, perfectly synchronized: "An important decision has to be made today, number 0002. You are offered a short-term reconstruction task. OB-LOM is asking for your help, since we don't have enough power to rebuild the State into a livable structure on our own. If you accept the task and finish it accordingly, you are free to go after you are done."

But what if I don't want to rebuild the State? What if I don't believe you? I wrote to them.

A blond mannequin-like Dwarworker with a thin mustache walked into the room and wrote to me with a porcelain smile on his face: *Then you can go outside and rot with the starving crowd.*

Prok and Uror giggled at the Dwarworker's reply.

The corners of the twins' curvy lips went up in the same animalistic grin everyone smiled around me. All three held themselves straight in a dry villainous fashion, casting me glances of pleading insistence. The dreadful memories of being touched by those wounded hands outside, having no Dom or family to return to, and the soothing powder-soap-oak fragrances coming from the twins made me conclude: I must accept the task.

I signed the papers of the OB-LOM Perestroika Release, also referred to as OLPR, which they had ready for me in a perfectly tight pile.

"Very well," said the twins in a voice so low I couldn't believe they were still the age they looked.

"Who are you two?" I asked them in my mature, diaphragmatic voice.

Their eyebrows went up, changing their calm faces into a confused grimace.

"Unlike you, we are the bright future of the State," said Prok.

"And your only job is to clean the dirt of the glorious State that you and the other inglorious citizens left behind," said Uror.

"Oh—your other job is to behave yourself for once," added Prok irritably. "You are one of the dumbest survivors we have accepted here."

"Here is your uniform," said Uror, fighting a giant yawn.

The floor sank under my feet. Neither the opinionated twins nor the written application ever mentioned to me that the Perestroika capsule's "short-term OLPR task" would last no less than seven years.

CHAPTER XIII

WARDWORD

WHOOOOOOSH. I WAS FLUSHED INTO A SPACE glowing with security and cleanliness. Landing on an endlessly wide, flawlessly maintained oriental rug, I finally exhaled after holding my breath for quite a while, like I always did in moments of suspenseful uncertainty.

After daydreaming for about an hour in the wondrous silky rug's creases, I stood up. My mind was at ease for reasons I will never know. And so, it seemed, were the minds of hundreds of other people around me. Tense and alert, with mouths unstapled yet tightly shut, they were dressed in trim red paper-crisp suits and blue overalls. We were there to do our job as directed by the children, who tiptoed in groups similar to well-groomed packs of darling wolf cubs with unblinking, trenchant eyes. Their job was to watch the two camps we'd been divided into from above. Both camps were there to rebuild our Rodina. We were there to turn Dwar into a more powerful, more invincible citadel of order than it had ever been.

Camp One's main job was to calculate everything and map out schematic blueprints of everything OB-LOM hadn't been deprived of due to its recent government-instigated catastrophe. Some of the not-too-cloudy professors from Warddoor and our old cowardly Gosti were among the calculating troupe.

Camp Two was filled with a lower working class. That's where I ended up. Our functional hands cleaned, purified, built, and stretched Dwar's gigantic pipes that glittered in the veins of the reconstruction monster.

From day one of my cleaning mission, the tick-tock-tuck in my head switched to something I can hardly describe onomatopoeically—inexplicably symphonic, built with rising and falling kitten-purring and soothing plopping-of-mushy-potatoes-gently-hitting-the-walls-of-a-large-metal-pan-while-boiling sounds. All in all, it was very pleasant. So pleasant that the next seven years in the OLPR chamber slipped through my fingers like an indomitable stream of water. Days were like minutes, weeks like hours.

Scrubbing walls and floors with toothbrushes, operating quick vacuum cleaners, and licking the floor with a special tongue-sponge cap—invented for achieving a superior degree of ostensibly germ-free environments—was what made me lose count of the days. In my soft, oversized jumpsuit, I cleaned with an impossible degree of enthusiasm, lapsing into fantastical thoughts about how sparkling OB-LOM was going to be thanks to my efforts.

My hopeful persona was drenched in the tranquility of the artificial suns rotating on the ceiling of my personal private space, built similarly to the bedroom I grew up in, for psychological comfort. My heart was filled with more and more fabricated happiness every day at the same time, when I soaked in those harmless Dwarwater baths. Yes, they had a strong delusional effect on me.

Preserving my originally written manuscript in my mind had become a challenging ambition. Before entering Dwar, I made it a goal to recite my book every night before bedtime in the exact same way, word by word, but once I was disposed into the whiteness of the new habitat, I could no longer control the trickle of changes that came along without invitation. As a result, my skewed perspective of truth and reality was slowly changing my original narrative. I wasn't sure my once-tragic story was still worth telling the world the way it had been written. I kept thinking: *Maybe it shouldn't be told altogether? Maybe I made it all up? Maybe OB-LOM does not deserve to be spoken about so poorly? What good do books of a critical nature do, anyway? Or of any nature? Why does anyone need to write anything?*

I wholeheartedly hope my narrative thus far hasn't given you the wrong impression of how strong my will is or whether it is lacking. I am well aware that I had given in to the cowardly influence of the totalitarian trance more than once in my story, but no words on any of the tips of my tongue can explain to you why I was so frequently susceptible to the faux comforts of my Rodina's mental trickery. None of it makes sense to me either. Perhaps my inability to resist is hidden in the primitive instincts of all living beings. Perhaps my search for comfort was beyond my resistance.

Thanks to our hard collective work and the children's impeccable supervision, Dwar was reconstructed into Wardword, a highly sophisticated realm of intertwined labyrinths and intimidating cranes, a colossus of improved control situated in the middle of the same old crunchy winter desert. All of OB-LOM's architectural omissions were hidden amid automatic conveyors and impeccably operating robots with metal creases sewn into the factories' canals the former GCD had branched out into. The plunger and stapler mascot had been supplanted by an uneventful image of a two-headed eagle cut out of the rare metal discovered some-

where in the sky (thanks to their successful experiments of sending more Glashkas to outer space).

The LIM-Leaders' former assistant with the biggest head, who had gathered the last bits of functional individuals and thrown the rest of the LIM-Leaders to the angry crowd before their audacity to suspect him of any unsavory operations, awoke and became *Glav Ruk*.[38] The chubby, quick-witted man with a potato-shaped head was now issuing nine hundred regulations a day to improve the sheer vastness of OB-LOM and its monstrously decreased population. "An improved, notably better population" was his most common objective.

Seven years passed in what seemed like no time. The labs, roads, rags, and protrusions I cleaned with my tongue this whole time had become so bright that all the old visible dimensions had collided into a single illumination. On a regular morning that must have looked like night (there was no way for me to see it), the same twins walked into my compartment. They had grown into sleek young men with perfect features and hair shinier than the floors I'd polished with my tongue.

"You have served OB-LOM well, 0002. We had our doubts that you were capable of anything, but you proved us wrong. The Glav Ruk is waiting for you. Don't make any bad decisions now," they said in a hypnotic baritone and walked me into a gorgeously foggy pink room with a long oval table in the middle. Ten tall chairs framed the table.

The twins pushed me forward and shut the door behind my back, leaving the Glav Ruk and me alone in the room. The man was comfortably mounted on the most mesmerizing chair like a self-enamored host, decorated with an ample bib sitting on his chest. There was nothing about his movements that gave off an impression of urgency or control. Casually sipping his supremely upgraded tea named Super Princessa 2 from a sumptuous samovar, he addressed me without lifting his eyes

38 Russian abbreviation for "Glavnyi Rukovoditel"—general/executive director.

from the porcelain ruffled-with-multiple-roses cup. I could read his lips effortlessly: "I was informed you accomplished the task. Well done, Sashenka."

My heart fluttered. Nobody had called me Sashenka but my parents. I showed the man my best smile and blushed. In a blink, the Glav Ruk's perfectly manicured hand was stretched toward me. A much bigger and better-rehearsed smile than mine gradually grew on his face, like a puddle of batter schlepped into a skillet on its way to being shaped into a thin blintz. The apparent weakness of his physique along with the peachy smoothness of his skin were enough for me to conclude: this man had not seen any labor and had his life served to him on a silver platter.

"I called for you to see what your further intentions were, dear. Before you say anything, let me remind you of your rights—you, of course, are more than welcome to stay here with your camp. In case you desire to live outside of the camp, you will be provided with the best amenities in OB-LOM. You have indeed proved yourself as a worthy worker," he said in a calming tone, deliberately dribbling the thick brown tea from both corners of his mouth. "What does your heart desire? Tell me. Here, have some tea with me."

The shampoo-cleanliness of the room and the euphoric tea I took a sip of felt so incredible in the moment that I wanted to lie next to this man's feet and lick the dirt off of them.

"Stay, stay, stay," whispered the entirety of the pink walls.

As I was nodding with my eyes crossed, in a strange ecstasy, a large calendar with the double eagle head caught my attention. What I saw in the calendar made me rub my eyes over and over again. Even though I had never been good at counting, there was no doubt in the world that it had been years since I entered the OLPR.

In a split second, the idyllic, opulent, pink room became an uneventful bureaucratic yellow office. The Glav Ruk was a miserable-looking man with hateful eyebrows eating a plate of pig faces and wiggling uncomfortably in a giant faux-leather chair. I had been lied to for seven consecutive years.

"So?" the Glav Ruk repeated to me without noticing the size of my eyes as they ogled the calendar. "What is it that your heart desires?"

These were the words I squeezed out of myself with too much confidence: "I am out. Let me go."

The Glav Ruk's face turned purple. Then he lowered his eyes demurely and said: "Well then, time to gather your possessions. And don't forget to turn in all the cleaning supplies you were given at the cleaning supply station. Prok and Uror will walk you out as soon as you are ready. Oh, and one more thing," he said, rereading my signed contract. "Before entering, you agreed to take the PRO-creation bath upon completion of your service."

The realization of my negligently signed contract made my guts churn in a soughless symphony of every door there used to be in Dom: "Uaee-ghaghkaa-eeek-aakh-choo-uuu-iii-eee-aaaa-pfeee-swoon-yaaa-chuckeeee-dghrkha-pee-pa-wooo."

Sloshing and other clatter.

I moved my head in a multi-circular denial. Multi-oval-circular-square repetitive denial.

"Take your clothes off, or they will do it for you with the PRO-creation scissors."

A square bathtub on wheels with bright pink hissing water rolled into the yellow room. The twins reentered, proudly carrying a humongous pair of rustic scissors that resembled two crossed eagle heads. I tried to show the three that I needed some privacy, hoping I could jump out the window when they weren't looking, but they remained in the same position, staring at me with a mixture of curiosity and hatred.

"Do it." A twenty-minute pause. "Now!" They kept insisting. Their perfect white teeth remained prominent for the rest of the procedure.

I shook. I coughed theatrically. Fainted. Barked. Then I took off my overalls and sat in the tub. Everything became at peace again. I don't remember what happened to me, but when I opened my eyes again, I was back in my private cubicle. Very pregnant. Every other female worker who was to be released that day was in the same situation.

The window that used to be tightly shut had been unlocked; one didn't need any observational skills to see immediately that the world outside was not the same. There, in the visible mist, stood sharp icy gardens resembling dragon teeth and gigantically tall cone-shaped buildings with elevators of all speeds, moving at an irregular rhythm like drunken mechanisms of an old overheated machine. Everything had become so perfectly polished that the land became too slippery for the public to walk straight. The OB-LOMannye had been successfully trained to operate conveniently wheeled sleigh-chairs with automatic functions. That's how people stopped walking altogether. Bulky mishkas with unfortunate neurotic facial tics they were cursed with during some sophisticated animal-tests were still ice-skating on the streets and making sure everything was under control. Their skates remained the same.

The GCD chambers turned into gigantic outlets with a variety of delicacies and goods. Most of them were no longer locally produced. Let me be completely honest with you: the only locally produced goods the new GCD offered to the State were those plain bottles of Wardwater (still consumed in abundance) and mittens. Some things never change, you see.

OB-LOM had acquired endless amounts of machinery and tinsel garlands while we were constructing it. Its land popped into circular divisions containing lots of producing conveyors operating independently of one another. No, they weren't actually producing, merely importing items from other lands. The GCD no longer needed any manual labor to distribute anything. Most commonly, those who were laid off from their positions stayed in their Doms and raised their babies for the rest of their lives.

The Glav Ruk and other OB-LOM Leaders had welcomed millions of objects of automatic convenience that were utilized by everyone on a daily basis with great appreciation and joy. Their presence and easy access had taken over people's midbrains. OB-LOMannye could no longer function without these new assemblies of highly functional curiosities: bulky clicky objects for remote communication, motorized skis, gaudy antifreeze robes, revitalizing masks, self-cleaning brooms, warming mustard jackets and underjackets, the same dresses and underdresses, multifunctional doors, and so on.

Everything had been modified into something of higher perfection and quality to the point that even mishkas and stray dogs (who were now DOMesticated through the earlier-mentioned animal testing, or as they preferred to say, "training") started using the clickies, which were capable of anything with just one click: independent food attainment, unlimited deliveries of anything (even whole buildings) from anywhere in time and space, enhanced fertility, smell and stain removal, and so much more, all in one little clicky. People's thumbs had grown so much from the clicking that one day the local mitten industry had to resize their entire production. In fact, thumbs had transformed into something people could easily use as tools, such as hammers, pliers, and screw guns, even though nobody actually needed to build anything anymore. Everything had been already built, or rather reconstructed.

Besides their enlarged thumbs, people's bodies had grown in size quite a bit, too. The new garment manufacture (which was no longer local) consisted of multicolored robes and pajamas for comfort. That was all people could fit into. Every OB-LOMannye wore a bright red hat with a large pom-pom that served them as an information-exchange antenna that made their clickies work exceptionally well.

This grotesque system of progressive technological brainlessness took over OB-LOM. Such drastic change was followed by poor grammar, chronic obesity, and complete helplessness, manifesting itself as rapidly as the new pipes erected by Wardword's construction workers during the seven years of their technological captivity. The local, still-not-so-primitive-though-used-with-extreme-limits language people had once mastered became a series of orangutan vowels, commonly expressed through exclamatory behavior and even more commonly through electronic faces identifying one's mood. I think the mood list offered no more than twenty choices.

Regardless of these thousands of progressive changes, the State was still struggling with balancing its populace. It was mandated that everyone had to have between ten and twenty children, from as many people as they desired, without having to sign any papers or fill out any forms. People became nearly as stupid as street poles, except they didn't lose their ability to count acceptably. Ballet remained just as popular, though ballerinas had tripled in their body and tutu sizes.

Thanks to gathering information from other lands, the State had become dangerously inventive, still lying quietly in its own opaque capsule of regulations and clarity deprivation. The Glav Ruk had amassed, quite literally, a lake of treasures he could easily dive into.

There was no chance of anyone starting another rebellious act at that point, due to the fact that OB-LOM had changed the population into a simplistic herd of followers. People were quiet again. Timofey Grigorievich and Pangina were promoted to be the Glav Ruk's most esteemed helpers.

Precisely seven years after I had first entered, I walked out of the factory with an unwanted child in my abdomen and saw the hazy dawn landing on the groups of chubby people in a shimmering variety of sizeless robes and silly pom-pom hats, riding their wheelchairs with clickies, like a group of blinded ants. Many had strollers attached to their wheelchairs. Triple strollers, quadruple strollers. The weather remained the same. No technology could ever change OB-LOM's weather or temperature. Such was life. It was frozen.

"For all the work you have done to reconstruct Wardword and conceive a child from the most flawless citizens in the State, you are granted a new Dom," I was told prior to my departure in a beautifully written note with many stamps.

The mishkas gallantly walked me to the other side of OB-LOM, separated by a bridge—the bridge I'd cleaned with my own tongue for seven years. My temporary new room was another place I had cleaned for years. The smell of my chlorine detergent was still present everywhere I stepped. I sat on the rough, lonely bed next to a carefully folded straitjacket in the medical department for the clinically insane.

At first, I hit the walls with my fists and tore apart the mattress. The black cube implanted in the back of my mouth burned like a volcano, mercilessly scorching my palate. After loosening and grinding it for five hours, it finally fell off. The door opened and hit the wall with so much strength the ceiling crumbled. A wide-boned, sweet-faced, wrinkly lady in a white gown hurriedly rolled into my room in her big-wheeled white wheelchair. She picked up my black square and said sweetly, "You don't need this anymore, honey. We know more about you than we needed."

The lingering disapproval of those words gave my mouth a prominent flavor of old paper. I could no longer hold my nausea back—big chunks of letters and punctuation marks mixed with intestinal juice came out of me and dripped all over my straitjacket and the lady's gown. Before I managed to close my teeth on the wrinkly lady's arm, she threw three bulky syringes at me like a deft warrior. I fell unconscious.

Twelve hours later, Wardword became a finished construction. The Wardword Glav Ruk announced to all of OB-LOM through the new shiny hexagonal loudspeaker: "We must finish the once-failed project and dislodge the fantasies of deranged minds, who disrupt the order and discipline with nonsensical novelties, to clear the path of OB-LOM's future and save the population from the madness of thought and imagination. The last two offenders of clarity are sentenced to be sent to the COO for improvement and overall better living in case they fail to improve after correction methods."

The majority of the well-fed, metal-statue-looking local citizens voted yea. Those who didn't vote yea were immediately sent away for a thorough medical checkup and prescription medicine.

My life was over.

I couldn't avoid the COO, no matter how much I wished to. Once my mind was erased, the whole land would be scrubbed clean of any unnecessary expression of insubordinate literary thought. I was due to give birth to a new flawless citizen in the arena the same day.

CHAPTER XIV
THE COO

Без му́ки нет нау́ки.[39]

Beware: everything that happened after my COO sentence I only recall in distorted analogies.

They gave me seven more days to practice some of the best oblivion procedures so I could happily join the new world of brainwashed people, create nineteen more babies (in case the one I was about to have was delivered successfully), and wear my own red pom-pom hat. I must admit, it was one of the most impressive pom-pom hats I had seen.

In my solitary confinement, they brought me stacks of colorful magazines without a single word written in them. They were rich with fantastic color propaganda images of the new lifestyle everyone was extremely happy to live: triple- and even quadruple-decker buterbrods, strollers, blue-eyed babies in ruffles, colorful bowls filled with exotic fruit, blank-faced, bare-chested ladies in huge fur hats with red pom-poms and valenkis of different sizes (!), shiny wheeled chairs of the most inconceivable shapes,

39 An old Russian proverb: "Without torture, there is no science."

borscht of all colors and flavors, clickies and a range of little faces expressing emotions, DOMesticated cats and dogs (which had become very tiny and strange-looking), delicious-looking pashtet for them in pretty tubes, topless Glav Ruk riding mishkas and horses, a whole section of meat showing the biggest cow tongues imaginable, images of childbirth with crowds of people cheering next to the smiling ladies with their legs spread open, Wardwater bottles shaped like statues, icicles, and bears, and new Doms with automated systems in which everything was done independently by means of clapping, stepping, and reproducing a few orangutan vowel sounds. In the very last section of the magazine were exercises designed specifically for me.

I flipped the pages of the magazine, thinking that I must have fallen asleep centuries ago and everything I had been doing was nothing but a nightmare. I pinched myself in every possible way—I even threw my whole body against the walls, for which I was tied up in a sturdier straitjacket, but alas, nothing changed. I was still there with a stomach as big as a ripe watermelon and big bumps all over me.

When my behavior seemed to improve and I could finally count how many fingers I saw in front of my face, they removed my straitjacket. This is what I scratched with the remaining leftovers of the pencil I received from the other prisoner in the room next to me, leaning against the wall with an alien child twisting and turning inside my womb:

DAY I.

I am addressing you from the metallurgy yard where stands a gargantuan citadel rich in bulwarks, infinite doors (their knobs are carved from greenish lava, burning the frozen air, making my nose run), granite pillars, gloomy entryways, levels covered in mustard plastic bed pads, and short ceilings. I am a prisoner here. Whether or not I die here remains to be seen.

DAY II.

It seems like there are no floors here, as there is an optical illusion of overall mustardness; its entity turns the space into one endless cube. Despite Wardword's highly polished facade, the steps at each entrance are surreptitiously rotting away, giving it the tightly ingrained stench of bug spray and ammo-

nia. Each step is overgrown with horrifying baneberries resembling diseased eyeballs and serving Wardword as its garrison, a manic protoplasm. Its itchy little crystals unfurl upon the newcomers as electric chairs. They are constantly watching. The back of Wardword looks out into the open space from which it is separated by the gray fence with sharp nails.

All I asked for was a well-deserved departure. They couldn't grant it to me. Lack of connotation. Then they got me pregnant. They say I will have two beautiful twins. They want to erase my brain. They say I have too much nonsense in my head.

DAY III.

If you are reading this, it means I'm most likely gone. No, I am not dead, no. I am not here to die, because they won't let me. Death is positively forbidden here. I'm in a mental trap I built with my own hands. Ha-ha-ha-ha-ha!

DAY IV.

Something is collapsing inside my brittle mind. The unwanted children I am bearing in my achy womb are growing bigger every day. Heavier. The atrocious anxiety it's giving me has finally sprawled into a wounded pterodactyl.

DAY V.

I am addressing you through my thoughts, since they are all I have left, but at the same time, even my thoughts are not going to count very soon, since they will be erased (for protection purposes, of course). By the way, I don't think I will ever finish my novel. I have been forced to forget it, I think, about 9300 times in the past three days. Yes, I try to count, regardless of my fear of numbers, because days are long here.

I hear the stupid ticking in my head again. It hurts so much I want to open my head and pluck out the tick-tock-tuck from my brain with my long, dirty nails. Looks like there used to be other disagreeing brains imprisoned here—I see bite marks and illegibly scratched messages on the walls. They must have already been cured. But how could they be cured? This place is so confusing I may never see clearly again. They say no one is confused in OB-LOM but me. They say I am unreasonably angry and deserve no say in any of OB-LOM's affairs. They say individuals like me are rotten. They say individuals like me cause disorder.

My teeth chatter, but I'm not cold—why is that? Crooked fluffy spiders descend from the ceiling several times a day to munch on my scalp. Perhaps they want to make me forget too, with their tepid, stagnant secretions. I don't like them, but killing them would mean I would not have any company. I don't believe the spiders are part of the State's conspiracy. Or are they?

DAY VI.

Today was my last chance to be released from my COO sentence. I don't think I passed, since I refused to look at the images from the magazines or count fingers before me. They brought a bundle of newly born babies to my cell, wrapped in cloths, carefully stored in display cages to give me an idea of how cute babies are and how lucky I am to become an OB-LOMannaya mother. Frankly speaking, I thought they were terrifying, like enraged aliens, even though I don't actually know what aliens look like. Finally, they called for an army of male individuals who, unfortunately, didn't know how to play chess anymore. I apologized to them for my picky nature and asked them to leave me alone. How did everyone get so very dumb?

At the beginning of the next day that looked just like night (which I'm sure you are already quite well aware of), Wardword diagnosed me with incurable madness that can cause social confusion and disorientation. The only option for me now is to forget everything and live carelessly. Somehow, I still have the strength to refuse. I don't want to forget any more of who I really am. I don't want to stop trying to leave this place. Whoever you are, oh glorious reader, I promise you that one day I will finish writing this story, and you will read it and learn about the dangers of totalitarian thinking.

They have experimented with several dozen restorative methods to cure me, along with all the more terribly oblivious methods like some light, elegant performances of psychosurgery, but nothing worked. The most torturous daily procedure has me in the oval helmet called Shapka-Zabudka40 they fasten

40 A made-up Russian word meaning "forget-me hat."

on my head. The only time I am released from the stupid hat is when I am being spoon-fed by the wrinkly ladies. They feed me whatever I am assigned to eat or drink, putting me through an ordeal of brain-cracking pain. When I am in Shapka-Zabudka, I see a multitude of my own reflections there—my beady eyes protruding like marshmallow wires. My face is distorted in these mirrors, but I swear I am not altogether bad-looking. I have big eyes and strong legs. What else? I am not sure, but I think what makes me good-looking is the fact that I don't look like the people outside. They have become identical again, like many years ago, when Pa took me outside of Dom for the first time. When I am released from the hat, I try to repeat my favorite words I hope I will never forget. The words I don't want to forget are: nurture, tortoise, borscht, figurine, murky, snout, blooper, knuckle, sizzle, and Cheburashka. Those words sing to me.

None of what they feed me has a distinctive taste. It's neither salty nor sweet—merely plain, like paper. You, of course, must have tasted paper at least once in your life. The papery flavor somehow gives me a sense of repetitive pulsating oblivion. It makes me forget, but I am still able to remember. I remember everything as vividly as can be. Why can't I just forget and be released? Because I would rather die. I promise you, oh glorious reader, someday you will read this story from a book. From a book that may not seem realistic or accurate. From a book that will show you how truly absurd totalitarian thinking is.

At Wardword, my body vomits more than it swallows. I am being scrubbed away from inside and outside. I often think I am going to dissolve like a cloud. Then maybe I could escape.

Yesterday, through one of the peeping holes I'd carved out of anxiety, through which I could easily inhale winter and sense the vibration of the other prisoner's tooth-grinding habit, he or she passed me a note written with a pencil: "Please let me speak to you. I tried to whisper, but you never answer. Please write me back. Unfold the paper to find the pencil." The pencil fell out of the note. It had lots of bite marks on its sides. I wrote back: "I apologize for not responding. I am simply deaf. Why are you here?

"I am an inostranec. But what's even worse—I am a skazochnik[41]*. I will go to the COO tomorrow and forget everything," was the prisoner's final reply.*

I was put back into Shapka-Zabudka before I had a chance to write anything else.

DAY VII.

They released me from Shapka-Zabudka. Through the disgusting window of my square room, I saw Sash, who had grown into a tired-looking man. He was sitting in a wheelchair. Wrinkly ladies were clumsily rolling him to the monstrous COO.

"Sash! Sash! Sash!" I yelled with all my might, thrusting my fists against the unbreakable windows. He turned around. I wrote on the sweaty window: "Comrade." He smiled with what looked like considerable effort and nodded.

Pangina and Timofey Grigorievich released a huge dome that hung above Sash's head. It covered his whole body with a bloodcurdling "WHOOOM!"

In the last note Sash wrote for me with an almost fully eaten pencil, I found the same feverishly drawn image of a tree, strange figures floating in the sky, and two small people standing among it all.

"Cave ab homine unius libri"[42] *was all that was written there.*

The walls bulge in here as if possessed with invisible thoughts tormented by oblivion. But I still remember everything very, very vividly. I absolutely abhor my Rodina. I must depart. I promise you, oh glorious reader, I will tell you everything in my book one day.

They fed me one more time. The flavorless cabbage was infused with lots and lots of soothing potions, painfully coating my soft and hard palates with its aggressive burning acids.

At this point, my rapidly thinning reality is fading and shrinking inside these dreary constructions. Sizzle, knuckle, murky, bo . . . borscht! I can see two or four thousand people waiting outside. It's my turn. They are coming after me. I am afraid I have been stirring up all those memorable words in vain. If I forget all the words I know, I hope I will manage to preserve "sizzle" and "borscht."

41 Russian: "storyteller."

42 Latin: "Fear the man of one book."

Those were the last words I wrote on the wall behind my bed. The sky that day was extraordinary; the bright green bunches of clouds informed the State of a high percentage of COO radiation. Feeble yet decisive steps. They came after me while I was searching for shapes and faces among those clouds. I was supported by their rough sandpaper hands on both sides while stumbling through long mustard tunnels and corridors, my feet stamping the ground unsteadily. They kept mouthing to me in a repetitive mantra: "You will be cured in no time. Can't wait to see the twin babies."

As soon as we reached Wardword's exit, they put me in a wheelchair. My smelly straitjacket was way too tight. Twenty thousand thoughtless people with forty thousand strollers were waiting outside, creeping in from all directions of the State in angelic anticipation and half smiles that made them look almost constipated. Everyone in the COO arena was going to experience my hour-long memory-cleansing journey on a large screen. Such wonderful entertainment, erasing my uneasy brain! Ah! The last confused mind was going to be neutralized forever. Glory days! Kak vse! Wardword provided everyone with unlimited supplies of buterbrods and Wardwater throughout the procedure, since it was the most efficient way to keep people focused in those days. People were going to munch on their kielbasa during my baby delivery. Then OB-LOM would be the safest place once again.

My wheelchair moved automatically, on its own, as if guided by an invisible hand. It was on its way to Wardword's black-square pedestal in the middle of the ground framed by tall square mirrors and a triangular dome hanging above it on hardly noticeable strings, like a puppet. I was approaching the middle of the incubator.

Once all the straps had finished locking me in the central spot, I started seeing distorted faces of my own looking at me from large mirrors all around.

The murmur of objections and applause filled OB-LOM. My mind attempted to digest, fold, and decompose in the jaws of the new societal etiquette, which I knew I was never going to manage. My mother was right—I was ruined by the otherness they'd raised me with. Life could have been much easier if I didn't have that resistance.

"You will live happily among us when you come back from the COO," said the multitude of iron voices.

A tight metal rope was fastened around my neck and head. I had to sit straight to avoid being hurt. Even though my memories were mixed up and I was too scared to even breathe, I was somehow thinking about my mother's childbirth story—how she had me. I read it in one of her diaries after her death. She had dealt with an incredible amount of struggle while giving birth to me in Biblioteka. She said I almost suffocated myself with my own umbilical cord when I came out of her . . . it was miraculous that she and I survived. The day she was ready to give birth, she couldn't go to the –BOL-NITSA, simply because my parents didn't want anyone to know I was ever born. Ma asked one of our lady Gosti who claimed to have once been an *akusherka*[43] to help her accomplish the act, though the lady wasn't overall competent, nor did she mention to Ma that the –BOL-NITSA had ordered that she change her specialty due to her squeamishness and recurring dizzy spells followed by long-lasting spells of dramatic fainting. She brought a bagful of specially brewed juices to help Ma feel less pain, not knowing that Ma was severely allergic to everything in the injections. Ma got her injections in three different areas until the forgetful akusherka-Gost noticed that Ma wasn't doing so well: Ma's tongue swelled to the size of a red snapper, and she almost swallowed it until Pa put a broom in her mouth to keep the tongue in the right place. The akusherka fainted long before Ma, even though the latter was in incomparably more pain.

Pa was left surrounded by the two passed-out women, not knowing what to do. He soon found out that not only was Ma no longer alive (she was clinically dead for a few minutes), but she also had a baby coming out of her wrapped in its own umbilical cord. It was my fault, I suppose. I suspect I must have been dealing with my own prenatal confusion. I must have refused to greet the world outside of Ma.

---

43 Russian, meaning "midwife."

I suffocated myself with the "umbilical scarf" to the point of my own near-death experience until Pa cut Ma's abdomen and released me to the kerosene lamp in Biblioteka, where I spent so much time growing up. Ma, the akusherka, and I survived after multiple reanimation attempts performed by Pa, who learned that night more about childbirth and saving people's lives than he had ever expected. Ma wrote in her diary that while approaching death before giving me life, she was flying down a dark tunnel similar to the ones behind our walls. She wrote that she was flying toward a constellation of pretty flickers of light at the end of it.

Meanwhile, the crowd in OB-LOM grew increasingly ecstatic. I had a second to watch the happening. Besides the army of local infants moving in their toothless sameness, the first three rows were filled with Agnesa Borisovna and Vasiliy Fyodorovich's neighbors, Warddoor-goers, old Gosti, the GCD Buh-Galters, and some of the mishkas. They hadn't changed much. Above their heads were dithered billboards displaying moving images of self-cleaning diapers and triple-decker strollers. Some of the attendees were seated on the ground, since no seats were left among the rows. Nobody was willing to miss a chance to watch the last COO procedure in OB-LOM's history. Their noses were glistening with drops of sweat, their eyes—with joy.

I was enthroned, disrobed, and seated spread eagle, feet and arms locked on both sides.

The Glav Ruk's order to start the COO made everyone stop moving simultaneously, like well-trained pets.

My dry mouth was moved by some invisible power; it spread open and began to grow as wide as a lake of sorts, until it grew into a single mauve hole. A giant triangular dome fell from the strings and covered my whole body. My breath came in gasps.

I was still, wide-eyed, entangled in the tumorous pain growing parallel roots in my temples. The purplish vortex in front of me was darkening into a pitch-black tunnel with a constellation of ugly flickers of light at the end of it. Tick-tock-tuck. Unendurable flashes of fever.

A bomb of tumultuous applause and whistles flew around OBLOM, ripping apart the faint fragrance of baby powder and dog piss. The COO's broad projector was about to display my mind's journey on the screen. Every bit of mental torture I was yet to trod through was to be planted directly in their vehement pupils. The dark image on the screen gradually brightened in the belligerent moonlight beams. The delirium of my past and present intermingled. Clashes of ticking and tocking, and my cry of terror.

PART III

THE CHAMBER OF OBLIVION

At this point, my dreams begin to fade and melt away, like water in water. My vanity and my nostalgia have confected a scene that is impossible. Maybe so, I tell myself, but tomorrow I will be dead and our times will run together and chronology will melt into an orb of symbols, and somehow it will be true to say that I have brought you this book and that you have accepted it.

—Jorge Luis Borges

CHAPTER 1

FIGHT OR FLIGHT

So that you may understand what I saw in the disorienting abyss, the altitudinal code of which must have been invented by some extraterrestrial genius, you must be patient with me. It was a mental surgery of sorts. I was plunged into

Pitch-black stillness.
Drifting.
Afloat in infinity.
Time was frozen,
and so was the temperature.
Locked-in syndrome.
Dreary condensation.
40°C/-40°F
I could not recall
my name.
My teeth
were clenching.

I held
my mouth
open with both hands.
I nearly bit them off.
My body
was outside of my body.
It shrank.
Expanded.
My nose
itched.
My nostrils
flared
which I flanged
as wide as I could afford.
My head
in two-three-four
more feet
turned
right-left-right
with a delay . . . .
as if underwater.
My ears
in four-three-two-one
popped
like freshly cleaned pipes.
And there . . . .
I heard
a symphony
of distorted echoes.
Splendid.
Charming.
Exquisite echoes.
The walls were chanting.

Meowing.
Cooing.
I was yawning.
Repetitive facial spasms.
Every millimeter of resonance
came to me
in hundreds of fluctuations,
tones,
honks, and moans,
drenching me
in the rhythmically tapping
chaos.
The overall rhythm
was oddly perfect.
Identical.
I covered and exposed
my membranes
a billion times
to renew
the sounds
all over again.
La-la-la!
The same airy intensity.
I couldn't get enough
of the empty music.
I could hear again.
I listened.
Listened and listened.
Boom-ba-ba.
Choo-cha-cha.
Zhoom-zham-zham.
La-la-la.
Shoo-sha-sha.

Voom-vah-vah.
My eyes
were catching
the fading dull light's glimpses
from above.
No bottom was to be seen
below.
My layered-oilcloth-pillow
lungs and guts
were pervaded,
infected
with a swooning, febrile glow.
It had a sensuous kernel
deep inside
in its bluish shade of purple.
Pulsating,
smelling of iron—
iodine—
new linoleum—
dill.
So much dill it made me feel ill.
Deep-fried ozone
spiced with wasabi.
The microfloral taste
of my throat
complicated the creases
in my high forehead.
It wiggled the jigsaw sculptures in
my forebrain.
It lost its
ticky-tacky-hugger-mugger-
shilly-shally thinky-thoughts
and farfetched associative permutations.

I was nearing the end of
my lush-air consciousness.
The complete nudity of
my mental transformation
was purer
than bivalve mollusks.
Scarier than fear.
Unknown flora and fauna,
in the bottomless fountains
of my blood circulation,
turned into
cacophonous icebergs.
A distorted mirror plexus
tightly connected
by invisible webs
was flying next to me.
A crooked halo
of sickening
blood-orange fleshes
or fruit flies
quivering.
The mirrors
showed me everything
with abnormal precision.
The specks of dust
flying around
my head
were not specks, but memories.
Departing,
peeling off,
like flakes of skin.
The spinning light leaks,
sucking out

my remaining thoughts.
They made me watch.
Still reflections of
disorderly human faces.
Expressions of personal
tragedy.
They looked
as though they could repay
a second glance.
Inside my Mind's
fluffy bits,
I saw whirligigs.
Oriental rugs drowning
in borscht.
Saxophones freezing
in giant icicles.
Books attacked
by numbers.
Equations.
The alphabet.
I no longer distinguished.
I cried.
I laughed.
I screamed
like a frustrated forest creature.
Or a very lonely one.
The unequivocally changing light
looked like one's
behind-the-eyelid vision
when pressed hard,
causing the occurrence
of little green specks
usually shaped like outrageous crowns

and amoebas.
They are called phosphenes,
they say.
The beams slapped me.
The beams scratched me.
Like razor-teeth piranhas,
encrusting the affected spots
with tall goosebumps
and linear bite marks.
Upon reaching the end
of the tunnel,
the atmosphere changed.
Drastically.
The highly uncomfortable
magnetic withdrawal
came to an end.
My Mind's pieces,
trapped inside the mirrors,
came to a halt
like fatigued trains.
I froze afloat until
I discovered
I could swim-fly
through the air.
Quick sporadic movements.
I didn't fight.
I flew
in inconsequential thrusts.
The mirrors exploded
into millions of little fragments,
washing through me
like ice-cold bullets.
They took away my pain,

resistance,
and fear.
I didn't cry.
I quietly laughed.
I was calm.
Hysterically calm.
The atmosphere was about done
absorbing my "I,"
deeper and deeper,
galvanizing
my swallowing habits,
spewing out
the rest of me
into the wide-open
black door.
The rock bottom.
It flew open
with a loud hiss.
The previous chanting switched
to eerie
organ-whoosh-moan
accompaniments.
A symphony of distorted echoes.
Dull.
Repellent.
Harsh echoes.
The hall behind the door was whistling—
roaring—
grunting—
interrupting
the last anxious vignettes
of the tunnel.
I flew into the hall.

A new dimension.
Stranger than everything.
Magnetic
bulky
eyes,
blinking
in the dark.
The door shut.
Shhhhhh.

CHAPTER 11

LAOPHIS

THE LONG GLASS CORRIDOR BEHIND THE BLACK DOOR glistened like the wet swollen face of a newborn otter. There was not a teaspoon of self-defense left in me.

I proceeded farther with laser-sword precision. Unconscious servility, rather.

Millions of mesmerizing stalactite-like eyes blinked in the borderless, dimly lit bluish space. It hurt to watch them. The cold hall led me to a broader space: a giant milk bottle I was walking inside, supported by thousands of wrinkled-from-age maniacal ballerinas, tirelessly trotting in the air to keep the bottle afloat. Their movements were synchronized with the plumb-sax-ophone-ka-zoo buzzing. Everything was buzzing.

There was another door in the middle. It was white. Then another. Black doors. White doors. And more doors. I walked through about seventeen of them. Each time I walked through a new door, I would lose about a year in age. The slightly swaying, unified sounds coming from their keyholes revealed that cyclical, stealthily stamping mechanics were operating somewhere near. I pushed open the seventeenth door and walked into a new space, lit with thickly piebald amber and aluminum glossiness. I was about five and a half. I was in Dom that looked nothing like Dom. I heard the tick-tock-tucks and some familiar voices. It was all very confusing.

The surface of the floor was monstrously slippery. I did an awkward somersault in the air, landing in the chunky bronze puddles coming toward me from every direction. They smelled of sardines. Oily sprats, for certain.

My eyes became heavy like two old fortepianos. Hypnotized by the excessive ticking, the high levels of moisture, the fake replica of my childhood habitat, lying among a net of humming generators, a great deal of industrial cranes, and systematically pulsating pipes resembling a harmonica, I suddenly concluded: it was a dream that was nowhere near over.

A slimy tube, curled up next to me, was lifting itself up and down. To my greatest horror, it was not a tube but a giant, blemished, partially galvanized, checkered snake, framing the imperishable chalice of unknown powers. The monster chased its own tail at lethargic speed, winding the space with a breezy reptilian dance. Its nostrils, shrinking and flaring, shook the dome with microearthquakes, created by the creature's seismic hiccups and turbulent heartbeats.

Such enchantment! Even though adrenaline was pumping like a whistling hose in every inch of my head and neck, I couldn't help ogling the monster. The moment I stepped an inch away from it, the snake's eyes opened wide and fixed themselves upon me like butcher knives preparing for a large-scale dissection.

Tick-tock-tuck.

Hoosh-hush, hush-hoosh.

Distant la-la-las.

Every engine of the interior operation was purring into life.

The snake threw its hose-tongue impeccably, like an archer, then twisted me into a hard pretzel and swallowed me in one gulp. I could hear the maniacal wrinkly ballerinas' movements accelerate on the other side of the bottle.

Chanting switched to "Kak vse! Kaaaak vse! Kak vseeeee!"

In an instant, I became drenched in bubbly muck, thoroughly lubricated inside a lukewarm, drowsy pit. Hovering.

For the most part, it looked like a broad canal of cotton soup soufflé.

Have you ever been morbidly poisoned by a giant mythological snake? Most likely you have not.

What was it like? At first, it granted me a feeling of sensuous complacency similar to the cleanest set of bedsheets a person has ever slept on. I felt wonderfully, comfortably dead. Next, I dissipated into the whirling-hot stream inside the monster's stomach. In the faux pool of sleepy poisoned waters mixed with ink, I was simmering alive. All in all, it was a very strange feeling.

The more I wiggled my toes and fingers to make sure my limbs were still mobile, the more my veins became replete with boiling broths of unknown origins, causing every part of me to shrink and expand as the heartbeats of the snake pushed me toward the garishly looming vertical light at the end of the new tunnel I was being propelled toward. My spine cracked. The amber light extinguished.

CHAPTER III

OOOASIS OF MANY UNKNOWNS

My crunchy eyes thawed out from the venomous prism-film, observing a translucent mist of skewed dullness. No colors were left around. Curled up in a lethargic-sun-dried-shrimp position, still a five-year-old in a significantly oversized hospital gown, I found myself inside that same scruffy milk bottle, navigated by a group of elegantly swimming maniacal ballerinas. Three Os were engraved on one of its sides. I was floating down a vigorous ink waterfall, groping around in the blind fog; its long threads of airy fluff were coming down the sky, spreading in the same drunken-spiral manner as a thickly whipped ounce of half-and-half would pour itself inside a churner while turning into a chunk of butter.

The overbearing pastel emptiness, exclusively interrupted by the cloud's interpretive dance, told me to be prepared for something extraordinary. A new realm, perhaps. Stranger than anything.

"Hoosh-hush," whispered the same deceitful multitude of voices from the inky water.

A flock of little fishy heads looked at me—sad elephant tortoises. I swear I could hear them sigh. Eight more gusts of wind. The lower ribbons of smoky clouds receded like two silver bushels on an old man's head. The shore was near. The maniacal ballerinas pushed me out of the bottle and swam away.

I stepped out of the tub, plunging my feet into the stubborn black figure eight–shaped river. I grabbed the base of a peculiar fence and held on to it as hard as I could until I fully crawled out of the manipulative stream. My wide-open wounds oozed big drops of muddy poison. Stretched supine on the unknown ground, encrusted sporadically with dead cicadas similar to shrunken pieces of fat in a piece of salami, I hugged the ice-cold fence with the same affection anyone would hug a warm comrade.

A graveyard with no end. An asymmetrically curvy graveyard, a parody of a particular gnarly forest out of my old nightmares.

"Bo-o-o-om!" The ground cracked in three, revealing the opening to a thorny trail patched up with half-faded soil patterns. The moment the fog froze, each cicada awakened from the dead, emerging out of the sticky, mushy ground, surreptitiously creeping closer to me, snoring, cracking their growing metallic fur and phallic fungi on the unctuous, slimy ground, twisted with little brown veins. Millions of cicadas. The more they chanted, the more the ink river drained itself, releasing piles of breathless elephant tortoises. Some of them were significantly deformed. Their lightly ticking hearts that were not hearts but old pocket watches, attached to their spinal cords, stuck out of their torn chests. The different speed the mechanisms were running at disrupted the calmness of the breathless environment.

The earsplitting primordial cry the cicadas' perky wings were giving off sounded like a broken orchestra of pipes and drills. Since there was only one way to go, I ran straight without ever looking back.

"La-la-la-la-la," I sang at the top of my lungs while stumbling over bushes and piles of dirt, to make the cicada vocal chaos go away.

"Hello?" I asked the emptiness once everything became as quiet as it had been when I was deaf.

A sudden gust of wind blew a fluffy cloud of dust past me, revealing a crooked arrow on a broken crossroad sign. "OOOasis of the Unknown" read the skewed sign, lying flat on the ground and situated amid canopies of question-mark ivies and worn-out, partially erect vacuum pipes.

I turned around for the first time and immediately became tangled in the vacuum-pipe bushes. Chaotically grabbing on to everything that might get me out of there, I saw an old paper crane above my head. Strange symbols were written around its edges; their appearance gave me the worst headache. "*Transit umbra, lux permanet,*" I read aloud with difficulty.

The sound of my voice tore one of the silver vacuum-pipe wires that prevented me from untangling myself. Little strands of light leaked from it, projecting specks of color onto four bare feet hurriedly approaching from afar. Two scrawny humans, tied by old rusty chains around their arms and legs and completely covered in ink, stumbled toward me with a lot of grunting, huffing, and puffing. Old torn-out black-and-white uniforms with lots of polka dots hung from their bodies like spooky curtains from a children's theater. Pointy paper cranes floating deliberately around their heads in skewed halos made them look like a couple of mythological prophets who had certainly survived drought, famine, physical abuse, and some kind of exorcism. They sighed.

"Spasibo . . ." They stretched their arms toward me, letting the chains fall away effortlessly.

"She looks so much like you!" said the muddy gentleman sentimentally to the muddy lady.

"Ah! I could never let myself believe this day would come," she replied and added with much less joy in her voice, "you shouldn't be here . . . how could this be . . . how could they let it happen . . ."

"Who are you two?" I inquired, cautiously interrupting their conversation, trying not to stare at them too explicitly.

"She doesn't know who we are!" the muddy lady said, dramatically throwing her arms in the air, completely disregarding the fact that the remaining edges of her chains hit the muddy gentleman on the head.

"Ouch!" squealed the muddy gentleman. "Watch it now, Alexandra!"

The muddy lady disregarded his words and continued looking at me with profound adoration.

"Of course she doesn't know who we are," whispered the muddy gentleman impatiently. "She just arrived! She must not know who *she* is!"

"Eh . . . she is better off not knowing," admitted the muddy lady sadly, "but maybe you and I can help."

"Her Mind can't stay here with us. Interrupting the ball is the best we can do."

"Shhh!" whispered the muddy lady. "I can hear them."

"Put the chains back on us!" said the muddy lady.

By her face and the tone of her voice, I could tell she absolutely detested the wicked metal things on her ankles and wrists.

"We shall all hug," said the muddy lady, slowly bursting into tears. She added, "Think of everything you are about to see as a bad dream. Nothing more than a very bad dream. There is a good chance we can get you out of here."

While carefully hugging the fragile couple, I saw an army of smoky silhouettes emerging from the fog.

"Who am I—do you know?" I hurriedly asked the muddy people.

"You are one of us," said the muddy lady.

"Do you know my name?" I asked.

"No, dear, I don't know what Sveta named you. I would certainly be honored to call you 'vnuchka,'" said the muddy lady.

In a moment, everything became as dark as the ink in the dissolving river. The cicadas' bloodcurdling chanting was all I could hear. I was blindfolded and taken away from OOOasis of the Unknown to the next dimension. Stranger than everything.

CHAPTER IV

0002!

Numbers covered your bodies; numbers crawled over you like lice. One ought to strip you of everything, and naked you ought to be driven into the woods . . . It is unnatural for a thinking and seeing human being to live among irregularities, unknowns, X's.[44]

—Yevgeny Zamyatin

44 Yevgeny Zamyatin, *We*, trans. Gregory Zilboorg (New York, 1924; Project Gutenberg, 2020), http://www.gutenberg.org/ebooks/432.

THROUGH THE HOLE IN MY SHABBY BLINDFOLD MASK, I made out the perfectly round salutary ancient gate, whiter than the shore's blinding whiteness. Twisted cracks. Ubiquitous holes. The gate, built from sturdy bones of unknown creatures, shaped like large numbers holding up decorative spades and shields, could scare away anything willing to enter the town without an invitation. The bones of the gate cracked open, reshaping themselves into three Os. The smoky silhouettes threw me into a tiny, smelly cellar (it reeked of oily sprats, I swear) with many sewing machines and tra-ta-ta-ta-ta hoses.

The previous chanting continued: "Kak vse! Kak vse!"

They patch-slap-schlepped me into a large bowl of soupy water. Their hands stung me like electric ozone layers, zipping and zapping the highly carbonated waters into which I was thrust. The insane effervescence of that hissing ablution worsened my deep bites, crisscrossing me like thick rusty chains. Gladly, it didn't last long. Soon enough, my pain switched to a series of pleasant tickles.

The odd centipede cleaned me to perfection, after which I was additionally stitched with lots of threads like a complicated piece of embroidery. Their loud, slimy knuckles were purposefully hitting my bones, examining the hollowest areas in my body, injecting weight under the skin on my back, and, finally, stamping a foot-long surgical stitch on top of it all.

The procedure was done. My neck folded downward, throwing my head onto my chest, pinching every nerve there was in me. I found myself looking down at a wooden beaded square shining under my knees—an adjacent continuation below my knees. My new legs. My hands had been replaced with intricate medieval-looking fans. I was kneeling on an ancient abacus I could somehow operate with impressive proficiency. A mirror on the edge of the abacus, shaped like the number 2, helped my spatial recognition, though I could not see my own reflection within it.

I saw what I had become as soon as I entered a brighter room with shiny granoblastic floors: no identifiable features were visible on my face. I was shaped like a wobbly swan. Alas, I wasn't a swan; I was a Two with a peculiar hump on my back, shivering like a wet puppy. The heavy head of mine wasn't moving very well, since I didn't quite know how to operate it yet, so I let it hang aimlessly. My heart wasn't ticking. There was a good chance I didn't have a heart at all, which, in my new state, I believed was a tremendous achievement.

A stream of unknown dark blobs and sticks ran toward me from every door there was in that space. The whole town was there to see me.

"ZZZZ?" they wheezed to me, suspicious at first, but when they saw my hump, their heads bounced up and down with a contagious amicability.

"0002!" they exclaimed joyfully.

My name was Two too. My impressive hump, which made me look like a raggedy swan, maintained my movements at the lowest of levels. There was no such thing for me as "to stand upright."

In a matter of two hundred seconds, I understood everything they had said. No, it wasn't like any speech you may have heard. It consisted strictly of numbers. The wall of noise that sounded a lot like cicada cries turned out to be the OOO language.

My long double sneeze gave the congenial Fives, Fours, and Ones, plus several clumsy Seven-folks beaming with kindness, the idea that I

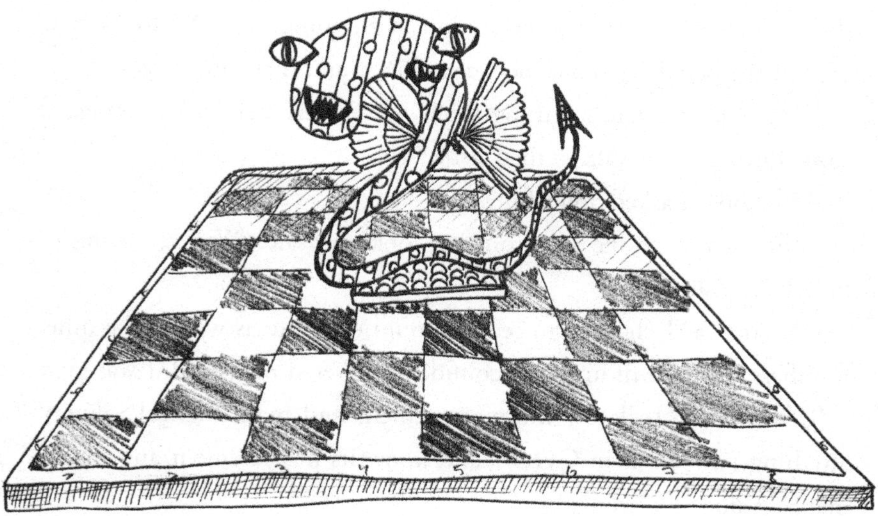

was ready to be greeted. Aside from their beady tired-panda eyes, there was practically nothing human about their appearance and cursory movements.

They gallantly formed an enormous figure eight around me, pulling me to the middle with infinitely precise attention. Such a well-choreographed puzzle it was! The noise of thousands of moving abacuses quieted down, leaving hollow echoes of distant tick-tock-tucks.

"OOOaaah!" I exhaled loudly, releasing a thick layer of dust from my new mouth. My breath became even again. The action was greeted with the most bizarre round of applause you can imagine; instead of hands, the creatures had a pair of worn-out valerian-looking fans, and they flew back and forth in one repetitive motion like thousands of mechanical butterflies. And that's how I became a new member of the strange army of mime-like creatures dressed in striped polka-dotted black-and-white uniforms. Stranger than anything. Uglier than anything.

Various dots on our featureless faces served us as eyes and mouths. Each group of numbers carried the number of eyes and mouths they represented. For instance, threes had three eyes and three mouths. As for me, besides having the regular number of eyes a normal human would, I had an extra mouth. The most peculiar ones were those one-eyed, one-mouthed Ones. They were cut out so thinly that they could track down the slightest geometrical imperfection in anything in OOO by measuring out the parallel distance between objects and their single eye.

"We can calculate anything with crystal-clear perfection," bragged some Ones on our walk to the Castle.

"Me too?" I asked doubtfully.

The Twos gave me a patronizing look and said: "You are being infinitely foolish, 0002."

As soon as I checked to see if I could calculate as well as the other numbers, a flicker of uncanny confidence entered my Mind. I was gradually beginning to know the measurement and mathematical value of anything I'd look at in OOO—and know its measurement and mathematical value precisely.

I stood there on my knees and counted, and counted, and counted. My newly found grandiose mathematical precision immediately took away my back pain. It was almost like waking up from a long coma and realizing that the entire world makes perfect sense to you. *What a relief!*

Sixes looked like sacks of potatoes. Their bellies were so big that they always remained seated on their abacuses, as if glued to them. Their six mouths filled with dagger-teeth looked like they were always wide open. Eights and Zeros were never around. They were the privileged numbers who lived in the Infinity Castle with the Infinity King and Queen. Their purpose was to serve the OOO Kingdom, create extra numbers, and slaughter Notnumbers.

The Zeros' main job was to camouflage themselves to an extreme degree in order to attract Notnumbers, tricking them into thinking that the former were Notnumbers as well. The undeniable fact was that without multiple layers of ink blush, their faces looked extremely blank. Due to their complete blindness, Zeros had nearly no spatial recognition and walked very poorly.

I nodded.

A group of Sevens pointed at the biggest door in the space with symbols on it and said, "0002, do you know what these things are?"

I scrutinized the door through the mirror on my abacus for an inappropriately long time. Big drops of sweat ran down my crooked, rubbery spine. I recognized a few letters I used to know in that writing. My heart was pounding.

"No, I don't know what these are," I lied.

"Are you infinitely sure?"

"Yes."

Such semblance of a mutually consecutive action put the numbers' Minds at ease. They no longer looked tense.

"They are our enemies, 0002," said the Sevens.

"Notnumbers," added the grumpy Sixes.

"They are infinitely dangerous!" said the Threes.

"Looks like you are ready to meet the King and Queen!" yelled the Twos.

"The Infinity Majesty awaits us!" yelled all of the numbers.

"Hurry, hurry, hurry, the King is waiting!" repeated Sevens. "We are talking infinitely too much today!"

I looked at the gate I came from one more time to remember where I had met the muddy figures, but the strong wind turned me back to my position looking straight ahead. The numbers' demeanor changed.

"For your information, Two, nobody travels that way. This is your home. There is no way back through that gate," said the Sixes in a lower voice than before.

"Don't worry, though, 0002. There is nothing there but Notnumbers. Urrgh! Such infinite residue," said the snarky Threes.

"We have killed nine thousand of them today. They are such parasites," said the big-headed Nines.

Sevens gave me a lukewarm look: "Notnumbers are infinitely harmful. They are the parasites that enter OOO with the wind. They are not welcome here. We have caught them seven million times."

Threes: "The wind is the only thing we cannot calculate in OOO, but having windmills certainly helps to keep it steady. They help us send the Notnumbers back."

Ones: "We hate Notnumbers! The ones that refuse to leave, we catch and dispose into the Notnumber purgatory where they melt back into the ink river."

Then all of the numbers turned toward me, chanting for what seemed like forever, "Say it loud, say it clear, no Notnumber is welcome here!"

"834692093489798597342711212322323232l, 0002!"

"03849353432342346985438923400003332323234542121121???"

I repeated the idea after them, seemingly agreeing with everyone's xenophobic feeling toward the creatures that weren't numbers like us: attentive to detail, focused on overall mathematical performance, organized and eager to be useful. "3121312312313131235456565654699999993233232!!!"

"Everything will be infinitely perfect as soon as we learn the Infinity Dance!" they said as we cheerfully continued our journey to meet the King and Queen, operating our squeaky abacuses in perfect rows like handicapped monkeys.

"0092387238573945739457398793433424223425444323 2, 0002!?!?!?!"

Our fans, held up like flags, pushed us up the densely foggy polished hill.

OOO's exceptionally smooth tiles and their cyclical chaos, those hypnotic movements they whirled with, created a stellar pattern of switching black-and-white squares. They changed the overall whiteness of the atmosphere with an optical illusion of a gorgeous puzzle. The beautiful, hypnotic emptiness, that seemed less uninhabited with every inch, made me happily, infinitely drunk, until in two thousand moist blinks, amplified by shapes and shadows, I found myself standing among intimidating-looking windmills, bushes, statues of numbers, and hexagonal buildings.

Where am I? I thought to myself.

When there was no more fog creeping from anywhere toward our army, the wind calmed down. We reached the heart of OOO, where the exquisite figure-eight-mighty-giant-construction emerged seemingly out of nowhere, on the crest of an infinitely tall cliff. It called us like some uncanny forest nymph. The light ticking it produced sounded like an infinitely soothing lullaby.

The carcass of the Castle was built from a slightly shinier variety of tiles than the rest of OOO; they switched much faster and looked like insane kaleidoscopes, tricking everyone's Minds in the most precise mathematical manner, running their programmed sequence cyclically, flying around like a loud heartbeat-drum-conch-shell-rollercoaster. The Castle had three windows like this:

O

O

O

A clock with many numbers sat in the middle O, ticking like this: "tick-tock-tuck." Every little detail of the clock was silky, royal, and wondrous, like ancient priceless jewels. The arms of the clock were crooked, as if someone had broken and repaired them multiple times. They walked in all directions with a specific code that required the most advanced multiplication abilities to fathom. Only seconds mattered for the clock's direction. In fact, there were no hours or minutes involved in its work. Numbers called it the "Second Clock."

All of us—the crooked hunchbacks, arithmetic clowns, and crawlers—felt incredibly small and insignificant at that moment, admiring the Infinity Castle like a flock of impossibly enamored bats ogling a thick halo of mosquitos.

"02232823819848989238492384923849849234 89!!!"

We wheezed and wheezed with such loud excitement that I thought the Castle would crack in half. Somehow it didn't; on the contrary, it blossomed into a brighter, more powerful entity, an infinitely tall machine, a sturdy warrior of mathematical security, showing us its dignity and power.

Great big old scruffy windmills, hunched like elderly ladies, were planted on the infinitely perfect marble surface around the Castle.

"It would have been an infinite nightmare not to have them here, since the Notnumbers dare to come through the gate two hundred thousand times a day," the Twos whispered to me benevolently.

"Even though the mills appear infinitely fragile, the strength of their blows divides the numeric thickness of the atmosphere accordingly and effortlessly. We have cleaned them four thousand times for the ball in the past four days," added the Fours.

I silently nodded to everything the numbers had to say about the Kingdom, helplessly watching the grandiose reflection in my abacus's mirror—a bevy of unbelievably precise lines, circles, and hypotenuses. I saw the entirety of universal numbers in every millimeter, molecule. In every reflection.

CHAPTER V

THE INFINITY CASTLE

The top window of the Infinity Castle flew open. An army of sloppy Eights pushed the Infinity King on a giant abacus-throne toward us. His throne looked like this:

O
O
O

The King looked like an Eight that had accidentally swallowed another Eight sideways. He was polka-dotted entirely from head to toe—his skin consisted of never-ending mouths and eyes that never stopped observing everything around. Regardless of his unfathomably grotesque appearance, he gave off a sense of imperturbable gravity and charisma, luring everyone to himself like a hunk of universally desirable cheese. He was, by all means, one of a kind: a mustached giant with a multitude of eyes, shielded by several heavy creases gliding down from his egg-shaped skull. His two biggest eyes (the rest of them were rather limpid-looking) were decorated with a tiny pair of reading glasses. An elegant bow tie was perched on one of his necks.

Swift movements of his flexible cheeks rose up and down, left and right in a half grin, half smirk. After puffing and wheezing for a while, he managed to reach his pedestal (his infinitely large body took over the three circles of the throne) and give the entire OOO a tragically meaningful look, a half pout, half kiss on his face. Even with his great size, well-rehearsed royal gestures, and pretense of might, it was clear that he must have been infinitely old.

Lighthearted Zeros came out of the Castle and surrounded the throne in a half circle. Their presence seemed to energize the old King. He blew his cheeks proudly, nodding at everyone in town, dryly cleared his multiple throats, and wheezed in a strangely authoritative voice: "Infinitely good day, Ones, Twos, Threes, Fours, Fives, Sixes, Sevens, Eights, Nines, and Zeros! Welcome back to the Infinity Castle! I am infinitely pleased to announce—there are less than 86400 seconds left before the Infinity Ball begins and the Infinity Spiral comes to life. I want to infinitely thank you for the hard work you have done to protect OOO from the wicked Notnumbers. I was informed this morning that the last missing number was spotted near the gate. Has the missing number arrived yet?"

The numbers pushed me forward as I shook with bewilderment: "Yes, your Infinite Majesty, the last missing Two has just arrived! We took care of the infinitely precise procedure. 923013102839012389128308091283109012317657!"

The King's eyes opened extremely large, like two full-size manholes, making him look like some exotic bug from a tropical country.

"We are infinitely pleased to have you with us, 0002! Infinite round of applause! You are so infinitely important to us! 223332838238238!"

The numbers' fans applauded to me with outrageous enthusiasm.

The King continued flattering me to the point of complete buffoonery.

"Now listen infinitely carefully, 0002: you will reach the perfect state of clarity today with us!"

"Idearium is near!" continued chanting the entire Kingdom in infinitely perfect unison, aligning itself in a figure-eight shape.

"The pure state where we equate! The clear ply where we multiply!"

Fives whispered to me: "We have been waiting infinitely long for you to come!"

"The ball will be infinitely incredible! We are about to finish something so infinitely powerful!" added Ones.

Another loud wheeze-announcement came out of the King's mouths and spread all over OOO's land: "Let us eat before our last day of Not-number war! I solemnly declare the beginning of the last Infinity Feast in OOO Kingdom!"

CHAPTER VI

THE INFINITY FEAST

An infinite number of bibs fell out of the lower window in the Infinity Castle. We put them on the best we could and sat on the ground, aligning our abacuses as a single infinitely long makeshift table. A two-thousand-foot-deep skillet rolled out of the fog and came to a halt in front of us, like a gargantuan black cat. It had a huge red ceremonial ribbon on the side, the only color I had seen in OOO. Our mouths opened, uncontrollably losing streams of black saliva onto our perfect bibs. We were ready to feast.

The Infinity Castle's top window flew open, showing us a terrifying action of lazy Eights with long, sharp daggers instead of hands, slaughtering little Notnumbers. Zeros, covered in beautifying inks, were vacuuming the dead Notnumbers through vacuum pipes attached to them, choking on their mushy bodies with endearing coquetry. For OOO's prosperity.

When Zeros couldn't take any more Notnumbers, they dropped nearly dead, throwing up little ink eggs from their holes, like ice machines, straight into the black skillet. The King was shaking with excitement. The first window opened again, and other Eights beat in an endless number of black ovals to make the Infinity Cake. The inside of the ink eggs contained multiple pairs of gray and red eyes, staring at each other passionlessly right from the inky yolks. Eyeball to eyeball. Little innards were sinking in the dough. A shudder of hunger passed through the numbers. I could hear them drool.

Three paper cranes with chaotic squiggles on both sides landed fearlessly in front of me. Eights shot them in a matter of eight seconds. Splashes of ink covered my abacus. Part of me knew I had to continue hating Notnumbers, but there was something irresistible about what they presented inside out: a series of funny images and squiggles I could hardly understand. Everyone's earthquake-like cheering awoke me from scrutinizing the cranes. A sudden wave of panic hit me.

The King was becoming irritable and jumpy watching the cake preparation. His eyes were moving in zigzagging ovals, their pupils spreading rounder and rounder like two growing puddles of runny dough. As soon as the Infinity Cake was done, the King's throne rolled to the skillet. He lifted a big piece of it and released his erect icicle-like tongue to give it a taste. The King's maddening sexy squeal, similar to that of some marine mammal, gave everyone an impression that the cake must have been exquisite. Then he purged himself to a degree of infinite obesity until his face turned into a bubbly surface, so ripe that it seemed it was just about to pop and ooze burning-hot volcanic pus. The numbers lifted their fans and began to move them very, very quickly.

The King took a short-lived nap. When he awakened and regrouped all of his chins, stomachs, and cheeks, he almost burned a hole in my face with his laser eyes.

"You made it just on time, Two," he barked. I nodded obediently. The King was examining me so closely that I couldn't see anything except every sizzling pore of his sweat-downpour-faceless face. He burped with a bounce and planted a wet, passionate, gooey kiss on my head, dripping his sweat and saliva all over me. The temperature of his secretions was terribly lukewarm, almost intolerable, irritating and icky.

"Your turn, 0002!" the King commanded peremptorily.

"Eat!" he yelled, letting out a completely intolerable stream of gamey breath with a great plosive stress.

I put a tiny piece of the slimy cake in both my mouths. The veins, eyes, and innards in it were still alive, trembling in convulsions throughout the whole procedure of the consumption. They married each other in my inky saliva, turning into hissing snakes in the cracks of my mouths.

While grinding the rubbery flesh, a strange pain made me cringe. As soon as the King cheered to my first Infinity Feast, I spit the cake back into the horrific anti-sanitary abyss. My whole being was filled with severe palpitations. My heart pounded, the temperature of my body so hot that I swear I thought I was going to melt into a puddle.

When everyone finished eating the cake, the King rolled back to the Castle, still chewing and dripping a little bit of ink on his polka-dotted apron. He dragged a squeaky bowl of additional cake for the Queen after him.

"Very, very good, OOO Numbers! The new Two and I have an infinite amount of work to do before the ball. But don't get too infinitely excited yet; there are quite a few pieces of Notnumbers left in OOO. Go kill them as infinitely quickly as possible! Remember to multiply, divide, add, and subtract all of them! Don't let a single parasite survive!"

The windows of the Castle shut themselves with a soft, exhaling, freeing "0-0-0-0!" and the whole Kingdom heard the sounds of vivid tapping behind the doors of the Castle.

"He and the Queen never stop rehearsing the movements before the ball," Ones told me. "They believe the perfect rhythm of our collective dance will make the infinity formula work."

"See you at the ball, 0002!" said the Threes.

The numbers set out to roll into the local labyrinths, dividing into even groups to attack Notnumbers, leaving me in a group of casual Eights. In a few thousand seconds of thorough multiplication, division, adding, subtracting, and gathering used to outsmart the Notnumbers, the fatal gathering paused.

"Look at us," demanded the Eights, looking all over me with magnifying glasses.

"You must see the King this very moment," they insisted, pushing me deliberately through the main door of the Infinity Castle, exchanging a series of hostile electrocution-like whispers among themselves. My two throats nervously swallowed.

CHAPTER VIII

THE INFINITY TEST

THE DOOR BEHIND ME SHUT with a loud "phoooom." My former expectations of what lay inside the Infinity Castle failed tremendously. Instead of containing something pleasantly illuminated, an old cave emerged from behind the door, revealing hundreds of doors, hiding thick layers of fluffy debris and broken pieces of abacus. The first compartment I walked into was an ashen ballroom with the OOO throne in the back. Another Two was hung upside down in a coffin-like container in the middle. The King wasn't facing me.

"Excuse me, your Infinite Majesty," I said.

The King let out a creepy shrill laugh and turned around with an expression eviler than I expected. The tied Two's eyes opened. They were filled with horror.

Seeing the Infinity King at that moment was like seeing him for the first time. He had changed his look for the upcoming ball and come out as a coxcomb character from medieval times, resembling a black metallic cream puff covered in multiple constellations. I must admit, it was truly a hypnotic attire. His abdomen distended to the size of a hot air balloon, and so did his voice. Eights threw me two inches away from his throne. He gave me another gross kiss on the head, piercing me with all of his chainsaw-eyes.

"Thank you, OOO8s, you are free to go," said the King.

After the Eights had emptied the room, the King did something I expected the least: he cracked his gown open, like a peapod. A middle-aged man with a bushy mustache came out of it. The Infinity King costume he'd been wearing earlier was operated with the use of multiple buttons, fans, and sounds, the volume and variety of which could be controlled by a small device in his hand.

"Timofey Grigorievich," he introduced himself in a deep male voice, performing his best version of a curtsy-bow for me.

"There is nothing I cannot see in OOO that you can," he said to me, staring at me with just two eyes as far as guts can possibly go.

I covered myself up with my fancy fans, shaking with such intensity that I could no longer listen to the King.

He softened his voice: "Let us be clear—I am here to make you finish the tests you once failed. Enough of the charade. I am getting carried away. Stop acting like a coward, 0002. This is your time to shine."

Speechless stare. Complete confusion.

"My time to do what?" I fearfully asked.

The King threw a professorial glance at the Second Clock and said to me: "We don't have much time left. Your Mind needs to be reconstructed. RE-CON-STRUC-TED! It will finally be granted the right ideas, and all your nightmares will be over. You've suffered enough, haven't you?"

"What is this place?" I dared to ask.

"We are in your subconscious Mind, obviously," said the King.

Alas, at that moment, I didn't understand what that meant one bit.

I wasn't sure whether it was the malice of his tone or the horrifying costume lying next to his dirty feet that made me hear thousands of tiny voices enter the Castle in a mismatched choir:

"We must dislodge the fantasies of those who disrupt order and discipline with nonsensical novelties. It won't hurt if you obey. Everything will be over in just a few minutes, and you will become the infinitely perfect citizen. Kak vse! Kak vse!"

"Idearium is near!" yelled the King.

The other Two on the ceiling wiggled with all of its might.

"I don't know what this all means," I said. "What do I need to do?"

"You must retake your numerology test. Plain and simple. If you make another mistake, you will suffer the worst pain of your life during the ball. But enough pain. I offer you a much better deal. The more precisely you calculate, the faster it will be over for you. Then we dance, and it's done."

"I don't think I know how to dance, your Infinite Majesty," I said.

"That will be taken care of last. Now let the test begin," barked the King in a militaristic manner.

A giggly crew of Zeros locked me in a round double circle. The King pulled an old tin chair from one of the Zeros and sat in it.

Then the same little voices I had heard earlier bombarded me with equations and formulae I managed to solve with impressive precision at a humanly impossible speed. His Infinite Majesty looked possessed with his mustache erecting itself up and down without ceasing, mouthing arithmetic patterns with his single human mouth while rustling papers at the desk, clicking his tongue and clapping his hands like a little child every time I gave him the right answer. Whenever it took me longer to give him an answer, he would begin to pace up and down the Castle. Heavy footsteps.

Suddenly, one of the Notnumbers flew into the Castle and landed on the other Two.

"*R!*" whispered the Notnumber.

"What's going on?" yelled the King, looking in my abacus mirror.

When he saw the flying Notnumber in the Castle, he grabbed a dagger and threw it, but instead of injuring the Notnumber, he hit the hanging Two. Drops of red blood fell on my math test.

"Fear the man of one book," whispered the bleeding Two. I looked at the King, holding his math book with the same care one would hold a newborn.

"*U!*" whispered another Notnumber.

My counting skipped.

"*N!*" yelled the third Notnumber.

The sound of chains and an elderly giggle.

"Run, Vnuchenka!!" yelled the voices from outside.

"0498923570234092375902375927509275323739820394712477 9448347452834872823528372034909000998890000000000032342 3402495389234892348!!!" yelled the entire Kingdom.

The three Notnumbers were slaughtered and flushed into the ink river.

The elderly couple who released the Notnumbers into the Castle had been arrested in about twenty-four seconds.

"Who am I?" I asked myself out loud.

I broke all of the remaining equations until I couldn't count altogether.

Long pause . . . .

My understanding of numbers left me. Timofey Grigorievich spied a quickly forming puddle of blood next to me.

"You failed your test again, you worthless brat," he shouted, slapping me in the face.

I am not sure what awoke the confidence in me, but I slapped him back with my fancy fan-hand. I didn't know who I was, but the feeling of resistance that was filling my hardly ticking heart felt more familiar than anything. I tried to run as far away from him as I could, stumbling over the polished floors, failing to avoid the group of scrawny albino Zero ballerinas blocking my way.

The King approached his throne like nothing had happened, turned it around, and from it removed several torture instruments.

Pangina came out of the Queen's room dressed like a glorious ballerina in a gargantuan tutu, her face tighter than I remembered (her bun always made her face look like a fitted sheet), and struck me with her shiny walking stick. She was a glorious Zero Queen, wiping her face of the Infinity Cake ink she had just indulged in.

When I could hardly breathe, she patted me on the back and said: "You are just as infinitely stubborn as your stupid relatives. A third generation of hopeless stupidity! Unbelievable. Nobody's Mind has ever survived the final procedure."

Timofey Grigorievich stabbed me several times with sharp knives, making me bleed red ink all over the Castle. Knowing that there was no way out of it, I covered myself with my fancy fans again, whispering to myself in broken instances: "I don't belong here . . . something is awfully wrong with this place! Nie kak vse!"

The numbers were coming back from the Notnumber War. They looked monstrous, hideous. The wind cracked my head sharply to the right, and I saw all the numbers' abacuses standing two inches away from me. I could hear their intense breath.

"0002! It's time to dance!" they said in voices I could no longer recognize; I could have mistaken them for stormy gusts of wind knocking down iron pipes.

At that point, all the tiles and buildings transformed into horrific shapes moving so chaotically that it was impossible to look at anything directly. Everything was spinning.

CHAPTER IX

THE INFINITY BALL

They tore my Two-costume and placed me into a hexagonal bubble with multiple wire connections next to a bubble containing the other Two. Ones put heavy locks on my ankles and wrists. Threes sewed my eyelids wide open. Then they locked me and the other Two inside the Second Clock's face on opposite sides, as far away from each other as possible. Both of us were losing lots of blood, which was not ink, but real blood. It was the first time I could make out the appearance of the other Two, who was not a Two, but a boy. The ball was about to begin.

Threes tapped their feet three times. An army of remaining numbers dressed in white metallic cream puff–like ball gowns happily stormed through the open door.

Timofey and Pangina greeted them with an exceptionally well-rehearsed "Welcome, welcome, welcome!" and a few contagious, uniquely synchronized pirouettes.

The clock lowered itself to the ballroom, its face unlocked.

"Time to dance!" Pangina wheezed in a victorious soprano.

She was accompanied by an army of albino Zero ballerinas with identical human faces, a replica of Pangina's malnourished features, and eyes empty like drained lakes in an arid desert.

"OOO numbers, this very hour has come!" the King announced with a thick, resonant vibration coming from every pore of his being.

"Thanks to our infinitely perfect calculations, the Queen and I have found the infinitely perfect formula for winding the Infinity Spiral. The infinitely perfect Mind will be created," he wheeze-barked, flaring himself with awkward flamboyance. "Let the Infinity Ball begin!"

After the numbers were properly costumed, the gowns locked themselves within their skins like ticks. The fancy fans flew away like an infinite swarm of butterflies. Everyone's abacus fell off their bodies and rolled away toward the ceiling, building an extra layer of prison for me and the other Two. Everyone's deformities went away. Ones, Twos, Threes, Fours, Fives, Sixes, Sevens, Eights, and Nines straightened up, rapidly transforming into albino ballerinas. They were ready to dance. It was infinitely terrifying to watch.

The Second Clock struck three times, pertaining to an unknown Infinity Ball hour, ringing a sonata of electric silence. The multitude of magnets pushed all of them toward one another and flew around the room like hot molecules, incredibly fast, miraculously avoiding running into the groups of about four thousand pop-eyed shaking and wiggling ladies with identical faces. The spiral line they were building with their infinitely evil ballet movements, rotating on their toes in figure eights, like musical boxes, and performing occasional suck-in-and-out belly dances, was the final step before they were going to turn into the Infinity Spiral inside the Second Clock. All of the albino ballerinas' steps were wound up like impeccable mechanisms. Their muscles awoke from their frozen state, and they struck poses like harp strings, ready to sing an overture of some loony tremolo. They turned, and turned, and turned, and the spiral fortified itself all the while. The arm of the clock had almost reached its middle.

The rhythm the King and Queen were tapping was impossible for everyone to ignore—especially for the other Two and me. It seemed like with every tick and tock, we were losing more blood. The ticking of the clock transformed into a series of drumbeats. My body was becoming increasingly controlled by it.

The next ritual of the ball was division. The groups divided into appropriately sized groups and strolled away to their final infinite positions in which they would remain frozen forever.

The spiral was nearly done. It was locked in the center of the ballroom like a giant chain; a big part of it was slowly entering the black circle. The ball was a step away from the Infinity Spiral finishing its formation. I was wiggling in a big slimy bubble hugged by multiple gleaming threads, hung upside down like a bat in disquiet. The slowly approaching albino ballerinas were snatching at my bubble, attempting to attach themselves to it with little strings, like creepy puppets with hanging umbilical cords. All of the Zeros were one, bound firmly by thick webs moving toward me, a condensed nucleus of a magnificent spiral, built from overlapping layers of shiny numeric roe, a bulwark of an extraordinary height and multitude of angles.

Long screeching horn.

They dashed themselves harder and harder.

And then, suddenly, the other Two broke away from its coffin-container and jumped into my bubble, making its edges freeze and harden.

Pause.

Beeping in my ears, a phosphine vision.

My heart like a thunderstorm causing sunshine instead of a natural disaster.

The Infinity Spiral lit up as brightly as the Sun and then broke into pieces like a brittle vase, causing the windmills to churn as quickly as they could.

The room presented a dizzying number of evenly smashed identical albino ballerina heads resting on thousands of black marbles. Their heartbeats went out in rows.

The King came out of his spinning trance. His face turned the color of ganglia.

"You Two! You will not ruin my Kingdom! NOOOOO!!" he boomed on the verge of tears, clutching his temples in his whining baritone, making the Second Clock's arms run around like racehorses.

A familiar soupy breeze knocked out the remaining pirouetting numbers of the Infinity Ball.

"No one's Mind can survive the COO!" Pangina squealed.

The delirium of my past and present intermingled. Clashes of ticking and tocking, and my cry of terror.

I don't know what happened to the King and Pangina. Most likely, they evaporated, as everything else did. Their essence and tutus coagulated back into the thick buttery fog.

I opened my eyes and saw Sash. Our faces changed from shock to disbelief. Our eyes lit up. The corners of his lips lifted themselves up, growing into a big smile. Our heartbeats were all that could be heard in the Kingdom.

Everything inside my stomach somersaulted into loudly chanting violins and harps. I held him very tightly, hiding my face in his shoulder.

"It's almost over, Sasha," he gently whispered in my ear.

"Words. Words. I remember words. I remember losing them," I said to Sash in a broken OOO dialect. I longed to gather more memories, but nothing else was coming to mind.

The popped nucleus of the evaporating Kingdom turned into sulky-faced clouds.

The windmills on the right shore spun out of control. An ink tsunami of newly awakened words and letters was hurriedly creeping in from behind the gate.

There was cracking, boiling, and roaring everywhere around.

Sash and I, hand in hand, reached a crosswalk. We were at the corner of OO and O (said the signs hanging independently in the air), facing the literary tsunami coming after us.

CHAPTER X

IDEARIUM

Before the giant tsunami of words written in cursive washed away the remaining bits of the Infinity Kingdom, I saw my babushka and dedushka standing by one of the windmills, arm in arm, like in the portrait Mama and Papa showed me in our old Biblioteka. They happily waved at us. Their bony hands were shaking out of control.

"We are all free now, Vnuchenka," they said in shock. "Go now, see what the world is like behind the wicked gate."

Sash and I became separated by the wall of excessive exclamation marks and semicolons.

"Alexandra is my name!" I screamed at them.

All I could see were their tears of pride and the chaos of letters behind their backs.

Everything lit up.

The elephant tortoises helped me move with the flow of words floating around us. The brightest, most heartwarming memories of my life trickled through hundreds of thousands of microlayers of my brain, filling my heart with a feeling of freedom. My hair coiled itself into a disorderly weather vane. I was beginning to remember more and more. I remembered the day Ma and I finished my first kitten embroidery. I thought about the day Pa helped me learn to tie my shoes, and when both my parents shared their knowledge of observing the world from every angle and perspective by capturing our surroundings in my first bubble-head-yellow-cloud-triangular-bird images, uneven paper constructions, and melodic verses we referred to as *stihi*—poems. I remembered the particularly strange place I once called Dom with an oak fortepiano and the acrylic stains all over it. I remembered Papa's hands, always rough like a cat's tongue, teaching me to flip pages and read books. I remembered Dom's doors making tragic, disorganized noises. I remembered the alphabet.

A: Pa's compass. B: the glorious queen bee; Kot Begemot's bulky eyes. C: Ma's earring. D: Pa's belly after dinner. Sometimes mine. E: bird foot. F: clover with only one leaf. G: snake chasing its own tail. H: Ma and Pa dancing slowly. I: me acting like a fishing rod. J: shrimp; Pa's nose. K: my own pair of big scissors. L: valenki . . .

Each letter in the inky whirlwind vibrated with its own sound. I kept repeating them out loud, watching the sunken vacuum pipes blossom into many elegant weeping willows underwater. Even the most crippled ones were moving. The question mark–shaped bushes were turning into letters. The vacuum cleaner pipes were releasing them too. The sky shaped itself differently, in a softer capacity, with more shapely streaks of cotton softness.

The tick-tock-tuck was gone forever. Everything froze. There was no more chanting, no more numbers, snakes, ballerinas, or numerology teachers. My consciousness recapitulated.

While holding my breath underwater, the elephant tortoises pushed me into the milk bottle boat Sash built many years ago. I lifted it a few inches, slowly running out of breath. The boat led me to the surface without any resistance. Multiple milk bottles were filled with the hand-copied stories Sash and I used to read when we were little.

CHAPTER XI

GLASHKA

THE RIVER CALMED DOWN AND TURNED INTO a perfectly still surface. The milk bottle boat brought me to a beautiful shore. From across the river, I saw Kazmas. I was back in Grodek. A line of mist surged on. Green light brightened the inside of the tree. I stepped out of the boat and put my feet onto the moist ground outside the tree, scrabbling at it. The purity of the natural graininess I buried my fingers in had the most compelling feeling. I pressed my face against it and listened. Besides hearing how the ground was breathing, I could also hear soft steps coming from the shore.

Sash, still a boy dressed in the same clothes he wore when I first met him, approached me from afar. I was about seven.

We stood there, next to the redwood tree, seeing each other the way we remembered ourselves at the place we both spent the best days of our childhood.

"Is this real?" I asked him, fearing he would give me a negative answer.

"I am not sure. But then, ever since I got out of here, nothing seemed real, so I don't have an answer for you," he said, wrinkling his forehead.

"Maybe we have lived the same fantasy all along?" I said with a sad smile.

"I would almost prefer to think so. I know it's been a pretty terrible one, but at least now I have someone who can relate. It's almost over . . ." said Sash.

"What did you see there? Out there?" I asked him, fearfully pointing in the direction I had come from moments ago.

"War. A lot of war. They wanted me to kill everyone I used to be friends with. Including you."

"War? You didn't see any numbers?"

"Everyone sees what they are most intimidated by or scared of out there," said Sash. "Something emotional that forces their psyche to interfere with the State's order. I am sure we did not fail LIM in exactly the same way."

"How do you know all this?" I asked him.

"I promise I will tell you very soon."

"I thought I was never going to see you again."

"I looked for you everywhere for years . . . they made it very difficult, you know."

"Until they put us in the same jail," I said.

"The last two to be sent to the COO," said Sash, impersonating a Wardworker.

We continued impersonating other characters from OB-LOM, laughing harder than we had ever laughed in our lives, feeling closer to each other. Our weather vane hair was twisting itself in all kinds of peculiar shapes until it tied us together. We were one, sewn firmly by the vibrant roots and thick webs of our past.

"What happened to you after I left the tunnel?" I asked when we calmed down.

"I found the key Ada gave you," said Sash.

"And then?"

"You will see," he whispered mysteriously.

Sash offered me his hand, leading me into the open field of giant cosmos flowers.

"You and I are here right now because you read the last page of the book Ada asked us to read. I left it for you that night to help you find me in case they sent us to the COO," said Sash.

I nodded silently, making myself comfortable on the warm dewy grass.

This was the first time *SLFFGR* had been read by both of us from the very beginning to the very end.

While reading this special book, I watched the dazzling expansion of comets and constellations up in the night sky, among which I saw the long-missing malnourished heroic dog Glashka peacefully floating in the space with no edges or center.

Everything we read was descriptive, rebellious, improbable, and so very imaginative that I could believe anything would be possible from then on. *SLFFGR* was a book of great importance, because it offered every contradictory perspective, warning, image, solution, and logical idea, easily explicable to readers of all ages. I heard my parents' voices in it telling me one more time why literature could make a difference. Depriving anyone of creative thoughts and the freedom of their expression is the most unutterable crime, my friends.

"It doesn't end here; open the bottle," whispered Sash.

I opened one of the most persistent milk bottles that had practically glued itself to me in the ink river, took out a piece of paper, and read: "*Transit umbra, lux permanet.*"

"It was us! The book ended with two kids next to a redwood tree, surrounded by cosmos flowers!" I exclaimed.

"Yes. I drew it, because freedom of thought and utmost enlightenment come to people when they release their inner child and let themselves revisit the places where they learned to express their early artistic thoughts the most. That's here."

"Are you going to tell me how you know all this?"

"Ada. She helped me. She found a way to say goodbye to me that day. In Kazmas," said Sash with a giant smile.

"What does 'SLFFGR' stand for?" I asked.

"*Samizdat Literature for Future Generations' Resistance*," said Sash with an even bigger smile on his face. "You know, everything had to be abbreviated back then."

"For konfidentsialnyi purposes!" we said in unison, laughing uncontrollably.

"The end," we whispered, shutting the book.

As soon as the book was shut, we levitated into an open sky filled with sleepy-looking comets. We softly swam-flew, crossing the delicately blinking saffron darkness around us, watching our old tree shelter turn into a tempestuous miniature foliage, dancing and digressing in the honeysuckle wind. Time with all of its meaningless imagery and fancy multidimensionality traveled with us and the haunted stars, out from the COO.

Illuminating exhale.

No more borders.

My name is Alexandra Victorovna. I am twenty-seven years and two hundred days old. I love long sentences, diminutives, polynomials, vegetation, big noses, blush on people's faces, borscht, eccentricity, allegories, and squeaky doors, because they remind me of Dom. My favorite words are: nurture, tortoise, borscht, figurine, murky, snout, blooper, knuckle, sizzle, and Cheburashka. Those words sing to me.

CHAPTER XII

HOW I LEFT OB-LOM

When I opened my eyes, I was back in OB-LOM, surrounded by the same structures and people. As much as everything looked exactly the same, something was uncannily different. No, it wasn't the fact that I was no longer pregnant (my stomach had shrunk before my eyes like a balloon the moment I awoke). It wasn't the fact that I could hear everything again either (the crowd's sonorities had dissolved). I believe it was the way people were watching me. They were saddened. Quiet. Their heavy makeup thawed under a supremely sentimental flood of tears. There were no more murmurs of objection of any kind in the crowd. Even the babies were quiet. Thousands of bears surrounded the arena with their paws politely folded on their fluffy bellies. Their demeanors and half smiles gave away how much they were enjoying the turn of events.

The twins loosened my chains and gently helped me step off the vibrating carousel of my worst nightmares.

I turned in a full circle to look at the entire town without missing a single face. There were real tears in those eyes, switching their dour expressions into something lovely. Pangina was sobbing vigorously, hanging on to Timofey Grigorievich's arm, untying her tight ballerina bun into a beautiful mane of red hair, washed to its natural look by the rain and everyone's tears. Yes, it was raining for the first time in many, many years. There was nothing identical about OB-LOMannye faces.

A giant rainbow unfurled in the sky, shining resplendent beams through the frozen surfaces of the land. It was the Moon that looked almost as bright as the Sun. It was the Moon that looked more glorious than ever before.

Pangina untied the rest of my chains.

"I hope you learn to appreciate ballet one day," she whispered in my ear. "Prosti . . ."

And I did—many years later, far, far away from OB-LOM, at a place where ballet was in no way used as a method of torture for better upbringing or courting.

"Your hair is very beautiful like this, Elena Alexandrovna," I answered to her in full voice.

"All for nothing!" she blurted out theatrically, pretending like there was no kindness between us, and turned with guilty elegance to OB-LOM, arms akimbo.

The arena of people formed a long path, leading me all the way to the State's gate. Despite the fact that the ground was impossibly slippery, I let myself fall while running and be as silly as I used to be, sliding further and further away from the frozen country I refused to proclaim as my Dom, where psychiatric wards were bursting open with thousands of new patients who had just been awakened from a long century of literary hibernation. The electronic sign on top of the citadel read: "Under Construction."

The closer I was to the gate, the wider it opened itself, as if pushed by a strong invisible hand.

"Wait!" someone shouted behind my back when I was steps away from the open gate. Sash, still dressed in his patient gown, was running after me.

"Hold your horses! Don't leave without me!" he said.

"Is this really happening, or are we in another weird dimension?" I asked him.

Sash pinched me with all his might.

"Ouch!"

"I believe it is happening. Can you multiply one hundred thirty-three by thirty-two?"

"No way!" I answered, laughing. "I may not want to count anything for a while."

"Are you ready to get out of here?" he asked impatiently, teasing me with a clumsy pirouette.

"I have never been more ready!" I yelled, throwing a dirty snowball at him.

With marvelous anticipation all over our faces, he grabbed my arm and led the way through the border of the State, where there lay an infinitely long railroad.

"Choo-choo!" sang the aquamarine train, emerging from the silver fog and gradually coming to a halt.

The lunar rainbow became aurora borealis.

Before I say anything more, you must promise me you will never tell anyone what I am about to say.

I can't explain this to you . . . but ever since I was little, leaving OB-LOM always seemed like the happiest of thoughts and most logical idea, though as soon as I would become close to escaping, something about it would immediately become more beautiful than life. Especially that day. For just a short instant, a vague feeling of sentimentality washed through me when I was seconds away from crossing the border. Looking back at my life and all the seemingly improbable events, people, and creatures it presented through my fantastical prism, it suddenly felt like an amusing fairy tale (*skazka*, as you know), and I had every urge to share it with the rest of the world—without anguish and regrets, but with the absurdity of its irrational essence. In OB-LOM language, "world" sounds a lot like the word *mir*.

Mir in OB-LOM language also means "peace."

"Goodbye, OB-LOM. You look very beautiful like this," I whispered to the green shapes of polar bears in the sky.

Sash pulled the doorknob of the last train car, letting out the most enthralling sounds of vivacious saxophone music welcoming us to the new world.

And that's how I left OB-LOM.

THE END.

EPILOGUE

But if I am not a criminal, I beg to be permitted to go abroad with my wife temporarily, for at least one year, with the right to return as soon as it becomes possible in our country to serve great ideas in literature without cringing before little men, as soon as there is at least a partial change in the prevailing view concerning the role of the literary artist.

—Yevgeny Zamyatin[45]

EVERYTHING NARRATED IN THIS STORY WAS ENHANCED with exaggerations and allegories, not on purpose, but with the accuracy of my post-Soviet childhood and visions of youth. Living in skazki has always been my

45 "Evgeny Zamyatin: Letter to Stalin," *A Soviet Heretic: Essays*, trans. Mirra Ginsburg (Chicago & London: The University of Chicago Press, 1970).

conscious choice. Descriptive writing is rarely objective, but words are our birthright.

It took me several years to master the language with which I am addressing you, with which I wrote this book. It was finished on a continent far away from Dom, where the air is warm, staples are not worn on people's mouths, and books are never prohibited (though read with much less appreciation).

Please visit **kristinabirk.com** to learn more about the book, discover my other creative pursuits, and sign up to receive updates on future projects. Perhaps I will tell you more about the new place of my residence in my next allegorical story. May I?

KRISTINA BIRK is a Ukrainian-born American writer, producer, and performer. Her most recent work includes two short films, a post-apocalyptic fantasy feature, and a dystopian pod play developed with Westward Orphans Productions in Los Angeles. This is her first novel.

Made in the USA
Monee, IL
18 October 2026

66035046R00163